Shivering Shih Tzu . . .

Something definitely wasn't right. With a growing sense of dread, I headed toward the dining room. I wouldn't have noticed the dog, but Seth, who was following like a stealth ninja, did.

"There he is!"

I jumped and backed into Seth, almost knocking both of us to the ground.

"I told you to stay put." My voice edged toward drill sergeant but Seth didn't seem to notice.

"Sorry." He was already on his knees, looking under the table.

"Is that Tuffy?"

I bent down to get a better look. A small ball of fluff was sitting under the dining room table shivering, its brown eyes shining. I nodded and kneeled next to Seth.

"What's the matter with him?" Seth asked, leaning toward the dog.

"Maybe he's afraid of you. I've never brought anyone with me before. I hadn't thought about it but he could be . . ." I stopped as Tuffy came out from under the table, crawled into Seth's lap, and continued trembling.

"He doesn't seem afraid of *me*," Seth said, and stroked Tuffy's head.

"No, I guess not. But something's wrong." I reached out to pet Tuffy, who usually was against all physical contact unless food was involved. He licked my hand and leaned closer in to Seth.

"*Stay here* with the dog. I'll be right back." I stood and scanned the room.

The hair on the back of my neck prickled, and my ears buzzed. I moved slowly toward the kitchen, old instincts kicking in. I hadn't felt this rush of adrenaline and fear since I'd returned to Crystal Haven. I couldn't say I'd missed it. As I reached back and felt along my waistband, I did miss the gun.

From the kitchen doorway I could see why Tuffy was quivering. Sara was sprawled on the floor: faceup, motionless, legs at an odd angle, eyes staring at the ceiling. . . .

Pall in the Family

DAWN EASTMAN

BERKLEY PRIME CRIME, NEW YORK

THE BERKLEY PUBLISHING GROUP
Published by the Penguin Group
Penguin Group (USA) Inc.
375 Hudson Street, New York, New York 10014, USA

USA | Canada | UK | Ireland | Australia | New Zealand | India | South Africa | China

Penguin Books Ltd., Registered Offices: 80 Strand, London WC2R 0RL, England
For more information about the Penguin Group, visit penguin.com.

PALL IN THE FAMILY

A Berkley Prime Crime Book / published by arrangement with the author

Berkley Prime Crime Books are published by The Berkley Publishing Group.
BERKLEY® PRIME CRIME and the PRIME CRIME logo are trademarks of
Penguin Group (USA) Inc.

For information, address: The Berkley Publishing Group,
a division of Penguin Group (USA) Inc.,
375 Hudson Street, New York, New York 10014.

ISBN: 978-0-425-26427-0

PUBLISHING HISTORY
Berkley Prime Crime mass-market edition / August 2013

PRINTED IN THE UNITED STATES OF AMERICA

10 9 8 7 6 5 4 3 2 1

Cover illustration by Daniel Craig.
Cover design by Judith Lagerman.

ALWAYS LEARNING   **PEARSON**

To my daughter, Ellie, with love.

Acknowledgments

Solving a mystery in Crystal Haven is a group effort, just as publishing the first Family Fortune Mystery combined the talents of many generous individuals.

Thank you to my editor, Andie Avila, and the entire team at Berkley Prime Crime. From copyedits to cover art, I am fortunate to work with such a talented, dedicated group.

Forever thanks to my agent, Sharon Bowers, and her enthusiasm for these characters. My gratitude to Clare O'Donohue for opening the door.

Clyde Fortune and the rest of the crew would not exist without the encouragement, critiques, humor, and friendship of my amazing writers' group. Wendy Delsol, Kim Stuart, Kali Van Baale, Murl Pace, and Chantal Corcoran—you are truly cherished.

I am grateful to Jamie Chavez for her editorial expertise and cheerleading.

Thanks to Barbara and Junior Morton for Tuffy's name.

Thank you to Brent and Nancy Eastman for all the techie assistance.

My parents, Ann and Bob Eastman, instilled a love of

reading and a self-confidence which is priceless. Thank you for a lifetime of comedic material.

Thank you to my children, Ellie and Jake, for support, tolerance, laughter, and love.

And to my husband, Steve, for believing.

1

I followed the shrieks to the living room, but didn't rush. It was early in the day and I was still caffeine deprived.

Mom, Aunt Vi, and Seth ducked and watched the ceiling. Occasionally Mom screamed when the small black shadow flew in her direction. They had already divvied up the equipment.

Aunt Vi's long red fingernails curled around a bedsheet stretched between her hands. Her brightly colored skirt swished over sturdy black shoes. She tossed her long silver braid over her shoulder.

My nephew, Seth, gripped my old butterfly net with thick leather gloves. At five feet six inches he was almost as tall as I was. He had taken to measuring himself against me on a daily basis, continually dismayed that he had not surpassed me yet. He flicked his head to the side to shake blond bangs out of his eyes. He did this so frequently it seemed to have become a twitch.

Mom wielded a large plastic bowl that she mostly used to cover her head. At almost seventy, she was petite and still beautiful. Her white hair was coiled in a tight bun, and her makeup was flawless, even though she still wore her robe and slippers.

They were after a bat. Again.

"Clyde, it's coming your way!" Vi threw the sheet at me.

I looked up and saw the bat swoop in my direction. I tossed the sheet at him but missed. More noise ensued as he looped around the room and headed for Mom. Seth held his position like a goalie in a very slow game.

I opened three windows and popped out the screens while the hunting continued. Seth took a swing with the net but had no luck. Vi readied her sheet again. Mom cowered under the bowl. This was home.

Some people run away from home to join the circus; I had left home to escape one.

Fortunately, my phone buzzed in my pocket. I waved it at the bat-hunting trio and stepped into the dining room. It was a text from Tish. She needed to board Baxter again. He'd been with us more than he'd been home in the month since I'd returned to Crystal Haven. I wondered once again why she was away so much.

Another scream and then a crash issued from the room next door. I took a deep breath and dove in.

"Nana Rose, stop yelling. You're scaring the poor guy." Seth frowned and followed the bat around the room with his eyes.

"What about what he's doing to me?" Mom turned to Vi,

and said, "I thought you said all the da—*arn* bats were gone." We all glanced at Seth. We had promised his mother we wouldn't swear in front of him. She still labored under the delusion that he was five years old.

Vi shrugged and glanced at the ceiling. "I'm pretty sure this is the last one." Aunt Vi is a pet psychic, and her pronouncements on all things animal are taken as gospel by my mother.

Vi insists each sighting of a bat in the house is a sign of impending doom. Then Mom consults the tarot cards to try to identify the coming disaster. So far, nothing. But that doesn't stop my family from predicting dire outcomes. In a tourist town where psychics and fortune tellers are more thick on the ground than Realtors, grim prophecies are routine.

"He's getting tired. Maybe he'll notice the window if he flies lower." Seth dropped his net hand to his side.

"Seth, stay on guard! He's probably faking." Mom continued to protect her head and track the bat.

The animal landed on the couch. I imagined I could hear its little heart racing. Vi threw the sheet at him, and he was off again on his loop around the room. On the second round he flew through the window and landed with a splat on the front porch. I ran to close the windows, and Seth darted outside to assess the escapee.

I turned to check on Mom. She took deep breaths and put the bowl down with shaky hands only after Vi and I assured her the bat had left the building.

"Maybe we need professional help," said Vi.

I had a few ideas about the kinds of professionals we would need, but I was pretty sure she meant animal control.

"Okay, well, Seth and I have dogs to walk—see you later."
I bolted out the front door and down the steps. I caught a
glimpse of the bat as it flew into the trees. "You coming?" I
called.

Seth gave a thumbs-up, climbed into my Jeep, and clicked
his seat belt.

"I wish we could start a morning without a major ruckus."
I sighed and turned the key in the ignition.

"Ruckus." Seth snorted. "You sound like Nana Rose."

"Take that back or you will never see your fourteenth
birthday."

"Now you sound like Auntie Vi." He grinned and shoved
his earbuds into his ears.

Before putting the Jeep in gear, I closed my eyes and
counted to five very slowly. My mother had suggested Seth
as my assistant because we were "at the same maturity level."
But, seriously, who doesn't act like she's thirteen when forced
to move back in with her parents at thirty?

Seth has been coming to Crystal Haven for the summer
ever since it was legal to put him on an airplane alone. My
perfect sister, Grace, hasn't stepped foot in our quirky home-
town since the day she left, and I don't blame her. Much.
She's made a good life for herself using her talents as a stock-
broker.

In Seth's other life he's a city kid and goes to an expensive
private school in New York City, wears a uniform, and plays
tennis. He has always loved coming here for the summer and
spending time on the beach and in the woods. Since I had just
moved back—*temporarily*—we'd been spending a lot of time
together.

"All right, our day just got more complicated," I said.

With exaggerated patience, Seth removed his earbuds.

"How complicated can your day be? You walk dogs and pick up crap. It's not like you're saving the world—anymore."

Seth was unhappy about my recent career switch from police officer to dog walker. I ignored him and continued. "We have to go get Baxter after we see our usual lineup." I waved my phone at him. "Tish texted, and she's going out of town again. He's coming to stay with us."

"Great, I love Baxter."

"Good, you're in charge of him."

Mondays are the hardest days, since the dogs have to get used to the weekday routine after spending all weekend with their owners. Our first stop was Archie's house. He is an Airedale with a pathologic fear of thunderstorms. Fortunately for us, the sky was a clear blue and he only needed a quick walk. Molly and Roxie were next. Molly is an Australian shepherd with anxiety, and her neighbor Roxie is a spoiled cocker spaniel with fear-biting issues. I had taken to walking them together, one being less anxious and the other less fearful. My favorite, MacDuff, followed. A Scottish terrier, he had become depressed when the daughter of the house had moved away to college. Vi said he had "empty nest syndrome" and she was working with him to find other "sources of fulfillment." So far, he was fulfilling his need to dig up his owner's yard.

After MacDuff, we drove to get Baxter. When we arrived at Tish's house, Baxter, who would have a frequent-flyer card if I wanted to encourage his repeat business, was waiting for us by the front door. His dark muzzle, comprised mainly of heavy jowls, pulled the rest of his face down to give him a perpetually worried countenance. His droopy stare brightened when he saw Seth. Baxter is a bullmastiff, which was another way of saying he's one hundred thirty pounds of drool. He adored Seth. He tolerated me because I usually accompanied Seth. Since he wasn't the only dog to ride in it, he hated my SUV. But I couldn't imagine anything better than a fifteen-year-old Jeep Wrangler for transporting dogs to their various destinations.

"Okay, on three," I said.

I was in the backseat of my Jeep with both hands on Baxter's collar. Seth had the other end, which was still firmly planted outside on the street. The dog was wearing his stubborn face, which consisted of jutting his jaw even farther forward, and I braced myself for a fight.

"One, two," I said, and Baxter lurched forward, his jowls flopping in my face and drenching me in dog saliva.

"We were supposed to go on three!" I said. I grabbed a dirty towel from the floor and wiped my face.

"I didn't push him. He did it himself," Seth said, and looked away too late to hide his smile.

"Get in the car," I said through clenched teeth.

We drove in silence to our next client's house. Seth had his earbuds screwed into his ears, but the corners of his mouth kept twitching upward. Baxter flopped his chin on my shoulder from the backseat, and I felt the warm wetness ooze down my arm.

I took my eyes off the road long enough to roll them skyward and wonder how I had ended up back in Crystal Haven with an enormous slobbering dog and an adolescent nephew who was either not speaking at all or talking so much it made my head hurt. *When will you teach me to shoot? Did you keep your flak jacket? How fast can you run? Do you think Baxter would make a good K-9 officer?* Much like with every other problem in my life, I blamed my mother. After my "incident" on the police force in Ann Arbor, I had called Mom in a moment of weakness. She had talked me into moving home for the summer. She made sense at the time, the way mothers sometimes do. *Come home, rest, take time to figure out your life.* My administrative leave morphed into a summer at home. I'd arrived in mid-June and it was already mid-July. At some point I'd have to decide what I was going to do come September. Within days of my return, Aunt Vi had used her connections to line up some "clients" for me. Many of her pet clients needed extra attention during the day. Even though I tried to argue with Vi on principle, her idea gave me a flexible schedule, a few extra bucks, and allowed me to spend the days walking other people's dogs.

The one good part about the summer was that I was spending it in western Michigan, mostly outside. Beautiful beaches and lush forests were all within a short drive. The tourist season guaranteed festivals and farmers markets and, after Ann Arbor, I needed a more relaxed pace. As we drove to Tuffy's house, I tried to focus on how much I loved it here.

It was close to eleven by the time I parked in the driveway of a small brick ranch on the outskirts of town. Tuffy's owner, Sara, was a part-time lawyer and often worked from home. I hadn't seen the dog in over a week. He was moody and spoiled and didn't like anyone but Sara. Plus, he's a shih tzu and wears one of those ridiculous ponytails on top of his head.

I nudged Seth. "Get your gear."

"What?"

"The pooper-scooper."

"Oh, man . . ." He slouched out of his seat, his bony shoulders sagging, and moved toward the back of the Jeep. As assistant dog walker, Seth was in charge of cleanup. He frequently pretended not to remember this aspect of the job description.

I stopped in front of the house and foraged under one of the spindly bushes flanking the front steps. I extracted the key from the fake rock Sara had hidden there and listened for noises inside the house. Usually Tuffy would be flinging himself at the door by now and barking furiously, as if I were an intruder he had never seen before, but all was quiet this morning.

"Just leave it by the steps and we'll go get him," I said to Seth, who was holding the scooper at arm's length.

I unlocked the door and stepped inside, bracing myself for Tuffy's attack. It didn't come.

"Tuffy?"

"Here, puppy," Seth said from behind me, and got down on one knee. He whistled. "Come on, boy."

Still nothing.

"This is weird, Seth. Stay here."

The shades were still down, and I threaded my way through the dimly lit living room, which was crowded with a sectional sofa that must have been purchased for a larger room, and a coffee table piled with books on spiritualism and séances. On the mantel, pictures of two college-age girls flanked a photo of the elusive dog. Sara's divorce had turned nasty over custody of the shih tzu. Had I been in her shoes, I would have walked away from the sectional and the dog.

Something definitely wasn't right. With a growing sense of dread, I headed toward the dining room. I wouldn't have noticed the dog, but Seth, who was following like a stealth ninja, did.

"There he is!"

I jumped and backed into Seth, almost knocking both of us to the ground.

"I told you to stay put." My voice edged toward drill sergeant, but Seth didn't seem to notice.

"Sorry." He was already on his knees, looking under the table. "Is that Tuffy?"

I bent down to get a better look. A small ball of fluff was sitting under the dining room table shivering, its brown eyes shining. I nodded and kneeled next to Seth.

"What's the matter with him?" Seth asked, leaning toward the dog.

"Maybe he's afraid of you. I've never brought anyone with me before. I hadn't thought about it, but he could be . . ." I stopped as Tuffy came out from under the table, crawled into Seth's lap, and continued trembling.

"He doesn't seem afraid of *me*." Seth said, and stroked Tuffy's head.

"No, I guess not. But something's wrong." I reached out to pet Tuffy, who usually was against all physical contact unless food was involved. He licked my hand and leaned closer in to Seth.

"*Stay here* with the dog. I'll be right back." I stood and scanned the room.

The hair on the back of my neck prickled, and my ears buzzed. I moved slowly toward the kitchen, old instincts kicking in. I hadn't felt this rush of adrenaline and fear since I'd returned to Crystal Haven. I couldn't say I'd missed it. As I reached back and felt along my waistband, I did miss the gun.

From the kitchen doorway I could see why Tuffy was quivering. Sara was sprawled on the floor: faceup, motionless, legs at an odd angle, eyes staring at the ceiling. The blood had spread underneath her and across her tunic, obliterating the brightly colored flowers.

2

"**Is she . . . dead?**" **said a small voice from** behind me.

I turned quickly to see Seth staring with huge eyes at Sara, and Tuffy trying to climb over Seth's shoulder to get as far away from the kitchen as possible.

Before I knew what was happening, my police training kicked in, and I pushed Seth behind me against the dining room wall. I peeked around into the kitchen and signaled him to be quiet. I was sure Sara had been killed, but I couldn't be sure the murderer was gone.

I stood for a moment and willed my heart to stop racing. Between the dizziness and the pounding in my ears, I was forced to lean against the doorjamb and take deep, slow breaths. The metallic tang of blood was so strong I could almost taste it. I was trained to deal with violence and death. I tried to remember what I was supposed to do next. My mind flashed back to that warm spring evening in Ann Arbor—the last time I had seen so much blood—but I quickly put a stop to that. I had to stay calm.

I cataloged the area to focus my thoughts. The back door was closed but not locked. A half-full coffee cup sat on the counter by a plate of untouched toast. Sara was wearing bright floral-patterned silk pants and a matching tunic. The pool of blood that had collected underneath her looked thick and dark against the beige tile. I started worrying about how she would ever get her grout clean—obviously, my shocked brain's attempt to distract.

I heard Seth breathing in my ear, and Tuffy trembled against my back. Otherwise, the house was silent. I signaled to Seth to stay put, and his wide-eyed nod assured me he would. I stepped into the kitchen, took a deep breath, and forced myself to feel for a pulse, knowing I wouldn't find one. As I touched her neck, I felt a surge of fear and rage and had to close my eyes until it passed. It was harder to ignore the rising nausea. Her skin was cold but still soft. We were too late to help her, but my exposure to death reports in my time with the police told me she hadn't been dead very long.

Keeping the back door in view, I returned to Seth and Tuffy in the dining room. We made our way quickly back through the living room and out the front door. I wasn't prepared to check the house without backup and with a thirteen-year-old in tow.

"I wish you hadn't seen that. I told you to stay where you were. Why don't you ever listen . . . ?" I began my tirade when we got outside but stopped as I noticed that Seth had transformed from an annoying adolescent to a little boy. He had the same look as the time he found a dead baby robin in the backyard when he was six, his first brush with death.

I couldn't remember the last time I had hugged him: a real hug, not just a quick airport hug. I had never embraced Tuffy, but I found myself holding both of them for a long moment.

"Clyde, I don't feel so good." Seth muffled into my shoulder.

I jumped back just in time to miss most of it. It only caught the toe of my shoe, but Tuffy wasn't as lucky. The dog glared at me from under his poufy ponytail as if it was my fault. The combination of all that blood and remembering Sara's lifeless body had my own stomach lurching in protest. I took deep breaths and held my hands together to keep them from shaking.

"We have to call the police," I said. I put my arm around Seth's shoulder and urged him toward the Jeep.

Baxter barked through the few inches of open window as we approached. We got in, locked the doors, and called 911.

We'd decided that being locked in a car with a vomit-covered dog was worse than a run-in with a murderer; even Baxter didn't put up a fuss when we left him behind again. I was hosing Tuffy off in the front yard while Seth sat on the stoop with his head between his knees when the police cruiser arrived. A young man climbed out of the car, managed to trip over a pebble, and walked to where I was drying off the disgruntled shih tzu.

"Hello, ma'am. I'm Officer Andrews." He flipped open a small notepad. "Dispatch sent me here to check on a report of a dead body."

I nodded and offered him my hand. "I'm Clyde Fortune; this is my nephew, Seth Proffit."

"Clyde Fortune? *The* Clyde Fortune? Are you Rose Fortune's daughter?" He looked from one eye to the other. I have two different-colored eyes, the one thing people always like to confirm for themselves upon meeting me. The left is pale blue, the right dark brown. Often people report this fact, as if I'd never looked in a mirror.

"Yes. Why?"

"My mother told me you went to Ann Arbor to join the police, but now you're back and everyone says you're finally going to join the family business."

"You are? Awesome!" Seth perked up at this news.

"Andrews? Jillian is your mother?" I studied his face: thin nose, brown eyes, and dark hair. He had the height and gangly bearing of all the Andrews kids. My mother and Jillian are best friends, and I had been in school with her oldest daughter. "I probably used to babysit you. Which one are you?"

"That's harsh, Clyde," said Seth. He shrugged and shook his head at Officer Andrews as if to say "you can't take her anywhere."

A slow blush crept up from under Andrews's uniform, spreading toward his hairline.

"Thomas. I think maybe you did babysit for us." His shoulders slumped.

"Sorry, that came out wrong. Listen, Officer Andrews, there's a dead woman inside." I swung my arm in the direction of the house. "I think that's more important than small-town gossip. And you can tell your mother I'm not going to join the family business *ever*."

"Why not? It would be so cool—" Seth began.

"Not now." I gave him my best glare, and for once it worked.

"Right, okay," said Officer Andrews as he made a note on his pad. "Are you a friend of the deceased?"

"Sort of. I'm the dog walker."

"The what?"

"The dog walker." I gestured to Tuffy.

"People pay you to walk their dogs? Here? In Crystal Haven?"

I just held his gaze. No one can do that for long; the eyes creep them out.

"Huh. Okay, show me." He sighed and pointed toward the house.

I didn't know if it was the puddle of vomit by the porch or the pool of blood in the kitchen, but Officer Andrews didn't have a strong stomach. Fortunately, he made it outside before contaminating the crime scene. He pulled himself together just as the ambulance arrived.

"I didn't expect . . . ," he said.

"I told them it was a murder scene on the phone."

"Dispatch just said a body was found. I thought, you know, a heart attack. I need to get the medical examiner out here, and the homicide detective." He began punching numbers into his phone.

"Okay, well, you know where to find me if you have any questions."

"Ms. Fortune, please don't tell anyone about . . ." He tilted his head toward the mess in the grass.

"It'll be our secret." I turned toward the car.

"Wait, I really don't think I can let you leave yet. The detective will want to talk to you and your nephew. He's a real stickler for details. I think you know him—Mac McKenzie?"

My head began to pound. I wasn't ready to face Mac. I had to get out of there.

I coughed to steady my voice. "I've been here for an hour already. I told you everything I know. I have a list of dogs waiting for me. My clients won't be happy if they come home to find out their animals haven't been taken care of and have been left to their own devices."

"But, I . . ." I could almost see the lightbulb over his head as he figured out what I meant.

"I'll give you the list of every place I'm going today. And you have my cell phone number. I can come right back as soon as everyone gets here or as soon as you need to talk to me."

"Well . . ." Tom watched the ambulance driver unload a gurney from the back of the truck.

"Seth, where's that list?"

"You have it," he said, as he and Tuffy wandered over to the cruiser.

"No, I don't. I told you to take it off the table." My hands found my hips of their own accord, and I realized I probably looked just like my mother.

"No you didn't."

"Yes, I—check your pockets." I crossed my arms to keep from frisking him.

"No, you . . ." He grimaced at Tom and began rummaging in his jeans pocket. "Oh, here it is." He handed a crumpled piece of paper to the officer.

Tom looked it over. "Archie, Molly, Roxie, MacDuff, Tuffy, Bonnie, Bear, Jewel, Crystal, and Hamlet." He stared at us. "What am I supposed to do with this?"

"What should we do with Tuffy?" Seth interrupted.

"I guess he'll have to go to the shelter," I said.

"The shelter! He can't go to the shelter." Seth bent to pick up the dog. "He just lost his person, look at him. He's devastated. How can you put him in a shelter?"

"Now *you* sound like Auntie Vi. He'll be fine. He'll have plenty of food, which is all he cares about anyway," I said.

"Clyde, we can't do that to him. You saw how traumatized he was. We have to take him with us. We're the only people he knows."

"He just met you and he doesn't like me."

"I'll take care of him. I'll do everything. We've already bonded. Look at him."

I had to admit. It was hard to resist two sets of soft brown imploring eyes. I sighed, knowing I would regret this.

"If Officer Andrews has no issue with it, I guess we can keep him until Sara's family is ready for him."

Seth and Tuffy hurried off to the Jeep before I could change my mind. I followed before Tom could make up his mind. He was distracted by the ambulance driver and the need to protect the crime scene.

I should have listened to that little voice that kept saying, "Shelter, shelter, shelter!"

3

Thanks to Seth, Baxter was out of the car again "because he was lonely and worried about us." After allowing Baxter and Tuffy to do the whole doggy ritual, which involved a lot of sniffing and walking in circles, we put Tuffy in the front and began to wrestle Baxter into the backseat. He stared at the house, carefully watching Officer Andrews and the paramedics. I made Seth pull from the front end this time, thinking I would avoid the drool. The dog made his front legs stiff and then turned and dripped on my arm, which he knew would make me jerk away. Fortunately, Seth was on it, and he pulled Baxter's face forward just as I let go. I gave Baxter a big shove from behind. The dog chose that moment to leap willingly into the Jeep, leaving me facedown in the dirt. Grateful that Officer Andrews was occupied with the ambulance driver and hadn't witnessed any of this, I glared at Baxter and slammed the door. He refused to acknowledge me.

Tuffy shivered on Seth's lap as we drove to my mother's house to drop off the two unexpected boarders. Baxter slimed both back windows until I cracked one open so he could hang his head out and inhale the passing scenery. Baxter recognized, as we turned onto my street, that we were almost there and began with tail wagging, low woofs, and running the length of the backseat to check both windows. He loved staying at my mom's.

I've been told by too many people to count that my family's house looks haunted. This statement is usually accompanied by a hopeful or terrified look, depending on the person, due to our reputation. A few blocks away from the downtown area of Crystal Haven, it's close enough for quite a bit of foot traffic but far enough away that it's definitely in the residential section. Surrounded by similar Victorian-style homes from early in the last century, ours stands out due to its size and general looming presence.

Painted gray and white—no bright, happy colors here— the Victorian has steeply pitched eaves and a large side porch that wraps around the back. The spires and vertical white accents on the front make it look even taller than its three stories. The large trees in the yard lend a shady gloom even on a sunny summer day.

I pulled into the long gravel driveway and thought yet again that if there were any dead to wake, the rocks pinging my undercarriage would do the trick.

We all piled out and headed for the porch. The front door swung open slowly as we approached. It creaks because Mom refuses to let anyone oil it. She thinks it adds ambience. Then, the door flew open to reveal my aunt. A deep purple shawl was thrown over her shoulders, even though it was mid-July. Vi is always cold and has a vast collection of colorful shawls to combat the "chill." Her twisted braid of white hair trailed down her back, her black eyes glittered.

"I knew it! I knew you'd be home for lunch," said Vi as she stepped forward. "I was just telling Rose to get some sandwiches ready, 'cause the kids are on their way."

I wondered how much the gravel driveway helped my aunt's intuition.

"We had a small mishap and need to drop off a couple of boarders," I said as Baxter trotted ahead of me and Seth followed behind with the shivering fur ball in his arms.

"Hello, Baxter. It's nice to see you again. I hope you enjoy your stay." Aunt Vi directed her comments to the dog. I waited for her to ask about his luggage.

Baxter sat and allowed himself to be petted and hugged by my aunt.

"Who do you have there?" my mother said as she bustled in from the kitchen, wiping her hands on her apron. She looked calmer than she had that morning. I assumed there had been no more bat sightings.

"This is Tuffy, he needs to stay with us for a couple of days, Nana Rose," Seth said as he sat in the middle of the entryway and cuddled Tuffy on his lap.

"He's not well. I can feel it," said Vi. "You smell awful, Seth." She was on all fours in front of Tuffy, ducking her head in her "submissive stance." She claims it puts the animals at ease.

"Isn't that Sara Landess's dog?" My mother looked to me.

I set my messenger bag by the front door.

"Mom, come sit down."

"What happened? I just knew that something happened,"

said Vi, slowly coming out of her crouch and leaning heavily on Seth's head as she stood.

"Seth, go get cleaned up while I talk to Aunt Vi and Nana Rose."

Seth nodded and carried Tuffy to the stairs, while Baxter followed like a large shadow.

I led the sisters into the living room. One of them had tidied after the bat incident. My mother and aunt sat on the couch; I chose the chair closest to my mother. It isn't a very restful room, dominated by competing patterns and colors, fringe and trinkets in an excess of Victorian style.

"So, what is it?" Vi demanded.

I looked at her and hoped she could hear my loud thoughts of *calm down* and *back off*. She didn't seem to be picking up on anything, so I turned to my mother.

"Mom, I'm sorry, but Sara's dead."

Her hand flew to her chest and gripped the amethyst and quartz amulet she wore around her neck.

"What? She was so young! What happened?" she said. Her eyes welled with tears.

"It looks like someone killed her," I said. I leaned forward to hug my mother, but she held up her hand, stopping me.

"How is that possible?" My mother twisted her apron in her lap. "She was the nicest person. Who would want to kill her?" The tears spilled over.

"We have to do something. We can't let them get away with this," Vi said, and patted my mother's shoulder. "Whoever did it has to pay!" She waggled her finger at me as if I were the culprit.

"The police were there when I left. They'll figure this

out." I stood up and paced in front of the coffee table, unable to sit still.

"Which police?" Vi asked, in a way that made me feel sorry for Tom.

"Officer Andrews took the call, and he was waiting for the medical examiner when I left."

"Tommy Andrews! He can barely write a parking ticket," she said, and turned to my mother. "No offense, Rose. I know you and Jillian go way back, but he's just a boy."

"They'll send a detective from the sheriff's office for this. They aren't a bunch of idiots," I said.

"Mac? He'll be looking into a murder in Crystal Haven?" Vi said. She pursed her lips and caught my mother's eye before looking away.

"Yes, Mac. I'm sure he'll do a good job. He had a great reputation when he was in Saginaw."

"Why did he come back here, anyway?" Aunt Vi asked me with one eyebrow raised.

"Mac and I aren't in the habit of sipping coffee and sharing our life plans. I assume he wanted to get out of the city. . . ." I'd wondered the same thing myself but didn't want to give my aunt any further reason to explore this line of questioning.

My mother was staring into space and mangling her apron. I sat again and put a hand on hers.

"Mom, I'm really sorry. I know she was special to you."

"Special" didn't quite cover it. Sara had been the star pupil in my mom's psychic classes. My mother had inherited some diluted abilities from my grandmother, and she generally stuck to tarot cards. I had inherited a bit more. What Mom lacked in personal ability she made up for by recognizing and developing talent in others. My entire childhood was testimony to her passion for discovering and developing "talent." It was also a lesson in how to spin even the smallest amount of intuition into a reputation as a fortune-teller. I wouldn't say my mother and aunt were frauds, but that was because they were family.

"Well, we have an eyewitness sitting upstairs with Seth. I'm going to see what he can tell us." Vi bustled off to accost Tuffy.

Vi's pet psychic abilities put her somewhere between a mind reader and an animal trainer. She has a huge following of people who bring their animals to her from all over the United States. I personally think her success has more to do with the treat bag she carries than with any sort of animal communication, but I'm the skeptic in the family. It's something we don't like to talk about at holiday meals.

"Vi has the right idea. We have to do something." My mother stood and wiped her eyes. She gestured for me to follow.

"Seriously, Mom? It's not going to help. You know I don't like . . ."

"She was my friend, and I need to do what I can to help her, Clytemnestra." My mother had transformed from fragile to steely, as usual. She only uses my full name in emergency situations. My grandmother Agnes had named her two daughters after her favorite flowers, roses and violets. My mother decided it would be clever to name her two daughters after her favorite roses. She loved orange roses, especially the Clytemnestra rose. My father must have intervened on behalf of my sister, and she was given the more normal name Grace. I can only assume that nine years later he was distracted when it came to naming me. In a town with its fair share of oddballs, my parents managed to guarantee I would be singled out as the oddest of them all.

"Just do this for me. It's not like I ask for much," she said as she led the way into her parlor. That could be debated, but now was not the time.

The parlor was like the living room only worse. It looked as if a demented decorator had spun in the middle of the room spewing Victorian-era knickknacks everywhere. The main color was lime green with deep red as a close runner-up. A small floral print covered the walls accompanied by a wide ceiling border of a larger floral pattern. A red and green striped couch shared the small space with red upholstered chairs sporting crocheted antimacassars across the headrests. The coffee table had a green-print fringed tablecloth, and the chairs, not to be outdone, had fringed throw pillows on them. This was my mother's office.

We sat at a small table flanked by two chairs. Mom pulled a deck of cards from a drawer on her side, removed them from a silk scarf, and placed them between us on the table.

"Shuffle and cut."

I shuffled. She had chosen her oldest set, a Rider deck from before I was born. The cards were worn and soft; they felt more like stiff fabric than tarot cards. I cut the deck into three piles using my left hand, placing each pile to the left as I had done so many times before.

She closed her eyes and placed her hands over each pile, "sensing" which one to use. I looked at the ceiling.

"I saw you roll your eyes at me."

"I was just looking at the spot where the wallpaper is peeling there. Maybe we can get Seth to climb up and fix it."

She glared at me the way only my mother can.

"Okay. Queen of Swords," she said. She placed a card in the center of the table. A woman was seated facing the right side of the card and holding a sword straight up. There were low clouds with blue sky in the background. My mother picked the "querent" card based on the person's coloring. I have dark brown hair, which is Swords. Sara was blonde, so she was Wands.

"But that's me." I pointed to the card. "I thought you were going to do Sara. She should be Wands."

"I can't do Sara. She's dead. I have to do your reading and see how you can affect this situation." Mom put her hand over the card to keep me from moving it.

"Okay, fine. But just this, Mom." I sat back, crossing my arms. "I don't want to hear about tall, dark strangers coming into my life."

"Always with the jokes. Fortunately, the cards don't care if you believe or not."

She laid out the cards in her standard pattern. She sat back, thinking. I leaned forward, not liking what I saw. For one thing, the Two of Swords was over the center card. It showed a blindfolded woman holding two crossed swords, which indicated a person closed off from others or someone who is refusing to become involved with others. My mother was sure to jump on that interpretation.

"Well," she began, "the Ten of Cups reversed indicates you have talents and gifts that you don't appreciate." The Ten of Cups shows goblets in a rainbow arrangement, which would be a happy card if it wasn't upside down, or reversed. She sighed and shook her head. "The Two of Swords shows you are purposely cutting yourself off from those gifts."

"Or it could mean I'm in a difficult domestic situation

and I have to protect myself from the interference of others," I said.

She looked up sharply. "When did you start reading tarot?"

"I think you did my first reading when I was about seven, Mom. I needed to know something to protect myself." Mom had been reading cards so long, that often her interpretations couldn't be found in any book, but I had learned enough to give myself some ammunition. I should have known better than to let a relative with a blazing agenda read my cards, but I'd been doing it all my life.

"Let's move on to the question of Sara," she said. "The Page of Cups represents Sara, she was developing psychic talents." She took a moment for a meaningful glance in my direction.

I was focused on the Death card in the "outcome" position. A skeleton in black armor rode a white horse through a devastated landscape. It didn't indicate Sara's death; this was another death or change to come. There were also Judgment and the Moon; the cards indicated I was fighting my psychic abilities to my own detriment. I was beginning to think Mom had stacked the deck. Good thing The Tower—people leaping out of a burning building—was absent or I would have locked myself in my room until the whole thing was resolved.

"Okay, that's enough. I really don't need to hear any more about my place in the universe according to the cards. I've always done the wrong thing in relation to the tarot."

She held up her hand.

"Wait, it shows the King of Wands in the near future. Honest, optimistic, a stern and strong-minded leader. You're going to have to deal with him."

"Why don't you finish up later, okay? Let's go check on Tuffy." I couldn't get away from the cards fast enough. The rest of them did not tell a tale I wanted to hear—fighting your inner self, psychic talents, all leading to death. It was always the same gloom and doom. The only good card was the Three of Cups—three people dancing and holding goblets overhead. At least I would have friends.

"You know, we wouldn't have to resort to tarot if you'd allow your own natural abilities to come forward, Clyde."

"Not again, Mom." I sighed.

"I just don't understand why someone with a gift like yours would choose to ignore it." She gestured at the cards.

"We've really done this enough, don't you think? It doesn't seem like much of a gift when all you see is death and destruction. I'm happier not knowing what will happen."

"That was a long time ago. You can learn to control it."

"Let's go check on Seth and Vi." I pushed away from the table.

We found them in Violet's apartment, a three-room annex off the main level of my parents' living area. The house had originally belonged to my grandmother and when she died, she left it to her daughters. Thanks to Grace, my parents had lost their house when the market crashed in 1987. Grace had one "talent" and that was the ability to predict the stock market. She claimed she saw letters and numbers in an almost constant stream and once she realized what they meant she began investing. In a snit over some fight with Mom, Grace chose not to warn my parents to dump their stock and they ended up losing everything, including their house. Aunt Vi was living with my grandmother at the time, and they had plenty of room. When Mom, Dad, Grace, and I moved in, we got the larger half and the upper floors. Everyone shared the kitchen.

In the end, I was glad we lost the house. Spending much of my adolescence living with my grandmother had been wonderful. She'd had a calm, serene presence that she hadn't passed on to her daughters. Unfortunately, she also had psychic talent that she passed on to me. She understood, better than anyone in my family, why I would want to block the messages coming to me.

Violet had not continued the Victorian theme in her area of the house. Claiming that her clients didn't need all that "claptrap," she decorated in a more modern, but just as colorful, fashion. Tuffy was sitting on one of the many client beds Vi kept scattered around her living room. Seth was sitting next to him and petting him gently.

Vi was rocking in her chair, knitting, when we came in. Baxter lay like a large lumpy carpet at her feet.

"Any luck?" my mother asked.

"No, he's too upset. All I could get out of him was 'bacon,'" Vi said.

"Maybe he's hungry," I said. Tuffy was always hungry, in my experience.

I received a triple glare from Violet, Seth, and my mother. Baxter didn't move.

"He's traumatized, Clyde. Give the guy a break." Seth leaned protectively over Tuffy.

"I just knew something was going to happen. The horses over at Miller's place have been agitated." Vi rocked faster and her fingers flew with the needles. "I was over there a couple of days ago, but they wouldn't tell me what was bothering them. My cat clients have completely clammed up. They're usually such a gossipy bunch. I should have seen something like this coming."

Seth's eyes grew wide; my mother just nodded. I looked at the ceiling.

"Seth, I need to finish with the rest of the dogs. Do you want to come with me or stay with Tuffy?"

"I think I'll stay with Tuffy." He curled himself around the dog, and I saw that he probably was just as upset as his new canine friend.

"Okay, I'll see you later." I turned to leave.

"What about lunch? I have sandwiches and brownies." Mom gestured toward the kitchen.

"I'm not that hungry, Mom. And I have to get to the rest of the dogs."

"Don't be ridiculous. You have to eat. The dogs can wait a few minutes. Seth, let's go." She walked toward the dining room, assuming we would follow.

We sat at the table—all of us. Seth pulled up a chair for Tuffy to sit in, and he began feeding the dog small pieces of lunch meat from his sandwich. Baxter didn't need a chair. He rested his head on the table and with his eyes watched each bite I took like he was following a tennis match. A wet puddle formed under his chin. My mother didn't eat, claiming she was too upset. I had taken about three bites when I heard my cell phone ringing in the front hall.

I found my messenger bag in disarray and covered in Baxter slime. I'd forgotten about the treats I'd left in there. Apparently he'd found them. By the time I'd waded through my wet bag, my phone had stopped ringing. I was muttering

Baxter's name just as I heard a chair topple and my mother shout, "Baxter!"

I ran into the dining room to see Baxter finishing off my sandwich. He caught sight of me and slunk over to hide behind Vi.

"He's sorry, Clyde. The sandwich just looked really good," Vi said, putting a protective hand on his head.

I scowled at them and hit the voice mail button on my phone.

"It's Mac. Call me."

I took a steadying breath and stood straighter. I hit call-back, and I could tell my blood pressure was rising by the pounding in my head. *Here we go.*

"Clyde, I need you over here now," Mac said, in greeting.

"Hi, Mac. It's been a long time. . . ." I tried for a light and carefree tone, but it didn't work.

"Save it, Clyde. You're lucky you're not under arrest for leaving the scene of a crime."

"Right. See you in ten minutes." I clicked the phone shut and took a deep breath. This was going to be worse than I thought, plus I'd have to skip the brownie.

4

The boats bobbed and clanged in the small marina as I drove along River Street. Turning onto Main Street, I was greeted by downtown Crystal Haven. All the storefronts were freshly painted in bright colors for the summer tourist season. Many stores had hanging signs along the street to entice wandering shoppers. Even without the spiritualist draw, it would be a tourist town. It's situated on the west coast of Michigan, south of Grand Rapids. This makes it close enough to Chicago for weekend travelers and not so far "up north" that it discourages day-trippers. About a mile inland from Lake Michigan, Crystal Haven is fed by a river that forms a small lake, which serves as a protected marina for boats traveling on the Great Lake. We have the usual Lake Michigan attractions: beaches, boating, fishing, and hiking. We also have the largest community of psychics outside of Lily Dale, New York. The early founders of the town settled in the late 1800s, when a large deposit of quartz was discovered and a small group of spiritualists flocked to the area, feeling the crystals would be attractive to the spirits.

While Lily Dale has remained a spiritualist retreat, Crystal Haven has branched out over the years to offer all manner of new age and spa-treatment services. My grandmother had moved here in the 1930s with her parents, who'd seen the promise of money through her "gifts." She had predicted the stock market crash, and her parents had managed to save most of their nest egg. By the time World War II broke out, she had become famous for her psychic readings and prophecies. WWII opened up a whole new set of clients who might have shied away from spiritualism in their pre-war lives. A steady stream of desperate parents and wives arrived in Crystal Haven to find out if their soldiers were alive and well. Eventually, the focus shifted, and Crystal Haven's residents realized they would need to branch out if they wanted to remain on the tourist map. The old guard was disappointed by this turn of events and routinely tried to block new businesses coming in that were not purely spiritualist in nature. However, there were enough young and savvy psychics on the town council to allow these "fringe" businesses to set up shop among the more serious spiritualist pursuits.

The split between old and new could only be detected by those living in Crystal Haven. Those listening to the vicious gossip. Aunt Vi's cat clients were particularly brutal, if she was to be believed. For the average visitor, Crystal Haven was a one-stop shop for crystals, talismans, readings, séances, massages, hypnosis, acupuncture, herbal medicine, and outdoor sports. We even have a golf course.

The small police station is sandwiched between a shop

selling crystals and palm readings, and a bookstore special-
izing in spiritualist titles. Its sign is small and hardly notice-
able among the larger and flashier store signs. Tourist towns
don't like to call attention to the need for law enforcement.

I parked and went inside, mentally preparing to see Mac
again.

Even the police station entrance is cheerful; it's painted
sunny yellow and features paintings of boats and beaches.
Occasionally, it's confused with a travel agency. I was surprised to see Lisa Harkness behind the reception desk. She'd
been a year ahead of me in school, and I'd always thought she
would get out of Crystal Haven the moment she got her
diploma. She used to say that real life was happening elsewhere. Still wearing the big, frizzy hairstyle from high school
and frosted eye shadow, she greeted me with a smile. She was
sporting a wedding ring and had a picture of two kids on her
desk. So that's why she'd stayed.

"Hi, Clyde. I heard you were back in town." She made a
few clicks with her mouse and spun her chair to look at me.
"Is it a nice change from the city?"

"It's good to be home for a while," I said. "Mac called
and wanted me to come right over."

"Oh, I know. He's been pacing around like a caged animal
ever since they got back from Sara's place. What a horrible
shame." She shook her head.

I cleared my throat and she glanced at me again.

"I'll tell Mac you're here."

When she hung up the phone, she told me to go back to
the visitor's office. The small Crystal Haven Police Department didn't have the expertise or manpower to run a homicide

investigation. Whenever something big came up, they sent a detective from the sheriff's office, which is about twenty-five minutes away. Fortunately, that hadn't been necessary for many years. Several doors sat closed on the left side of the hallway. The right side opened up into a large workroom where four officers had desks. I glanced in but it was empty. Lisa had said Mac was in the last office on the left.

The door was slightly ajar. I peeked around the corner to get a glimpse of Mac before he spotted me. I saw a gray metal desk with matching file cabinet, and a dead ficus tree, which must have belonged to the office's previous owner. It had been years since I'd seen Mac. He was four years older than me, so we were never in school together. He'd had Tom Andrews's current job for most of the time I was in high school. We both left town eight years ago, and I hadn't seen him since. He looked almost the same: short blond hair, with maybe a few more wrinkles around the eyes. He'd always been muscular, but now he'd become solid, mature, and more imposing. I wondered if he had forgiven me yet.

"Clyde, don't lurk. Come and sit." He hadn't looked up, and I jumped at the sound of his voice.

"Hi, Mac." I sat in the chair in front of his desk and rubbed my palms on my jeans. I felt like I was visiting the principal.

"Clyde. How have you been?" He tapped a stack of papers into alignment on his desk.

"Um, good. Thanks. You?" I wasn't sure what to do with my hands, so I held them tightly in my lap.

"Just great." He sat back and smiled, but it wasn't his nice smile. His gray-blue eyes were just as intense as I remembered. "Until someone gets murdered and one of my witnesses, who happens to be a trained police officer, strolls off the premises with trace evidence, leaving nothing more than a slip of paper with some dog names on it."

"I didn't touch that scene." Five seconds in the same room and we were already fighting. "And I'm not a witness to anything. We got there *after* she was dead."

"The dog, Clyde," he said, rubbing between his eyes.

"You think the dog is a witness?" I thought maybe Vi had been working on him without telling me. His steely gaze told me I was wrong.

"The dog was all over the house," he said slowly, as if instructing a new recruit. "Who knows what trace evidence it may have been carrying before you allowed it to become contaminated?"

"Oh." I glanced down to see what my hands were doing. "I don't think he would have been very helpful. We found him shivering under the table. He's not very brave. I doubt he went near the body or the murderer."

"Just have a feeling about that, do you? Or did it come to you in a dream?" Mac leaned forward.

He might as well have hit me. I sat back and took a deep breath. So. He hadn't forgiven, or forgotten.

"I don't have to take this, Mac. I came here to help." I started to stand but then thought better of it. "You know as well as I do that anything you pull off a dog is going to be contaminated anyway."

Mac pressed his lips into a thin line.

"I would have thought you'd have gotten over it by now," I said, and held his gaze.

He stared hard at me and then seemed to pull himself together. He took a deep breath, and I could see the tension release from his face.

"You're right, Clyde. Let's start over."

"Fine." I crossed my arms and held his gaze until he looked away.

"I need an official statement from you about this morning." He shuffled through the files on his desk. "Everything you did leading up to and including finding the body."

"Officer Andrews already has a statement."

"I need another one. I thought you wanted to help." He glanced up from his papers. "I also need to interview the boy. Is he old enough to give me anything useful?"

"He's thirteen."

"Grace's kid is thirteen?" He sat back, eyebrows up.

"She got pregnant right after she got married." I became very interested in a hangnail.

"Still, I didn't expect him to be that old. . . ." Mac rubbed between his eyes again.

"Mac, I'm really sorry about everything. . . ." I reached out and touched the edge of his desk.

"Ancient history, Clyde." He sliced across the air with his hand as if that settled it. "I need your help on this case. Let's not complicate things by dredging up the past. It's done."

"Okay." I pulled my hands back to the safety of my lap.

I told him everything Seth and I had done that morning, only leaving out the embarrassing part about wrestling Baxter into the car twice. I also decided not to mention Tuffy's testimony involving bacon. Mac liked the facts and wanted nothing to do with any intuition, or messages from other places.

I left out the part about the tarot as well; he already seemed tense enough.

"So, you're working as a dog walker?" It was the first time he had really smiled since I walked in. In this context, it was irritating.

I just looked at him, trying for the flat eyes Seth used so effectively.

"I heard about what happened in Ann Arbor," he said, rearranging the files on his desk. "You're a great officer. You can't let one . . ."

"Thanks for the concern, Mac." I gave him a look that said he had gone far enough. "By the way, why are *you* back here?"

"Maybe we can have coffee sometime and I'll tell you all about it." He grinned, but it looked more like a grimace, and as he stood up I noticed the cane leaning behind the desk. He caught me staring at it, and the set of his jaw dared me to question him.

"Let me know if you need anything else" was all I said.

"I'll need to interview the boy."

"His name is Seth, and he's really been shaken by this. Try to be nice."

A brief wounded look crossed his face, followed by his stoic stare.

"I'll have Andrews deal with him. He's always nice." Mac showed me his teeth, and he reminded me of a shark.

I was about to respond when Tom himself came careening around the corner of the door from the front office.

"Sir! We found him!" He stopped abruptly when he saw me, and his face turned bright red. "Oh, hi. I didn't know you were here."

"What is it, Andrews?" Mac growled.

"It's about the case, sir." He cut his eyes to me and back to Mac, raising his eyebrows.

"You can tell me in front of Ms. Fortune. She's still technically a police officer, even if she chooses to walk dogs instead."

"Okay." He smiled at me. "Well, we tracked the ex-husband to Chicago; he flew out of Grand Rapids this morning. We just got confirmation that he was on the flight and it landed safely."

"Do you know where he is now?" Mac asked.

"Well, no." Tom slumped. "He's there on business, and his office said since he made his own arrangements they don't know where he's staying." He hung his head as if he was expecting to be yelled at. "We have a list of the places he usually stays, and Lisa is calling them now to see if we can track him down," he said to his shoes.

"Okay, good work. We'll need to question him as soon as we find him."

Tom's head snapped up and he stood straighter, looking relieved.

"Have you located the daughters yet?" I asked.

"Charla went out to talk to them. She hasn't checked in yet," Tom said.

Charla Roberts was the acting Chief of Police for the Crystal Haven police force. She'd refused to officially accept the position since she stepped in when her husband, Dean, had died. She'd helped me figure out my own career path in late high school after a few minor run-ins with her in her official capacity. I adored her, but she wasn't very warm and fuzzy. I hoped she would handle Sara's daughters gently. For all the communicating with the dead that occurred here, Crystal Haven had minimal experience with murder.

5

I stepped onto the sidewalk outside the police station and into the familiar heat of July in Michigan and felt my shoulders relax. I had known coming back to Crystal Haven would be stressful, but I hadn't counted on Mac. The last time I'd heard anything he'd been working in Saginaw, on the opposite side of the state. Aunt Vi had informed me— *after* my bags were unpacked—that Mac had returned to the county sheriff's department as a detective. Because his mother still lives in Crystal Haven, I'd assumed we would run into each other eventually, but not like this. We had done an excellent job of avoiding each other when we lived a couple of hours apart in Saginaw and Ann Arbor. It would be much more difficult in a small town.

My stomach reminded me that Baxter had stolen my lunch. I turned left out of the station and headed to Stark's Bar and Grill. Alex Ferguson worked there and, provided he wasn't on one of his "improve the menu" tirades, I could get a good burger. Alex and I had been friends since the first day of high school. As I walked, I concentrated on the list of clients I needed to see that afternoon. I didn't want to think about Mac. Or about Sara. Or about my family. What I wanted was to whine to Alex about everything that had happened and have him pat me on the back and say "poor Clyde." Of course, there was zero chance of that happening.

I weaved my way through families pushing strollers, teens eating ice cream, and shoppers loaded down with bags of clothes and new-age trinkets. It was after one o'clock; the crowd was starting to clear outside the restaurant and the usual line out the door had disappeared. I stepped inside and squinted into the dim interior. The dark wood paneling, low lights, and dark green flooring made the restaurant feel cave-like. Alex claimed the owner, Joe Stark, kept it dark so no one would notice he hadn't updated the décor since the place had opened in the 1970s. A disturbing amount of olive-colored leather seating and mustard accents dominated the dining area. The place had been suffering a slow slide into oblivion with only a few loyal regulars keeping it afloat until Alex was hired on as the chef two years ago. It now had become a "must-visit" for the tourists.

I sat at my favorite table in the corner, facing the door. The server came to take my drink order. She was very thin and wore an oversize T-shirt and jeans. I asked her to put in my request for a burger and to let Alex know I was there if he had any time to spare.

She returned about five minutes later with a Diet Coke and something on a plate that did not resemble any sort of food I had ever seen. I sighed, and said, "New menu item?"

"No, Mr. Ferguson said he's trying it out. He wants to

see what you think." She lowered her voice to protect the other customers. "It's a tofu-eggplant stack."

My mouth went dry. I hate eggplant.

"Is he making a burger?"

"Um, I don't think so." She shrugged.

I poked at the layers of stiff white tofu and gooey eggplant. They were battered and fried. Even for Alex, I didn't think I could do it. I tried a small bite of tofu and didn't die.

I gestured to the waitress.

"Could you go put in an order for that burger and pretend it's for another table?"

Her eyes lit up as she saw the deviousness of my plan. They grew dim as she glanced at the mess on my plate.

"That should work. But he said he'd be out in a few minutes to get your opinion." Her furrowed brow said she had no faith in my ability to pull this off.

"It's okay. I can handle him." I smiled in my most winning way and even cut a slice of the stack to show her I was a good sport.

I quickly cut the food into smaller pieces and pushed them all around my plate. I put a few in a napkin and stuffed them into my bag just as Alex came out from behind the swinging door that led to the kitchen. He was slightly taller than me, with broad shoulders from kayaking on Lake Michigan. A few dark curls had escaped the gel he used and fell onto his forehead. He had the bluest eyes I had ever seen. He wiped his hands on his apron and scanned the room.

I gave a small wave. I pointed to my mouth and pretended to be chewing.

"Hi, what do you think?" he said as he pulled up a chair and assessed the plate in front of me.

I faked a swallow and took a sip of soda. "It's like nothing I've ever had before."

"I know. I really wanted to stretch the limits."

"You've done that. But do you think you might have stretched a little too far?"

"I know, I know. Stark thinks it's 'cuisine' if we wrap the steaks in bacon, or add bacon to a salad. Once I told him we could wrap water chestnuts in bacon, but that was too 'fancy.'" He waved his fingers to demonstrate "fancy." "I don't know how much more of this I can take." He pushed his hair back with both hands and then pulled it all forward again. No wonder the gel wasn't working.

"The place is doing great, Alex. That's all because of you. Stark will come around."

"Speaking of bacon, this morning he didn't even show up for the prep work." He took my fork and ate a piece of the eggplant without choking. "I had to do it all when I came in at ten, plus all my regular stuff, and the line starts forming at eleven thirty. I guess I'm lucky that all they want is burgers and sandwiches."

I stared for a moment in fascination as he ate some more of my food.

"Listen, have you heard about Sara Landess?"

"Did she and Tish have another shouting match? Or was it her and Gary?" He slurped some of my Diet Coke.

"She's dead, Alex."

He choked on the soda and spit most of it back into the glass. He took the drink napkin to mop his face and slid the glass toward me.

"What? What happened? A car accident?"

"No, she was murdered." I wrinkled my nose and pushed

the drink away. "Seth and I found her body when we went to take care of Tuffy this morning."

"Oh no. I'm so sorry. Are you okay? Is he okay? He's just a kid. Did he see much of it?"

"He saw enough." I nodded. "Tuffy's at my house now giving testimony to Aunt Vi," I said. Alex snorted and continued to mop up the soda.

"We have Baxter staying with us because Tish decided to go out of town this morning. Why did you think Tish and Sara had been fighting?"

"Oh, I don't think it's anything." He waved away the question. "Tish and Sara haven't gotten along since Tish tried to blackball her certificate last year."

All psychics working in Crystal Haven have to be licensed by the city council to practice within the city limits. I knew it could ruin their chances of starting a business if it didn't go through.

"I didn't know about that."

"It all blew over, and Sara got her certificate. Sara was really good. Tish was jealous." He shrugged. "She was just causing trouble."

"I wonder if Mac knows," I said, pushing the food around on the plate, hoping Alex hadn't noticed I wasn't actually eating it.

"What does Mac have to do with this?" He sat back, watching me carefully. Alex had been my biggest support when Mac had ended our relationship by moving to the other side of the state. He knew, better than anyone, how hard it would be for me to see Mac again.

"He's the detective in charge." I took a very small piece of tofu and ate it. This was torture on a mostly empty stomach, and Alex had ruined my drink. "He's with the sheriff's office as their homicide detective."

"Oh, right. I heard about that. Well, it's a good thing you're not on the Crystal Haven force, or you'd have to deal with him."

"Trouble is, because I'm a witness, I *do* have to deal with him."

The waitress approached with a Styrofoam container. I tried to gesture with my eyebrows to abort the mission, but she just kept coming. Alex noticed what she didn't and turned around.

"What's this?" he said.

"Just a take-out burger. For Seth," I said.

His expression told me he wasn't buying it.

"I guess you better hurry before it gets cold." He stood and walked to the kitchen without saying good-bye.

"You know I hate eggplant." My voice sounded whiny even to me.

Leaving Stark's place in the middle of the day was disorienting. The bright sun blinded me as I stepped out of the dark restaurant. I turned in the direction of my Jeep just as Officer Andrews rushed toward me out of a crowd of afternoon tourists and almost knocked the precious Styrofoam cargo out of my hand. We fumbled for a moment before I managed to get both hands on it and save my lunch from going *splat* on the sidewalk.

"Clyde, I'm sorry, I've been looking everywhere for you. I saw your car parked up the street and I've been in every store." He stopped to take a breath.

"What's wrong, Tom?"

He held up one finger while gulping air. I noticed we were attracting an audience.

"Everything's fine. I just really wanted to catch you before you went home." He glanced up the street toward the police station. "We can't talk here. Will you meet me at my mom's house in five minutes?"

I raised an eyebrow at him. "What's this about?"

"Not here. Five minutes, please?" At my nod he darted off up the street.

I didn't remember him being so skittish. Of course, the last time I'd seen him he was shooting cap guns and I was counting the minutes until I could take my money and run.

I drove to Jillian's house, which was located a few blocks away from the commercial section of town. I wolfed down half the burger before I got out of the car. The house looked smaller from the front than it actually was. With all those children, the Andrews family had needed space. Jillian also ran her business out of the house. She was a spiritual healer, and much of her work involved client consultations. A sign in the front window read: PSYCHIC HEALER, HERBS, AMULETS, CRYSTALS.

Tom opened the door before my finger was done pressing the doorbell.

"Hi, thanks for coming." He pulled the door wide and swept his arm toward the back of the house.

I had never been in this house without wishing for heavy-duty earplugs. When the Andrews gang was growing up, the noise level had always been just short of deafening.

"I've never been in your house when it was this quiet." I had fallen unintentionally into a whisper.

"Or this clean," Tom said.

He was right. The front room used to contain all manner of plastic dolls, toys, and ride-on vehicles. The sheer volume of clutter seemed to add to the noise. In the absence of children, Jillian had turned it into a serene sitting room with off-white furniture and neutral accents.

"Do you still live here?" I asked as I followed him down the hall to what I thought would be the kitchen.

He shook his head. "No, I have my own place a few blocks over. This was closer, and my mom had to run some errands. She left me in charge of her kitchen."

He pushed the door at the end of the hallway and we entered what looked like a witch's workroom. The walls were dark wood with exposed beams overhead that were cluttered with hanging herbs and grasses. Several blackened pots sat on an ancient stove. One bubbled madly and spit liquid onto the fire below. Tom moved quickly past shelves of glass vials and bottles, most of which contained powders and liquids that Jillian used in her healing work, and turned down the heat. Some people were just not satisfied with healing energies and crystals, and Jillian had always been known as someone who could mix up a few drops of something to cure just about any illness or distress. Just as he stopped the pan from boiling over, a teakettle began a steady scream.

Tom removed the kettle from the burner. The shriek died away. He began making tea as if we met every day in his mother's workshop.

"Sit, relax," he said.

I sat. I did not relax.

"What's up, Tom?" I said as he placed a heavy brown mug in front of me. It smelled of vanilla and damp leaves.

Rooibos. Jillian's favorite and something I had been subjected to since childhood.

He sat across from me with his own steaming beverage. He clasped the mug in both hands and inhaled the steam.

"Since I joined the force I've heard great things about your work in Ann Arbor," he said. "Your mother can't say enough about what a great job you did there. According to her, you're good at sensing where to find evidence, questioning witnesses, and figuring out how crimes were committed. She says you had an incredible record while you were with the police."

The room was hushed; even the bubbling pot seemed quieter. I didn't know what to say. I had no idea my mother paid any attention to my police work. Most of my conversations with her circled the question of why I wouldn't allow my "talents" to develop.

"She really said all that?"

Tom nodded. "I was hoping you would help me on this case. I've never worked on a murder before, and Detective McKenzie doesn't tolerate mistakes."

"What's with the cane?" I asked as I stirred my drink.

Tom shrugged and shook his head. "He doesn't talk about it. I heard he was shot during a drug bust. He transferred back here when the job opened up in the sherriff's office. Lisa told me the receptionist over there claims the cane is only temporary. All I know is he gets pretty grumpy if he thinks you're looking at it."

"Yeah, I noticed," I said.

Tom looked at me expectantly, waiting for an answer.

"I'll do what I can to help you, but I already told you everything I know."

"No, I mean, I want you to work the case with me," he said to his tea.

"I'm on leave, Tom. I can't do any official police work. . . ."

"I don't need official help. Mac already thinks I'm an idiot. I can't do anything right when he's around." His shoulders slumped. "I just need some extra insight."

"You want to consult with me on the case?"

"Yeah, consult. That would be great!" His eyes lit up as they met mine.

"Well, I suppose I could."

"Thank you!" He jumped up and stirred the pot boiling on the stove. It released an odor similar to cauliflower and dirty socks.

I buried my nose in the tea mug, wet leaves being preferable to whatever he was cooking. When I came up for air, I said, "You'll have to tell me what evidence you have so far and what new leads come up. You know if Mac finds out he'll kill us both."

"Right. We have to keep this between us." Tom sat down again and pulled out a little notebook. "What kind of evidence do you need? Something from the house? Clothing she was wearing?"

"I need whatever evidence you're using to solve the case."

"All of it? I don't think I can sneak it all out." He chewed on the end of his pencil. "Maybe I can get you in after hours. . . . Do you have to keep the items or just touch them?"

"What are you talking about?" I said a bit too loudly.

Tom looked up from his notebook.

"I don't want the items at all. I just want to know what they are so I have all the information," I said.

He watched me for a moment, and then a slow pink tide swept up from his neck to cover his face.

"Wait a minute. What kind of help do you want?" I didn't think it was common knowledge that I could "read" items—and sometimes even people—through touch. I had convinced my mother that I didn't have that ability, but she must have said something to Jillian.

"Just do what you did in Ann Arbor. To solve the case." Tom gave a palms-up gesture and knocked over his tea. Fortunately, it was mostly empty, but he made a big fuss over cleaning it up.

When he was done and I had him looking at me again, I raised an eyebrow, and said, "I used my brain and deductive reasoning, nothing more."

"You didn't use any other *skills*?" Tom asked, his voice rising to an unnatural pitch.

"No. I told you I don't do that anymore." I felt my jaw clench and reminded myself that I wasn't actually mad at him. It was my family that wouldn't let this go.

He put his head in his hands, elbows on the table.

"I'm sorry." He picked his head up and met my eyes. "We—my mother and I—thought you must have been using your other talents. That's certainly the impression your mother gave us."

This made more sense. Rose wasn't bragging about her daughter the police officer. She was bragging that her daughter the freaky psychic was passing herself off as a police officer. I was only annoyed with myself for feeling kindly toward my mother. I should have known that her single-minded obsession would not have been supplanted by a mere law enforcement career. She probably believed I was using psychic abilities to solve crimes. Little did she know it was the one time I listened to my "talent" that had landed me in my current mess.

"Tom, I'd be glad to help you if you still want my help, but only as a fellow police officer. I can help you sort through the evidence and maybe point you in other directions with the case, but I don't do psychic consultations."

He nodded glumly.

"I expected as much. Who would voluntarily take care of Baxter if they could do readings all day instead?" he said.

6

I glanced at my watch and groaned. I was late for
my afternoon clients—not that the dogs could tell time. But
I wanted to hear what Tom knew about the case. We finished
Jillian's potion cooking, and I convinced him to come with
me on dog rounds. Since my next client, Bonnie, lived only
a block away, I left my car at the curb in front of Jillian's
house.

Tom loped along next to me, stumbling on the occasional
ant or leaf in our path. He seemed to have trouble adjusting
his long-limbed gait to mine and kept speeding up and slowing down. His hands tried to keep up with his words as he
gushed about police work.

When we reached the top of a steeply slanted street, Tom
looked around. Probably checking for spies. We were almost
to Bonnie's house. The shady sidewalk was hushed and held
the lingering scent of lilacs. A group of kids played soccer

in the park one street over, but the area was otherwise deserted.

"Okay, what we know so far is that Sara was shot with a small-caliber handgun." Tom flipped a page in his notepad. "No one in the neighboring houses heard anything."

"Her house *is* pretty isolated," I said.

"There are no likely suspects, but we're looking at her ex-husband, Gary. They had a very messy divorce. Several witnesses have come forward claiming they were recently seen arguing."

"Are you sure he was even in town when this happened?" I asked.

"His flight left at ten a.m. from Grand Rapids. You discovered the body at eleven." He waved his hand in my direction and made a note in his book. "The ME is placing time of death at around eight a.m., give or take an hour."

"You'll have to see what kind of an alibi he has and what time he checked in for his flight," I said, slowing as we approached Bonnie's house.

"He checked in twenty minutes before his flight. They were about to give his seat to a standby passenger."

"You need to find out where he was before that." I pulled a ring of keys out of my bag, unlocked the door, and gestured at Tom to stand back. Bonnie was a standard poodle with an overexuberant greeting ritual.

A black blur rocketed toward me and, with a practiced side step, I grabbed her collar to avoid being knocked down. Unfortunately, Bonnie didn't stop as usual. She continued to run straight at Tom, dragging me along with her. When she hit him full force in the groin, he crumpled against the door-jamb and let out a high-pitched wheeze.

"Bonnie, off!" I said to the dog, who was now wiggling and licking Tom's hands and face.

"Yuck! Stop her!" Tom tried to stand, still protecting his injured area.

I pulled Bonnie to the hook where her leash was kept. She was so excited to have two visitors she could barely contain herself, nails tapping out a happy sound on the kitchen tile.

Tom, barely able to stand, held on to the doorjamb for support.

"Um, why don't you wait here and rest while I take her for her walk?"

He nodded and sank to the back-door steps. Bonnie took this as an invitation to begin the licking again.

I dragged her down the driveway to do her business.

We returned after Bonnie sniffed all of the usual spots and determined the neighborhood was safe from intruders. The poodle geared up for another encounter with Tom. Fortunately, he was standing and ready for her.

We locked her back in her house and continued up the street to Bear's house.

"What kind of dog is Bear?" Tom asked

"He's a mix of a bichon and a shih tzu. They call them teddy bears."

"Oh, that sounds cute. Are they big?" Tom limped and grimaced as we walked.

"About ten pounds." I slowed down a bit so he could keep up.

"Good."

At the back door, deep ferocious barking greeted us from inside.

"I thought you said he was little," Tom said. He hung back a good ten feet and held his open notebook just below his waist.

"He is. He just sounds big."

I opened the door to see Bear barking wildly; he finally calmed down enough to notice he recognized me. He wagged his tail and leapt straight into the air. Andrews approached to watch the antics.

"Hi there, Bear," he said. He bent forward to pet the dog. "Don't—"

But it was too late. Bear peed all over the mudroom floor. I quickly grabbed the dog to keep his feet from getting wet, snapped his leash on him, and handed it to Andrews.

"Submissive urination. He's letting you know you're the boss."

"Sorry."

"It's not your fault. Aunt Vi's been working with him for months. She's trying to get to the bottom of it but claims he's not much of a talker."

"He's one of your aunt's clients?"

Bear hopped on his hind legs to get closer to Tom.

"They all are. That's how I got this crazy job. I happen to be good with animals—most of them, anyway. She had a list of clients who needed extra attention during the day." I quickly stepped into the kitchen and rummaged in a cabinet for paper towels.

"And what's Bonnie's problem? Assault?"

"No, she keeps escaping from her yard and stealing things. She brings them home and hides them."

I cleaned up Bear's mess while Tom walked him, and they returned a few minutes later happily bonded.

"I think he likes you," I said to Tom.

"Well, *he*'s easier to like than that poodle." Tom grinned down at Bear, who seemed to smile back.

"Isn't this a sight? Crystal Haven's newest officer out walking froufrou dogs on the taxpayer's dollar," Mac said as he walked up the driveway, leaning lightly on his cane.

"Detective McKenzie. I was just . . . helping . . . the witness," Andrews said, and handed the leash to me.

He stood at attention, and I think he started a salute before he caught himself.

"They need you back at the station," Mac said. "I'll help the witness, if she *needs* help." Mac glanced from me to Bear and smiled at the dog.

"Yes, sir," Tom scuttled away in the direction of the police station.

I wished for a moment I could go with him. After the way things had gone that morning, being alone with Mac was not high on my list.

"Corrupting young minds now, Clyde?"

"Give me a break. I've known Tom forever," I said. I had put Bear back in the house and locked the door on his barking. "We were just catching up. You could be nicer to him."

"No one ever caught a murderer by being nice."

I scowled at him. "Well, I have work to do, and you've found your officer. I'll see you around," I said and started to walk away.

Mac followed at my heels. Even with that cane he could move pretty fast. He grabbed my hand to stop me. It brought back all the memories I thought I had buried. There was a time when I couldn't have imagined my life without Mac.

I still didn't understand what had happened between us, but I had thought I was over him. Maybe I was wrong.

"I was looking for you, Clyde," he said so softly that I turned to look at him.

"Why?" The word came out clipped, angry. I was furious with myself for letting Mac get to me, again.

"I need your help."

This was new. Mac never wanted help. I hoped he hadn't changed his feelings about psychic powers. I had had enough requests for psychic intervention already.

"I don't know how I can possibly help you," I said, but I was already imagining spending time with him, poring over the evidence, bouncing ideas around, figuring out how the clues fit into the puzzle, and, finally, identifying the guilty party.

"I need you to talk to your sister for me. I meant to ask you when you were at the station . . ."

My fantasy came to a sudden halt.

"What?" I felt a little dizzy. I would have grabbed him for support, but that would have made it worse.

"I thought you'd want to fill her in on how her son discovered a dead body." He looked away, unwilling to meet my eyes. "And then I need you to let me do my job."

In other words, stay out of it. He hadn't forgotten or forgiven me. My eyes burned, and I opened my mouth but no words came out

"Clyde, I'm sorry, I—"

"No problem," I interrupted, wanting to get away. "I'll take care of it, Mac." I turned and walked down the sidewalk and didn't wipe my eyes until I was sure he couldn't see me.

* * *

Gray-purple clouds that had threatened rain all afternoon finally made good on the promise. I'd driven across town to walk the last couple of dogs in a daze. The gathering storm matched my mood. I made it home just in time to avoid getting completely soaked. The delicious aroma of pot roast and carrots met me at the door—my mother was up to something.

I put my bag in the front closet and tucked my phone into my jeans pocket. Hoping to find dinner already in progress, I wandered toward the dining room. Seth sat alone at the table. The dogs were curled up together in the corner.

Asking about his day got me a summary of the dog testimony gleaned from many hours in Aunt Vi's company. Tuffy had not been forthcoming. He was sticking to his story about bacon. Baxter had reported that Tish had been "tense" recently. Although how he could tell the difference between tense Tish and normal Tish I had no idea. I wasn't buying any of it. My feelings about Aunt Vi and her occupation were well known in my family but, as long as I lived here with her, I had promised to behave and keep my opinions to myself.

Mom bustled in with dinner. My father followed with a bottle of wine, then came Vi carrying a stack of plates and a foul attitude.

Dad sported a swoop of white hair that rose straight up out of his head and gave him a perpetually surprised demeanor. I'm pretty sure that the shock of moving in with my aunt had never worn off. He is a dentist who still sees patients a few days a week and fills the rest of his time listening to his police scanner and forcing us to decipher 10-codes.

Tonight, he was fairly upbeat and sat next to me, humming to himself.

"You're in a good mood," I said, looking him over.

"We're having pot roast." He waggled his eyebrows at me.

"You don't really like pot roast," I said, and spooned carrots onto my plate.

"No, but you do, which means your mother has plans for you and not for me." He pointed to each of us and snapped his napkin open.

"Oh, Frank," my mother said. "That's ridiculous. Clyde had a terrible day. I thought she deserved a treat."

I knew then that I was in trouble.

As usual, the table grew quiet as everyone worked through the first serving. My mother turned on the dining room lights as the storm picked up. I sat between Seth and Dad. One was eating like he hadn't seen food in weeks; the other was pounding the wine and humming. It made for a distracting meal. Vi broke the silence. My father poured himself a generous second glass of pinot noir as she began her observations. Thunder rumbled in the distance.

"I've been working with Tuffy all day, and I can't get anything out of him." She leaned forward, glanced at Tuffy, and lowered her voice. "Shih tzu's are not known for their discerning minds. They bark at anything and have a generally overinflated opinion of their own power in the world."

My father muttered something to his wine that sounded like "It's not just the shih tzus. . . ."

Vi continued to educate us on the vagaries of shih tzus and their temperaments and finished by saying she was shocked she could get so little out of our particular house-guest. She glanced in his direction a few times, but he seemed to be ignoring us. Her conclusion was that he should be shouting his feats of daring and courage from the roof-tops but he wasn't, and she was getting nowhere.

Seth addressed himself to his dinner with the focus of a Zen master, and I kept checking to be sure he was breathing between bites. The storm outside was picking up steam, the thunder rumbling closer.

I interrupted Vi's monologue when she stopped to take a drink. "I heard today that Sara and Tish were having some trouble?" My mother glanced up quickly.

"Oh that was nothing," she said with a brisk flip of her hand, dismissing whatever I was about to say.

"I heard it was something," I said. "Tish tried to block her certificate. What's up with that?"

"What certificate?" Seth asked, coming up for air.

"The city council grants a certificate to newly trained mediums to allow them to practice within city limits," Vi told him.

She didn't tell him that without it the medium might as well pack up and move somewhere else. The law was passed decades ago and was still on the books, mostly because no one had had a reason to fight it. Whenever a new medium or psychic wanted to set up shop in Crystal Haven he or she had to interview with the city council and then pass a test that included giving readings to three council members. The certification process was not easy, but someone with Sara's talent should have had no trouble.

"Tish had a rough couple of years, and she and Sara just didn't see eye to eye on everything," said Mom. "Tish thought Sara was too showy, and Tish didn't care for the kinds of séances she was doing. But it was all within the regulations, and Tish had no recourse but to remove her concerns and allow the certificate to go through." She started to clear the table, a signal that she was done talking about this topic.

"What's the deal with Sara's divorce?" I asked, holding my plate as she tried to take it.

"What do you mean?" Vi glanced at my mother and then at me.

"I heard there was some trouble there, too. Sara told me she and Gary had a custody battle over the dog."

"His name is Tuffy," Seth said, and grabbed the meat platter from my mother. Tuffy's collar jingled as he lifted his head in response to Seth's voice.

"Tuffy. They fought over him, and they were seen fighting recently in town."

"Are you involved in the investigation?" My father had perked up a bit now that Vi was done talking. He swirled his wineglass and allowed my mother to take his plate.

"Only in the sense that I discovered the body and they've been asking me questions," I said, but I didn't meet his eye. My father could always tell when I was hiding something.

"When I heard on the scanner that you had found a 10-100, I thought maybe you could help them with the case, get back into the swing of things," he said, studying the tablecloth. We had been over this ground before. My family tiptoed around the question of why I was living with them again. They knew I had been involved in a shooting incident while on duty. But they also knew I was keeping something from them. My "administrative leave" excuse was wearing thin.

"I don't know that they want my help," I lied.

"What's a 10-100?" Seth said through a mouthful of potatoes.

"Dead body," Dad and I said together.

"I wish *we* could help somehow," my mother said.

"If only mother were still alive," Vi said with a heavy sigh.

My father rolled his eyes. Vi brought most crises back to wishing my grandmother were alive. Agnes Greer had left her mark on Crystal Haven and on her two daughters, who wanted nothing more than to continue her work. Aunt Vi had always been jealous that my mother had snagged a guy named Fortune. Not for any love of my father, just that his name was such good advertising. Her only compensation was that Greer carried its own weighty heritage in Crystal Haven. Greer's Woods, one of the largest public parks in the area, was named after my grandparents. Agnes's work as a psychic had brought fame to Crystal Haven and her donation of a large parcel of land meant that she had put Crystal Haven and the name "Greer" literally "on the map."

"I wish I could have met her," said Seth.

"Oh, she would have loved you, Seth," my mother said. Her eyes welled up.

"She could have helped with this situation," said Vi. "She could have contacted Sara for us and found out what happened. No problem." She snapped her fingers to demonstrate how quickly we would have had our answer. "Sometimes I sense her here with us." She looked up to the ceiling.

"Mother has never come back to us. We've tried so many times," Mom said, and wiped a tear from her cheek.

"Maybe *we c*ould get Sara to come," whispered Vi. "You could do it, Clyde, if you wanted to."

So this was the reason for the pot roast.

"I don't . . . ," I began.

The lights flickered as lightning flashed outside.

"Did you see that? It's a sign!" said Vi.

"A sign?" asked Seth.

"I think that was the storm," I said.

"Can't you feel it? Sara could be here right now, trying to tell us who killed her," said Vi.

"Cut it out, Vi. You'll scare the boy," said my father. He chugged the last of his wine, and glanced at the ceiling.

I couldn't help but look up, too. The room glowed with lightning. We all sat there for a moment, looking at the ceiling. I felt the hairs on the back of my neck stand on end. A loud crash of thunder shook the house. And then the lights went out.

7

"Wicked," said Seth.

"Oh, for Pete's sake, not again," said Dad. Despite his complaints, he loved it when the lights went out. He imagined himself as Mr. Fixit and had the whole electrical system in the house rigged with his own brand of circuit breakers. The fact that the house was almost one hundred years old and had switches that hadn't worked since his mother-in-law and her family moved in didn't bother him one bit. Between the wiring of the house and his police scanner, he was always off somewhere puttering, which conveniently kept him out of Vi's way. He jumped up and went to find one of the emergency flashlights he had stashed all over the house.

It was gloomy in the dining room with the storm outside and night approaching, but not completely dark.

Taking a stack of plates, I followed Vi to the kitchen and hoped that would be the end of the plea for spirit contact. But persistence ran in the family.

"Why won't you even try, Clyde?" Vi said as she took the plates from me and rinsed them.

"She's always been stubborn," said Mom, as if I wasn't standing right there.

"Well, she'll come around someday, Rose. Don't you worry." Vi patted my mother's hand with her own wet, soapy one.

I opened my mouth to reply, but they weren't done.

"I don't think she will. Ever since mother died she's been dead set against all of this." Mom spread her arms to encompass the whole room and possibly all of Crystal Haven.

Just as Vi finished putting the dishes in the dishwasher, the lights came on and we gave my father perfunctory applause for saving us from darkness once again.

Since I wasn't part of this conversation about my flaws, I went to the dining room to check on Seth and scan for any remaining dishes. I could still hear them in the kitchen.

"My cat clients have been very worked up about something. You know how they get when trouble is brewing. Whether it's a storm, a divorce, or teenage angst, they sense it. The aloof ones get all sentimental and the affectionate ones withdraw. It's like they can feel the emotional shifts and they don't know how to deal with it. Plus, remember the robin that flew in here last week? It was a sign," Vi said to my mother.

"I don't know . . . ," Mom said.

"And the bat this morning. And now this storm . . . ," Vi said.

I lurked in the doorway, eavesdropping.

"Sara is trying to tell us something. Do you really think

Tommy Andrews and Mac are going to be able to solve this?" Vi hissed.

"Why wouldn't they be able to solve it?" I asked.

They both spun to look at me, and were not quick enough to cover their guilty expressions.

"They'll be collecting evidence and samples and interviewing people, hoping to find a connection or uncover a lie," Aunt Vi said, not bothering to hide her sarcastic tone. Vi's opinion about fact-finding was almost as scathing as the rest of the world's opinion about psychics.

I had a hard time keeping a straight face. "Well, that *is* normal police procedure: to examine the evidence and find out who might have wanted her dead and go from there. That's how we solve crimes."

Vi shook her head. She waved her hand to dismiss the whole process.

"We just feel that in this case they should be considering Sara's talents and her unique connection to Spirit in their investigation," Mom said.

"You think she was killed by a ghost?" I asked.

"No, of course not. But Spirit can act in strange ways when a person is as connected to the other side as she was." Mom began wiping the counters.

"What do you want them to do? Have a séance and question whoever shows up?" I asked, willing my mother to turn around.

"Mac will never go for that, although it would be helpful," Aunt Vi said, considering this idea carefully as if it were actually on offer.

"I think I've been away too long. Or maybe not long

enough," I said, and left them to their plotting. This was an ongoing battle where my resistance was equally matched with their persistence. Between the dreams, the touch sensitivity, and the occasional flash of premonition, they were convinced I could be as great a psychic as my grandmother had been. The fact that I wasn't even a little bit interested in pursuing that career path did not deter them.

I found Seth in the room that used to be my sister's until it was clear she was never coming back. Now it had an undecided air about it—no longer Grace's room, not quite a guest room, but definitely gender confused. Her stuffed animals languished on shelves with her childhood books. Her various art projects and nature treasures that had been collected over the years decorated the walls and gathered dust on the dresser. Seth's current possessions were of the small and electronic ilk: iPod, Nintendo DS, cell phone, laptop. They cluttered the small desk along with a collection of fantasy paperbacks featuring dragons and swords on the covers.

Seth was on the bed with Tuffy and Baxter. How they all fit, I had no idea. The twin bed was a mass of fur and boy. Tuffy seemed to have stopped shivering, and Baxter sat alert in his guarding mode.

"Hey, the rain's stopped," I said. "Want to get these guys outside before it starts up again?"

Baxter heard "outside" and leapt off the bed causing the springs to shriek in protest. Tuffy watched him leave and then stood at the edge of the bed peering down, waiting for someone to tell him what to do.

"Sure," said Seth. "C'mon, Tuffy. You can do it." He

encouraged the dog to jump off the edge. Tuffy was not interested and had clearly been accustomed to more slave labor
than I was willing to provide. He danced from one front paw
to the other and fixed Seth with his imperious stare. It didn't
take a pet psychic to know what he wanted. Seth accommo-
dated him and lifted him gently to the floor.

"He's got your number," I said.

"I s'pose," he said and slumped out of the room, his two
shadows padding softly after him.

Outside, it had not cooled off but the rain left a clean smell
behind. We'd forgotten to turn the lights on and stood in the
semidarkness listening to the water dripping on the leaves
overhead. The dogs seemed to be getting along. They made
a funny pair, one so huge he could crush the other one. But
Baxter was very gentle with Tuffy, almost as if he understood
what a bad day it had been for the little guy.

"I feel like Baxter really understands what Tuffy is going
through," Seth said, as if he had read my thoughts.

"Yeah, they seem to be friends already."

"I hope they find out who killed that lady. It's not right.
She was just leading her life, and then someone comes along
and takes it all away. Leaving behind people and animals
that care about her," Seth said.

"I know." I put my hand tentatively on his back, not sure
what to do. "They'll do their best. No one wants to let a
murderer go unpunished."

"Clyde?"

"Yeah?"

"I was wondering . . ." He turned toward me, and I pulled
my hand away.

"There you are!" said a voice from the back door. I heard a click and the backyard was flooded with light. The screen door slammed and the porch steps creaked.

Alex walked toward us, only his dark outline visible with the porch lights behind him.

"Hi, Seth," he said.

"Hey." Seth raised his hand and let it drop.

"I see you have a couple of new inmates here at Chez Fortune."

"We didn't know what to do with Sara's dog, so we decided to keep him until her family can take him, and Tish called and needed to board Baxter with us for a day or two," I said, shielding my eyes from the sudden brightness.

"Makes sense," Alex said, hands in his pockets as he surveyed the yard.

"So, um, I'm taking them in before they get too wet," said Seth. When he whistled, the dogs came immediately to his side.

I watched, fascinated, as they followed him into the house. Neither one of them had ever done anything I had asked, whistle or no whistle.

"Hey, Alex . . ."

"Um, Clyde . . ." We both began at the same time.

"You first . . . ," we said together, and laughed.

"Should we just forget it?" I asked.

"Yeah, I'm sorry. I should have known better than to force you to eat eggplant."

"Well, I usually love all your food." I caught his look of disbelief. "Okay, I love *most* of your food. Some of the more exotic stuff can throw me a little. Doesn't mean there's anything wrong with it."

"Sorry, you had such a bad day. How hard are they pushing for a psychic solution in there?" He cocked his head toward the house.

"My mother made pot roast."

"Oh, it's on, then."

"I think it's only just begun."

The next day, Tuesday, Tish called in a panic about Baxter getting his heartworm medicine. She'd left a message and then shut off her phone. I had no choice but to go pick it up. Baxter got very quiet as we pulled into his driveway and lay down on the seat next to Tuffy. He pushed his jaw out and refused to look at me. I could tell he was gearing up for a battle. Apparently he and Tuffy had bonded more than I had realized.

"You stay here with them, and I'll run in and get his medicine," I said to Seth.

He gave me a thumbs-up and kept his head bobbing to whatever was on his iPod.

I knew Tish's house like my own, mostly because it *had* been my own. I had grown up here for the first eight years of my life. She had also been my babysitter off and on when I was younger, and I'd spent a lot of time with her. Much of my teen years were spent in the cozy living room that had once been mine, just hanging out, doing homework and avoiding my family. She was one of the few people in Crystal Haven who seemed to understand why a person might not want to have any psychic insight into events. When my mother got to be too much for me with her pressure to be a psychic, Tish stepped in and let me just be myself. She was from a generation between my family and me, a few years older than Grace but not as ancient as my mother and my aunt had seemed when I was a teen. Enjoying the absolute trust of my parents, she often became the chaperone to my teenage activities, straddling the line between cool and responsible.

I passed the oak tree that had been my favorite climbing tree as a kid. It had a hole near the first large branch. I used to write coded notes and stick them in the opening to be found by my imaginary friends. I remembered telling Mac about my fantasies of finding treasure maps or secret messages hidden there. Shortly after that, I began finding notes from Mac. He was better on paper than on the phone or even in person. He had to force me to check the hiding place the first time. After several very subtle hints that I didn't interpret correctly, he drove me to Tish's house, dragged me to the tree, and shoved my hand inside. After that, I checked every day and was almost never disappointed. I still had the notes, somewhere.

On the porch, I found the key under the mat and let myself in. I didn't linger in the living room but went straight to the kitchen to find Baxter's medicine.

Back outside, I locked the door and turned to replace the key, then let out a small yelp and dropped it. Cecile Stark, Joe's wife, who lived across the street, was standing right behind me. Petite, with blonde-highlighted, spiky hair, she reminded me of a scruffy terrier. Never one to make eye contact, Cecile darted glances toward Tish's front door, my car, and her own house.

"Oh, I'm sorry I startled you, Clyde." She tugged on her earring and glanced out at the street.

"I didn't see you standing there."

"I saw a car parked in the driveway and came to see if Tish had come back or if someone was looking for her. She's been away since yesterday morning," Cecile said, and did not back up. She had a habit of standing much too close.

"I just came to get some medicine for Baxter," I said, stepping back. "I'm taking care of him until she returns."

"Oh, that's very nice of you. He's quite a handful." She gestured vaguely toward the car. She claimed Baxter was a menace and was always trying to cause trouble for Tish if he ever got outside without a leash. Cecile claimed Baxter terrorized her cats but that's not the story Aunt Vi told. Vi said Cecile's cats were antisocial and all the other cats in town were afraid of them. They just seemed like regular cats to me. She continued to block my way off the porch.

"Is there something I can do for you?"

"No . . . I just wondered if you knew when Tish would be back." Cecile looked over my shoulder at the door. "She left in quite a hurry."

"Hurry?" I thought she had gone to a conference, but she probably didn't share her plans with Cecile.

"She looked like she was in a hurry when I saw her load up the car and take off before breakfast." Cecile finally took a step back. "I was surprised, as I get up quite early and I never see Tish until my third cup of coffee."

Tish hadn't called me until after nine. She'd said she'd forgotten to arrange for Baxter, and could I take him on short notice? Where had she been all that time?

"Well, I'm sure she'll be back soon. Do you want me to give her a message if I talk to her?"

"Oh no. No message." Cecile backed away and stepped off the porch. "It would be better if you didn't even tell her you spoke to me."

She darted back across the street and disappeared through the gate to the privacy fence that surrounded her yard.

Baxter let out a low growl as I got into the car. He didn't mean it for me. He was looking at Cecile's house.

8

Seth grew somber as we drove back into town. We had a lighter load of dogs to walk on Tuesdays and finished quickly. Baxter and Tuffy seemed to pick up on his mood and slumped in the backseat with lowered ears and droopy stares. I knew he was worried about giving his interview at the station. He'd watched too much TV about questioning witnesses and perps. I suspected he didn't want to have to relive and describe the events of the day before. He was probably trying very hard to forget them entirely. Grace had given her permission for Seth to be interviewed, as long as I acted as his guardian and stayed with him. She'd been very interested in whether or not I was buckling under our mother's influence and resorting to psychic resources. My abilities had always been the only source of jealousy for her, whereas I had had an abundant list from which to choose. She had normal-color eyes, had gotten the normal name, and the only thing she saw in her dreams was money.

The crystal shop next to the police station always left a large bowl of water out for dogs. The shop owner had even set up a stake near the sidewalk to tie leashes. Seth hooked the leads to the post and told the dogs to behave. Baxter sighed loudly and sat with his back to us. Tuffy glowered from under his topknot.

The police station was quiet when we entered. Lisa was behind the desk again, flipping through a catalog that featured flak jackets. She pushed a button on her phone, and Tom Andrews came down the hall.

"Hi. Come on back," he said.

After leading us into the large workroom, he offered chairs near his desk. Seth immediately slumped into one and allowed his hair to fall over his face. Tom asked if he wanted a soda. Seth never turns down an offer of free food or drink, so he perked up enough to mumble, "Sure."

Tom signaled me to come with him to the vending machines. Seth plugged in his earbuds and began drumming on his knees.

"Is Charla in today?" I asked while surveying the workroom.

"She's out on a call right now. She said she hasn't seen you since you got back," Tom said as we worked our way to the back of the room. "I wanted to let you know what we learned today."

I nodded and waited for him to continue.

"Sara's ex-husband, Gary, has an alibi. He was having breakfast with his daughter all morning and left straight from her house to catch his plane. She's confirmed this over the phone, but we still need to get her in here for an official state-ment." Tom began feeding coins into the machine.

"So now there are no suspects?"

"Not really. He was our best shot." He shrugged. Tom banged on the machine to get the soda out. "Gary did tell us that Sara'd been receiving some sort of threats through her website. He doesn't know whether she kept records or not. We're looking into it." Tom knelt on the floor to peer up into the dispenser. He gave the machine another whack. A can of soda shot out and caught him in the nose.

Ten minutes later, Tom, with an ice pack to his face, gestured us back out into the hallway. We followed him to a small room with a table and three chairs. Seth shuffled behind us as if he were being led to his own execution. He hesitated at the doorway.

"Dis id our inderbiew roob. Id's quieder here dan by desk," Tom said, the ice pack still on his nose.

"Are there people watching through that glass?" Seth asked, and pointed to the wall.

Tom turned around and looked at the mirror mounted on the wall as if he was noticing it for the first time.

"Doh, eberyone's out on calls ride now," he said. He leaned toward us, removed his ice pack, and lowered his voice. "We actually store our office supplies in the observation room."

"Then why are you whispering?" I said.

He snapped upright and pulled out a chair, gesturing toward the other two.

Seth sat, crossed his arms, and peered at Tom from underneath his fringe of blond. I sent him mental messages to sit up and pull himself together. He clearly did not receive them.

"So, Seth," Tom began. His lips stretched across his teeth, but he didn't pull off the smile.

Seth gave him the dead-eye look perfected by teenagers the world over.

Tom tried again. "Can you tell me, in your own words, what happened yesterday from the time you left your house until I came to Sara Landess's house?"

"You want to know everything?"

"Well, just summarize what you did until you got to Ms. Landess's house." Tom wrestled with his small digital recorder.

Seth reached out to turn it on for him.

"We picked up Baxter, walked some dogs, went to the lady's house, and found Tuffy. He was really scared, and then we saw the body lying in the kitchen."

"That's it?" Tom asked.

A crash and cursing sounded from the room beyond the mirror. Whoever it was, he wasn't editing himself for Seth's sake.

"I thought you said no one would be in there," Seth said.

"I didn't think anyone would be. I'll be right back." Tom jumped up, knocking over his chair as he rushed next door.

We heard voices. Tom's sounded pacifying and the other was a deeper angry rumble. Another crash. A door slammed.

Mac and his cane clomped into the room.

"Sorry about that," he said. He looked at Seth carefully.

Seth pushed his shoulders back and sat up a little straighter in his chair, glancing at me.

"Seth Proffit? I'm Detective McKenzie." Mac extended his hand.

Seth wiped his palm on his jeans and stood to take Mac's hand.

"Nice to meet you, Detective."

My mouth hung open in shock at these newfound manners. It was as if Seth had been replaced by some other teen. But I realized this was the polished, private-school-on-the-east-coast Seth. I was used to the summer Seth.

"Have a seat. Officer Andrews is needed elsewhere. If you don't mind, I'll take your statement."

"No, sir. I don't mind," said refined Seth.

"Excellent. Let's get started."

I still hadn't said a word and decided not to. They were doing just fine without me. I watched the ice pack sweat on the table where Tom had left it. Mac's interview led Seth through the morning, which touched on the bat-hunting episode and my brief wrestling match with Baxter. I was sure I didn't imagine Mac taking extra care over these extraneous details. Seth managed to skate quickly over his own puking and finished his story with me talking Tom into allowing us to leave the scene. He made it sound like I had bullied the guy because I used to babysit for him. Since this was Seth's testimony, I kept quiet.

I had a lot of time to sit and observe the two of them. Seth seemed older somehow. He'd pulled himself together to impress Mac; he was well-spoken with a larger vocabulary than I had been led to believe he had. I tried not to study Mac too much, but he was right across the table from me.

Based on my sweaty palms and racing pulse, I hadn't gotten over him. But I was determined to avoid him as much as possible, which shouldn't be hard considering the way he'd been acting thus far.

When the interview was finished, Mac led us back down the hall to the front. As we passed a large window into the workroom, I saw the reflection of Mac and me walking together. He brought his hand up as if to put it on my shoulder, then quickly regained his senses and pulled it away before touching me. What was he thinking? *He* left *me*. What would I have done if he had put his arm around me?

"Thanks for taking care of the permission part of things," he said when Seth had walked ahead of us.

I waved his thanks away. "No problem."

"I thought you'd want to be the one to tell her about it, and it saved me a catching-up phone call."

I knew Mac was not good on the phone. He saw the phone as a necessary evil and used it to convey straightforward information. I had been shocked when I'd received his first letter to me. There was a whole other side to Mac that most people never knew existed.

I turned to say something—anything—that would keep him talking, but he had already turned back down the hall. He made pretty good time for a guy with a cane.

"Clyde, are we going or what?" Seth called from the station entrance.

"Yeah, we're going. Here, take the keys and I'll be right out."

I turned to Lisa, who was pretending to read *Guns & Ammo*. She'd clearly not missed one instant of my conversation with Mac and was already firing up her cell phone for distribution of the gossip.

"Hey, Lisa, where's Andrews?"

"Oh, we got another call about vandalism in Greer's Woods." She flipped a page in her magazine, and clicked her phone off. "He went to check it out."

"What vandalism?"

"It's just kids. They've been digging out there for the past couple months. Some of it's in Greer's Woods, some on private property, some in the public park but all in the same general area. They dig holes and then fill them in."

"What's the point in that?"

"Dunno. It's kids."

Seth was starving after his "grueling" session with Mac, so we drove over to Stark's place. I knew I was taking a chance with Alex still sensitive about yesterday, but he would be more upset if he'd heard we'd gone somewhere else. And he would definitely hear. Crystal Haven has its own information superhighway, and it isn't on the Internet. Often the gossiper would be asked if he had gotten his information from a live person or from Spirit. I was still not sure which held the higher status.

We were just in time for the lunch rush, but I managed to get a parking spot close by. We got out and let the dogs have a quick walk along the sidewalk. Baxter was a minor celebrity in town; he knew more people than I did. Therefore, it wasn't completely shocking when a man came out of Stark's to pet him. He called him by name, and Baxter slobbered appreciatively.

The man was about my height, with a shaved head to either hide or embrace his receding hairline. He wore mirrored sunglasses, so I couldn't see his eyes. I don't trust people who hide their eyes. He nodded hello to Seth and me, and walked up the street. The whole encounter left me feeling weird.

"Do you know him?" I asked Seth.

"No, but Baxter does," he said.

"I feel like I've seen him before," I said as we encouraged the dogs back into the car. Fortunately, Baxter was sticking with Tuffy and didn't force us into our usual wrestling match right there in front of the lunch line.

"You've probably seen everyone in town before," Seth said.

It was cooler after yesterday's storm. But the line was long and I didn't want to leave the dogs in the hot car for more than a few minutes. I told Seth to stand in line while I ran the dogs back to the house. He nodded, stuffed in his earbuds, and stood behind the other hungry patrons.

I returned ten minutes later to find a bored, famished teen. After twenty minutes of listening to Seth describe the many stages of starvation he was enduring, we finally made it inside the restaurant.

We sat close to the kitchen and ordered two burgers.

Seth claimed he was breaking down his own muscle mass while we waited for our food. When the server brought the small bread basket, I feared for her fingers. Moments later she returned with an appetizer, compliments of the chef.

This was an underhanded trick, even for Alex. He could never get Seth to try any of his creations. But the thing she brought appeared to be a pizza. Seth adored pizza above all other food groups. He picked up a piece, sniffed it, and put it back down.

"I'm pretty sure there's fish in there," he said.

"Do you think it's anchovies?" I asked, suppressing a shudder in an attempt to be the adult.

"No, I think it's tuna," he said, and lifted some of the cheese with his fork.

"I like tuna," I said. "We could try it. It would make Alex happy."

"I could even eat anchovies at this point." Seth sighed and bravely took a bite. And then another—in three seconds flat, the pizza slice was gone.

I grabbed a piece off the plate before he ate it all. It was tuna.

"What's this?"

I looked up to see Joe Stark glowering at our pizza. When he noticed me looking at him, he flashed a dazzling smile.

"It's a new pizza Alex is trying out," I said, and pulled the plate closer to protect it.

"Of course. It's always something new with him, isn't it?" Stark nodded to us and strode in the direction of the kitchen.

Seth and I looked at each other and shrugged. Alex claimed Stark was a harsh taskmaster, but Joe was always charming to the customers. We were happily finishing off the pizza and complaining because it was too small when the burgers arrived, followed swiftly by Alex.

"Hey how did you like . . . ?" He looked at the plate. He glanced around for evidence we had hidden the pizza somewhere.

"The pizza was good, but really small," Seth said.

Alex sighed dramatically. "I'm glad you liked it, burger boy."

"Did you see Stark in the kitchen?" I asked, licking my fingers.

"Yeah, he was all worked up about an unapproved item

in his dining room," said Alex. He flicked his hand to dismiss it. "I'll deal with it."

I watched Alex to see if he was concerned. He seemed more worried about whether we liked his pizza.

"Hey, I had the strangest conversation today with Cecile Stark," I said to Alex.

"When has anyone ever had a normal conversation with Cecile Stark?" he said.

"She is a bit odd, even for Crystal Haven." I glanced around to be sure Joe Stark wasn't lurking in our vicinity.

"She came over while I was at Tish's house, wanting to know where Tish was and when she might be back, but I wasn't supposed to mention it to Tish. It was strange."

Seth had finished his burger and was eying mine in a dangerous fashion. I slid my plate out of his reach.

"I've learned not to take anything she says seriously. She lives in some other dimension even further removed from wherever the rest of this town resides."

"Be careful, Alex. That's the boss's wife you're talking about."

"Whatev," said Alex. Then he and Seth did a complicated fist-bump handshake.

"Have you heard anything about séances that Sara was doing before she died?" I asked when they were done grinning at each other.

"Séances?" Seth perked up at this bit of news. He loved any talk of spirits or ghosts. Even though he had been visiting Crystal Haven his entire life, he had never actually seen any "good stuff," as he liked to call it.

"I did hear about that. I think one of them got pretty wild. Diana told me . . ."

A server rushed up to the table. "Mr. Ferguson, there's an emergency. There was a small fire. Then Hunter got behind on the orders and they're freaking back there."

Alex jumped up.

"I'll call you later," he said over his shoulder as he went to rescue his kitchen staff. And appease his boss.

9

~~⚬⚭⚬~~

Alex's comment about Diana made me feel guilty.
I'd been back for almost a month and had not yet stopped by
Diana's place. I'd called her as soon as I knew I would be
returning to Crystal Haven, but we hadn't seen each other in
person. She'd been in and out of town all month, helping her
brother, Dylan, get ready for the round of regional outdoor
art fairs. But she'd been home for at least a week now, and
the longer I delayed, the more awkward it became—she and
Alex were my best friends. It wasn't that I didn't want to see
her as much as I didn't want *her* to see *me*. She always knew
things I didn't want her to know. She was unfailingly optimistic in the face of any setback and, frankly, I'd been enjoying my wallowing.

Seth loved Diana's store and had no interest in going back
home so we walked the two blocks to Moonward Magick.
The storm from yesterday was a distant memory, the sky a

clear cloudless blue, the streets packed with shoppers and spiritual seekers.

Moonward Magick is not the only Wiccan store in town, but it is the biggest and the best known. Diana is a very savvy Internet marketer. Between that and the fact that she plays to everyone's fantasy of what a witch supply store should be, she does a brisk business.

Incense hung heavy in the air, and merchandise crowded the dark wood shelves. Seth and I blinked in the doorway while our eyes adjusted after the bright sunlight outside. Diana had a huge selection of books covering every topic from psychic development and herbal healing to astral travel and tarot reading. Two young teenagers whispered near a section of stoppered glass vials and consulted a small black notebook. A young salesperson said hello and went back to her customers, a mother and daughter shopping for the perfect talisman for serenity.

"You need to wear it close to your skin, and you'll notice when you don't have it on," she told them. "I have this friend? And I can tell when she's not wearing her amethyst. She'll call me all in a snit, and I'll tell her to call me back when she's got her necklace on."

Seth went to the scrying section and began hefting the crystal balls—some as large as bowling balls, others smaller than tennis balls. He tried them in the various stands and seemed to have a preference for the dragons. When he turned to show one of them to me, he bumped into the display of semiprecious stones, spilling several bowls of them onto the floor. I rushed to help him re-sort the colored stones into their proper containers.

"Blessed be. I should have known it would be you," said a familiar voice from above.

I glanced up to see Diana, looking almost the same as she did the day we graduated from high school. Her orange curls were cut to just below her shoulders, and she wore less makeup now, having moved beyond her goth phase, but otherwise she seemed unchanged.

I jumped up to give her a hug and crashed into a rack of velvet capes. For its size, the store was really crowded.

"It's been too long," I said, hoping she wasn't mad.

"It has been." She hugged me back. "What took you so long? Is it Mac, or the fact you're living with your parents again?"

I stepped back; I had never quite figured out if it was touch or just proximity that brought out her ability to read me so well.

"Just busy," I said, gesturing toward Seth. "I've had Seth with me, and Vi's got me walking all her clients' dogs."

Her deep green eyes held my mismatched ones, daring me to try to wriggle out of this one.

I cut my gaze to Seth, who was still busy sorting rocks. She tilted her head—a signal of a truce, for now.

She walked toward the back of the store, past busts of Egyptian gods and goddesses in a display case, more bookshelves on astrology, kitchen magic, and paganism; shelves of bagged and bottled herbs; and books on herbal healing.

"Can we trust Seth not to destroy the place if we leave him out here unattended?"

I glanced back toward the front, where he'd finished with the stones and was looking at a display case of dragon statues. I shrugged, following her through a red velvet curtain.

Diana's office was the converse of her store. White

cabinets held her paperwork and computer, leaving the space open and clean-feeling. The room felt organized and efficient. Considering how cluttered her store was, it seemed some other person was in charge of her private space. She had always seemed to hold two opposite personalities in one body.

Diana's family had moved to Crystal Haven for the open and accepting attitude. Plus, the proximity to the beaches of Lake Michigan and the lush wooded areas of western Michigan were hard to beat. They were Wiccans, and after a bit of furor by the less educated, they settled in and used their knowledge of the town to run boat tours, walking tours, and ghost tours. Elliot Ward also opened a used bookstore and pursued his passion for finding treasure in the form of first editions and private diaries.

I was finding it difficult to navigate the social obstacle course and didn't share the suspicions and fear of my peers, so fortunately, we found each other in third grade and had been friends ever since. Diana was named for the moon goddess, and when she opened her Magickal store, after converting her father's dwindling bookshop, she changed her last name to Moonward. Diana's parents had died a year before that in a car accident, leaving Diana and her brother to make their own way in the world. Dylan left to pursue his artistic interests, and Diana stayed behind to combine her business sense and Wiccan lifestyle. Moonward Magick's success didn't erase the fact that at times she was a haunted daughter still missing her parents.

"What's going on with you? I want to hear everything." She sat back in her chair as if awaiting a good, long story.

I was afraid of this. It was going to be hard to talk to Diana without telling her everything, and I wasn't ready yet.

"Well, actually, I came to ask you about Sara Landess."

"Sara? Oh, that was terrible news. I can't believe anyone would want to hurt her. She was a really great person, always so nice. . . ." Her eyes became unfocused for a moment.

Before we got lost in the shock of Sara's death, I tried to redirect.

"I heard you went to a séance of hers recently."

"Oh yes! It was great. She did a really nice job. I didn't get any messages, though." She looked down at her lap. "You know I always hope to hear from my parents."

"I know." I looked at the picture of her parents propped on her desk. I'd never told her that I had known her parents would die. I hadn't known how, or even exactly when, I just knew they would never see Diana's success. It's the kind of thing my "gift" lets me see, the tragedies and catastrophes.

"Anyway, it was pretty exciting because Sara did have someone come through who had quite a bit to say."

Her cell phone rang. She glanced at the screen.

"That's my essential oils distributor. The last shipment came with half the vials broken. What a mess. Hang on." She flipped open the phone and held up one finger to me.

I listened to what didn't sound like good news.

"I'm sorry, Clyde. I have to go to the post office and file a damage report before they'll send another shipment. I guess I'll be looking for another source soon." She stood to gather her purse and keys.

"About the séance?"

"Oh, I'll tell you about it later. It's way too interesting to describe in three seconds. I'll call you."

I followed her out of the office to find Seth trying on robes by a mirror in the back. I watched as Diana turned the store over to her staff and rushed out the door with my only hope of moving ahead on this case.

I was in my room later that afternoon, surfing the Internet and reading Sara's blog for clues. She had a nice section about developing psychic talent, séances, and tarot cards. I had just begun scrolling through the comments section when I heard a car barreling down the driveway. Seth was out back with the dogs, and my mother and Violet were with clients. I jumped up to look out the window in time to catch a glimpse of Tish's white Tahoe pulling up outside.

I ran down the stairs to stop her from knocking on the door. We have the bell disabled so Vi's clients won't be disturbed and feel the need to bark and protect the house from visitors during their sessions, but Tish always "forgets" and begins pounding on the door seconds after trying the bell. I got there just as she was winding up for her assault.

"Tish, hi," I said through great gulps of air.

"Hi, honey. What's the matter with you? Are you having an episode?"

I had been known in my youth to have daytime visions of unpleasant events that left me breathless and exhausted, but I had found ways to avoid the visions, and Tish knew that.

"No, I ran down the stairs when I saw your car."

"Baxter's giving you such a hard time you have to race down the stairs to greet me?" Her laugh was a deep rumble. It always made me smile.

"No, he's been fine. He likes Seth," I said, standing aside to let her in.

Tish was the kind of person who filled a room, no matter its size. She liked to call herself a large medium. Everything about her was just a little bigger than it needed to be, except for her height. Her hair had been brutally teased. It stood out from her head, adding several inches to her five-foot frame. It was long and usually a blonde of one shade or another, depending on her mood. None of her clothes were the right size for her, and they swung to both extremes. In her daily life, she wore everything two sizes too small. This added an aspect of suspense: I constantly waited for her buttons to fly off or her zipper to give up its valiant effort. While working, she chose large, drapey fabrics seemingly worn right off the bolt. Today was a tight-clothes day. "Where is the big lug, anyway?" she asked, walking toward my mother's office.

I stepped in front of her and gestured for her to follow me toward the back of the house.

"He's out back with Seth," I whispered. "Mom and Vi are with clients."

"*That's* what all those cars are doing out there."

I gave her a look that said I wasn't buying the act. She knew what was going on, but was hoping to get a peek at who was here. Her one vice was meddling. She liked nothing better than to find out that there was a problem somewhere and then try to fix it. Unfortunately, her information often came from other realms and couldn't be proven. She had never messed around in my life, and for that I was grateful.

She shrugged. "You can't blame me for trying. Information is gold in this town."

"How was your trip?" I asked, hoping to steer her to the subject of why she had lied about her departure time.

"Oh, just wonderful! I love those retreats by the Oneness Institute. We had a healing circle. My teacher channeled her spirit guides, and we spent a lot of time in meditation with our own guides. Such a fabulous group of people. I wish they offered the retreats more often."

"Have you heard about what's been happening around here?" I led her into the kitchen.

"Oh my, yes. Such a tragedy. Sara Landess was very talented; Crystal Haven will surely miss her."

"How did you hear?" I waved a pitcher of iced tea, and she nodded.

"Jillian called and left me a message. We have to have our phones off during the retreat, but I got the message on my way back home. To think that all the time I was in communication with Spirit, I could have tried to talk to Sara."

I put a glass in front of her and took the seat across the table.

"Not that she would have wanted to talk to me. We weren't very close." She sipped her drink, her multiple bangles jingling with every move. "Our auras were such that we tended to clash, and something was happening to her in the past few months. She got very cloudy and gray. She used to be a brilliant orange, but that got kind of muddy."

I had to interrupt the flow of aura-talk or she would go on for days. "Tish, when you went to the retreat, why didn't you call ahead to arrange for Baxter?"

"I told you on the phone, hon. There was a wait list, and they called me at the last minute."

"You just packed up that morning and left around nine-thirty?" I picked up my own glass and tried to act casual.

"I don't remember what time it was." She studied her tea. "I was in quite a hurry, as you can imagine. Packing, cancelling appointments, arranging for Baxter . . ."

"You didn't see Sara on your way out of town, did you?"

"Of course not! Why would I do that? As I said, her aura was changing and I really didn't want to have much to do with that. I always say karma will catch up to you. I think hers finally did."

"You think she deserved to be killed?" I leaned forward, glad that no one else was hearing this.

"No, I didn't say that." She flapped her hand. "I feel terrible about her death, especially since we didn't always get along. In fact, I stopped and talked to her daughter Alison on the way home. Have you ever met her? She lives in Kalamazoo. We got to be friendly a while back over some things Alison had going on. She didn't want to tell her mother, so she came to me. You know how that can be." Her expression told me she knew very well how strained my own relationship with my mother was.

Tish could be a great listener. She had helped me through some unpleasant times. I was furious with myself for wanting to question her whereabouts on the morning of Sara's death, but I couldn't shake the feeling that she was keeping something from me.

I nodded. "That was nice of you."

"Well, anyway, sugar, I'd better be on my way. Is Baxter out back?"

"I'll get him for you. I think Seth is playing fetch with him."

I gathered Baxter's things and went outside to collect him. I was uncomfortable letting Tish go without getting more answers but couldn't see a way past it without openly accusing her.

I found Seth and Tuffy with Baxter in the far corner of the yard playing some version of fetch that seemed to involve Seth chasing the ball about as often as the dogs did.

Tish had followed me outside and when Baxter caught sight of her he loped across the yard and flung himself at her, almost knocking her down in his enthusiasm. He then charged back toward our small group, nudged Tuffy, and trotted back to Tish.

She waved from the back porch. Then they walked around the side of the house and disappeared.

"Do you think he said good-bye to Tuffy?" I asked Seth.

"Of course. They're friends," he said, and the look he gave me said, "duh."

10

With Baxter gone, Tuffy fell into a funk. We
brought him inside to the living room where all attempts to
cheer him with toys and treats failed. I was starting to fear
we would need Baxter to come live with us for the duration
of Tuffy's stay when I heard tires on the gravel again.

Mom opened the door with a loud creak, and quiet voices
floated in from the front hall. A moment later, she edged
into the living room, tight-lipped and pale.

"Gary Landess is here to take Tuffy," she said.

Seth put his arm around the dog in a protective gesture,
which caused Tuffy to renew his shivering. He must have
recognized his name and figured something was up.

I left Seth and found a distraught Gary standing by the
door. His hair was thin on top. It stuck up all around his
head from running his fingers through the nearly nonexistent
strands. A wrinkled and stained gray suit did nothing to
improve his appearance. His puffy, red eyes darted around

the room as if he were being hunted by some unknown predator.

"Hi, Mr. Landess. I don't know if you remember meeting me." I stuck out my hand. "I'm Clyde Fortune. I took care of Tuffy for Sara while she was working." He stared at my hand for a moment before reaching forward to grasp it briefly with a quick, damp squeeze.

"I remember. I met you once—here, over the holidays, I think." He didn't meet my eyes and mostly examined the floor. "You were living in Ann Arbor then."

"I'm so sorry about Sara," I said.

He nodded and sniffed.

"You're here for Tuffy?"

"The police told me yesterday that you were taking care of him. Thank you. I thought I should come get him." He shrugged.

I imagined the two of them, Tuffy and Gary, sitting in whatever apartment he lived in, staring at each other.

"We're happy to keep him for you if you'd prefer . . . ," I began, thinking of Seth losing both of his friends in one day.

"No, no, I'll take him." He squared his shoulders, bracing himself, I assumed. "We'll have to get used to each other again."

I showed him into the living room. He followed behind, shoulders slumped again. Tuffy looked up as we entered and seemed to shake even more as he leaned closer to Seth.

Gary grimaced a smile, and said, "Here, Tuffy. C'mon, boy."

Tuffy leaned closer to Seth, his eyes darting from me to Gary.

I felt sad for both of them. I was surprised that he'd fought Sara for custody when clearly Tuffy liked Gary even less than he liked me.

"I brought a bribe. This always works," Gary said, producing a baggie with bacon in it.

Gary crouched down on one knee, and said, "Here, boy, I've got your favorite. Bacon!"

He shook the bag and then opened it to give Tuffy a good whiff. Tuffy stopped shaking. He sat up straight and sniffed the air. He jumped off the couch and cautiously approached Gary. Seth was sending me all sorts of warning messages with his eyes. *What can I do?* I shrugged back. Tuffy belonged to Gary now.

As Tuffy happily snarfed down a piece of bacon, Gary reached over and picked him up.

"It works every time," he said. He stood and stuffed the rest of the bacon into his pocket, settling Tuffy more firmly under his arm.

Seth and I walked with Gary and Tuffy to the door. Seth gave Gary the rundown of what Tuffy did and didn't like based on his twenty-four hours of experience. Gary nodded politely and tried to escape with his dog as quickly as possible.

We opened the front door to flashing red and white lights. The police cruiser was pulled up to the front porch, crushing my mother's favorite rose bush under its back tire. Gary was caught in the bright spotlight trained on the door. I spotted Tom Andrews inside the car, placing his bullhorn on the passenger seat. He must have reconsidered its use when we stepped onto the porch.

Officer Andrews walked around the cruiser, tripped over the roses, and got tangled in the thorns. After extricating himself, he bounded up the steps and approached Gary, who stood with his mouth open while trying to keep Tuffy from struggling.

"Gary Landess?"

"Of course I am! You just talked to me this morning." He shifted Tuffy to his other arm and lowered his eyebrows at Tom.

"You're under arrest for the murder of Sara Landess." Tom tried to put handcuffs on Gary. Tuffy began to growl and show his teeth.

"Let me take the dog, Tom," I said.

But as I reached for him, Tuffy growled more and bared his sharp-looking canines. Gary clutched the dog tighter, as if that would save him from what was happening.

We appeared to be in a standoff. Tom held one of Gary's wrists, Gary held Tuffy with his other arm, Tuffy growled and looked like an armpit barracuda, while I fretted over what my mother was going to say about the roses. Fortunately, Seth was there. He stepped forward and put out his arms for Tuffy. Tuffy stopped growling and wiggled enough that Gary had to let go of him, allowing Andrews to get the other cuff on him.

"I have an alibi," Gary said, arms behind his back.

"Not anymore," said Tom.

He led Gary down the steps, and said, "You have the right to remain silent. Anything you say can and will be used in a court of law. . . ."

"I knew it!" Violet said at dinner that night.

We were gathered again around the dining room table, this time minus Baxter but plus Alex. I saw this as an improvement.

"I never trusted him, or liked him," Vi said around a mouthful of meatloaf.

"It would have been helpful if you'd tipped off the police before they questioned him and then let him go," I said, just because I was feeling irritable.

"Well, I had no proof. Now that Mac is in charge, no one will listen to anything my clients have to say." Vi's cheeks flushed pink in outrage.

My stomach dropped at the mention of Mac.

"It's true that things will be different now," said my mother.

"What do you mean, Nana Rose?" asked Seth.

"There was a time when Crystal Haven had no crime to speak of, and when we did, we knew who the culprits were." Mom looked from Seth to me. "We didn't need to go around investigating and snooping. It all got worked out. . . ."

My father reached over to pat her hand as she fought back tears. She was in a fragile state this evening. Gary's arrest on her front lawn had disrupted a difficult reading with a client.

I raised my eyebrows in Alex's general direction but covered it by taking a drink. My mother's volatile emotional states had been the subject of intense discussion over the years.

"Tuffy told me 'bacon.' That's what he said. I should have listened." Vi punctuated each of these statements with a fist to the table. "And then Gary waltzes in here and gives the dog bacon!" She threw up her hands and looked around the table. "You never should have let him go after that." Vi waggled her finger at me as if Tuffy had been somehow harmed by the evening's events instead of sitting happily on Seth's lap at the dinner table eating meatloaf.

"What did you want me to do? He's the owner. He came to get his dog." I reached for, and knocked over, my wineglass in my agitation; Alex caught it before it could spill but tipped his own water glass in the process. Mom jumped up to get a towel.

"You could use the senses you were given and realize when a murderer is standing in your living room," Violet said, ignoring the frantic activity around her.

"If you want to know what my *senses* are telling me, I don't think he did it." I had to lean past Mom and Alex and the mopping frenzy to look Vi in the eye. "I don't care what kind of alibi he does or does not have. It doesn't add up to me. The divorce was over. They'd already had the worst of their conflict. Why would he kill her now?"

"The tarot showed it was a man with money troubles that did it. I heard from Sara that Gary hadn't managed his money very well after the divorce," Mom said while she refilled the water glass.

"Well, I guess that confirms it. Tuffy said 'bacon' and your cards clearly identify Gary, so let's just bring all this evidence to the district attorney and we'll be set," I said.

"There's no reason to get snippy, Clyde. They're just trying to figure this out," Dad said.

Violet and I were staring at each other, neither one willing to back down.

Alex glanced from me to Vi. He hadn't been in the middle of one of these fights since high school. Seth and Tuffy stared with wide eyes.

"Stop it, both of you," said my mother. "I agree with Clyde. I'm surprised that Gary is the killer."

Violet finally broke the stare-off, a win for me.

"Let's not turn on each other here," said Dad. "The police know what they're doing. They've arrested Gary, and that's that." He poured another glass of wine, ending the discussion.

I was relieved that Dad felt that way. I hoped we could all go back to normal now that an arrest had been made.

"I know . . . ," Vi said, and drummed her fingers on the table. "We'll ask the pendulum."

"Not the pendulum." Alex groaned. He had not had good luck with the pendulum in the past. It was one of those things that Vi claimed anyone could do, but Alex had never managed to get that thing to swing. He was convinced that everyone else was moving it with their hands and he was the only honest one in the room.

"What's the pendulum?" asked Seth.

"Well, we could do that." Mom ignored Seth. "It *is* a yes or no question. Did Gary do it or not? I'll go get it." She hurried into her parlor and came back with a velvet pouch.

She carefully tipped the bag onto the table. A pointed crystal attached to a short chain slid out. Seth's eyes grew wide, my father's eyes closed, and he seemed to be talking to himself.

Vi produced a piece of paper that had a large plus sign on it. One direction indicated YES, the other No. Mom and Vi flattened the paper in the middle of the table and muttered to each other about the proper orientation.

"Okay, let's ask the pendulum," my mother said, surveying the table. "Clyde, do you want to do the honors?" She smiled as if she had offered me cake.

"No. Why don't you let Seth do it?"

Vi and Mom exchanged a glance.

"The boy has never done this. He doesn't know how," said Vi.

"It's not that hard. He can do it," I said, holding her gaze. Alex snorted next to me.

"Yeah, let me do it. What do I do?" Seth said, reaching for the crystal.

Mom covered it with her hand. After a pointed look in my direction, she turned to Seth. "Hold the crystal and concentrate on your question."

She handed the crystal to Seth, careful to touch just the chain, allowing only his energy into the crystal itself. Seth gripped the crystal and closed his eyes in concentration.

"What's the question again?" he asked, one eye popping open.

"Did Gary kill Sara?" Vi told the table as she cradled her head in her hands.

"Oh, right. Got it." Seth went back to concentrating. It looked painful.

Mom used her soothing voice, and said, "When you're ready, take the end of the chain and dangle the crystal over the center of the paper where the lines meet. Make sure it's very still and that you hold your arm steady. Then ask your question."

Seth stood and uncoiled the chain, allowing the crystal to swing free. He steadied it and hung it over the center of the paper. The room seemed to hold its breath. We all jumped when Tuffy let out a sharp yip.

Seth's pendulum began to swing from the jerking of his arm.

Vi looked at Tuffy, who was shivering again now that Seth had set him on the floor. "You're fine. This won't take long," she said to the dog.

Seth stopped the swinging crystal and held it over the paper again.

When it was still he said, "Did Gary kill Sara?"

The pendulum didn't move. We waited. These things took time. After several minutes, my father eased his chair away from the table and snuck off to the living room to read the paper and listen to his police scanner. After a few more minutes, Seth lowered his elbow onto the table.

Tuffy began a low growl but wagged his tail when Seth turned to look at him.

"There's something wrong. Ask again," said Vi.

"Did Gary kill Sara?" Seth asked, louder this time, as if the pendulum were hard of hearing.

At last, it moved. We all leaned forward to watch. It was subtle but clear. It swung back and forth about an eighth of an inch along the No axis.

"That can't be right. I'll do it," said Vi as she grabbed the pendulum from Seth.

They wiped down the crystal with the velvet, and Vi took her turn. She got results within seconds. Yes. We all decided on a tiebreaker. My best friend, Alex the traitor, voted against me, and I was chosen to hold the chain. My mother hadn't looked so proud since I had predicted old Mrs. Dunhill's death. She had been ninety.

I held the crystal and felt it get warm in my hand, then hung it over the paper and stopped its movement.

"Did Gary kill Sara?" I asked.

The chain was warm in my fingers. I focused on keeping my hand as still as possible. I felt a muscle twitch, and the chain started swinging. No.

Vi grabbed the pendulum from me and thrust it at my mother.

"You do it. You're the only one who really knows how. You'll be the final say," she said.

"But that was . . . ," Alex started. I shook my head in warning. He caught on and sat back.

My mother went through the whole process again. Her answer: No.

"Clyde, you have to talk to Mac," Mom said.

"What? Why?"

"It's obvious. The pendulum says it's not Gary." Mom gestured at the small piece of crystal. "Mac needs to know he has the wrong man in custody."

Alex grabbed his wine and took a giant gulp.

"You've got to be kidding, Mom. Mac doesn't believe in any of this. He won't care what the pendulum has to say."

"But be sure he knows to look for someone who buys bacon," Vi added.

Mom nodded solemnly in her direction.

"It's practically impeding an investigation if we don't tell him, Clyde." Mom offered Alex more wine, and he held out his glass.

"We could all be arrested!" Vi said.

"Arrested? Who will take care of Tuffy?" Seth held Tuffy tighter on his lap.

"No one is going to be arrested," I said to Seth. "Fine,

I'll talk to Mac." I had no idea how I was going to pull this off, but Mac would be easier to deal with than these two.

"So can we keep Tuffy?" asked Seth. We turned to look at him and the ball of fur that was our only witness to Sara's murder.

11

Wednesday morning started early for me. Tuffy woke up Seth with the sun and began whining to go out. After they crashed through the house and came back up the stairs, I was fully awake with no hope of going back to sleep. I got out of bed and went to my computer. I really wanted some coffee but didn't want to risk going downstairs and meeting my mother in the kitchen. She was a morning person. I was a night person. Just one more thing we had to argue over.

I checked my e-mail to discover that several friends were demanding I drive to Ann Arbor for a party that weekend. Not likely.

A message from a friend in the department said they were still investigating the last case I had worked. I skimmed the details, not really wanting to know. They weren't going to find anything that would fix what had happened. The decision about my police career would have to wait. I shut the laptop and decided to risk the coffee run.

I crept downstairs, avoiding the creaky fifth step, and peered around the wall into the dining room. No sign of anyone. I didn't hear any noise from Vi's end of the house, but she hadn't seen six a.m. in decades. I made it through the dining room and into the kitchen without incident. There was already coffee in the pot, which meant Mom was up, but where?

I quickly grabbed a mug and poured a cup, liberally adding milk and sugar. I was just starting to rummage for some cereal when I sensed a shift in the room. I turned, but no one was there.

Sometimes this house really creeps me out. My grandmother lived here all her life, and my mother and aunt swear she's still here, even though they'd never "contacted" her. Every once in a while, I'm sure they're right. You couldn't grow up in a town full of mediums and not at least entertain the idea of ghosts.

I stood there, waiting, feeling a cool breeze where there should not have been one, and then it was gone. I heard the *tap tap tap* of Tuffy's nails on the hardwood, and he and Seth came into the kitchen.

"Ahh!" Seth said. He jumped back and stepped on Tuffy, who squeaked and glared at me.

"What?" I said.

"You scared me. I thought I heard something, and Tuffy was acting scared, so we came down to check it out."

"He probably sensed I was about to eat," I said.

"Very funny. He's more sensitive than you give him credit for."

"What were you going to do if you found something? Scream at it?"

"No. I just . . . I didn't know you were awake, and then you were standing there and you scared me, okay?"

"Fine." I poured the cereal.

I dropped Seth back at the house after our morning rounds. I had some work to do and needed to be alone. I wanted to talk to Tish again and see if I could get any more information out of her. I was still bothered by the sense that she knew something about Sara's death. It was strange that the usually gossipy Tish hadn't asked any questions about Sara's murder or the investigation. And there was something going on between Tish and my mother. It wasn't like her to just breeze in and then leave. She hadn't even stopped to gush with my mom and Vi about her retreat. She used to spend every Friday evening at our house, but I had hardly seen her since I moved back home.

I went straight to the Reading Room. It was a converted city building that was used for psychic readings. The city council also offered workshops on tarot reading and psychic development, mostly in the summer months. Only the psychics that had been licensed by the city could give readings there, and it was a great way to get new clients. Tish was a regular on Wednesday mornings.

I approached the building with some caution, as I didn't want to meet Harriet Munson. She was in charge of organizing who was in the building and when. I had been involved in a small infraction of the psychic licensing bylaws as a teenager. Occasionally, I had come here with Tish and had offered my own brand of psychic advice before I decided to give it up forever. Harriet had never forgiven me for working without a license. And more than that, for telling her daughter that she should definitely pursue a career in acting instead of getting married. Harriet still didn't have any grandchildren. It would be best if we didn't cross paths.

I ducked inside the door behind a group of tourists and spotted Tish sitting in her usual place. She wasn't alone, but I had planned for that problem. Tish was very popular, and I knew it was unlikely she would be without a client. I tried to stay with the group and keep my head down. I hoped to sneak over to speak with her between readings.

I couldn't see who was with her, but she wasn't giving a reading. Normally, during a session, she sat fairly still and seemed serene. Instead, she was gesturing and getting red in the face, arguing with whoever was there. The man was trying to calm her down. I couldn't tell who it was. My group was heading in the wrong direction for me to listen in on Tish's conversation. I was about to break away from them when I spotted Harriet across the room checking in another group of hopeful tourists waiting to hear their fortunes or to contact a loved one. She hadn't noticed me. I was up on tiptoe to see over the person next to me.

Tish didn't look happy.

"Clytemnestra Fortune! What are you doing here?" said a high-pitched voice.

I slumped down off my toes and tried to blend into the crowd, which was much smaller than I originally thought, consisting of only four older women and me. Very few people still called me Clytemnestra. Harriet was one of them.

Harriet's short heels clicked their way over to me in quick, angry taps.

"Hello, Mrs. Munson. It's nice to see you after so much time." I tried for the charm angle.

"You know I don't approve of unlicensed psychics in the Reading Room," she whispered as she approached. She stood pointing her finger at me, bringing herself to her full five feet one inch.

The ladies had pulled away from me at her approach, but now they began to edge closer again at the idea that I was not just a psychic, but a rule-breaking renegade psychic at that. I kept one eye on Tish and her visitor, but I still couldn't tell what they were talking about. The acoustics were arranged to maintain privacy by several people working at one time in the same area.

"I'm just here to visit Tish. I'm not working. Actually, I don't do that at all anymore."

Harriet sniffed. My group moved away again.

"Yes, I had heard that." Harriet gave me the once-over, and narrowed her eyes in disapproval. "Well, as you can see, she's with a client right now."

I glanced over to see an elderly woman taking the chair in front of Tish. The man she'd been arguing with was just going out the door. My breath caught, and my mind raced— it was the same guy who had stopped to pet Baxter in the street yesterday.

"Okay, I'd better go, then. Nice seeing you, Mrs. Munson," I said, and hurried out the door after the mystery man before she could stop me.

I wanted to catch up to him and—do what? Accuse him

of petting Tish's dog? I raced out the door while glancing back at Tish and ran straight into Mac.

He gripped my arms to keep me from falling over.

Mac smelled really good. Like pine trees and fresh breezes off the lake. I tried to get my footing while he held me for a moment too long. Long enough to remember how much I liked being this close to him. From the way his eyes got soft, he was remembering, too.

"Hey, what's the rush?" he said, and set me back onto my feet.

"Oh, um, no rush. I came to talk to Tish and she's busy, so I'll just come back later," I said.

"I heard Andrews made his arrest on your front porch." Mac had dropped his cane during our collision. He bent to pick it up.

"Yeah, it was a bit dramatic. Gary was at the house picking up his dog." I rubbed my arms where his hands had been, still feeling the heat.

"Andrews could have picked him up earlier, but I think he wanted to impress you." Mac was standing too close. I had to look up to see his eyes.

"Impress me?" I stepped back and wondered where this was going.

"You mean you haven't noticed how he gets weak in the knees whenever you're around? You're slipping, Clyde."

We had to move aside to let a group out the door. Mac took my arm, and we stood in the grass off to the side of the walkway.

"Don't be ridiculous. We're just old family friends."

"Uh-huh. Well, I'm glad to have it over and done with. I wasn't looking forward to a long investigation in this town."

"Are you sure it was Gary?"

"I wouldn't have had him arrested if I wasn't sure. He lied about his alibi. He had a motive and opportunity."

"So? People lie all the time. It doesn't make them murderers."

"Just leave it alone, Clyde."

The air around us had become much cooler. Mac stepped past me and went into the Reading Room without another word.

With Mac out of his office, it seemed like a good time to visit the police station and see what I could learn.

Lisa smiled when I entered the station.

"Mac's not here right now," she said.

I sighed. "I'm looking for Officer Andrews."

Lisa flushed. "He's out, too. He's checking on a report of digging near Message Circle."

"Again?"

She nodded. "The crazy thing is, whoever is doing it is trying to fill in all the holes when they're done. I thought it was kids playing treasure hunt or something, but now it's been going on for long enough that I doubt it's a couple of eight-year-olds pretending to be pirates," she said.

"Where is it happening?" I said.

"Well, kind of all over in the park. Some of it is on private land, but not much. Sara complained that her land had some areas dug up about a month ago. But I shouldn't be talking about it. Charla always says I don't know when to keep quiet." She turned to her computer and pretended to be busy. Charla was right. Lisa never could keep a secret, which was bad for those trying to keep a secret but great for those trying to get information.

I decided to bluff. "My Mom told me about that—I think it's near my Dad's cabin. . . ."

Lisa was already shaking her head. "I don't think so. Isn't his place on the west side of Singapore Highway? She owned a lot that her father bought from the city back in the nineties when they consolidated some of the park on the south side of Greer's Woods." Lisa was drawing a crude map on a scrap piece of paper. "She and Gary split it in the divorce settlement. That's what they were always fighting about. He wanted to sell and she didn't, but the developers wouldn't take his land without hers."

"And that's the area that's being vandalized?" I indicated the area south of Greer's Woods.

"Not the only one. Also over here." She pointed with her pencil to a section that was adjacent to Greer's Woods. "You know the city council is not going to put up with trouble anywhere *near* Message Circle."

"They'll have Tom out there guarding it on his off hours next."

She laughed and nodded. The phone rang and she held up a finger while she answered it.

I wondered why I hadn't heard of this from my mother and aunt. They must have known that Sara and Gary had been fighting over the land. That would have only strengthened the argument that Gary had killed her. I'd heard about the developers wanting to put in a strip mall out along the coast highway. The town was very much divided on that score. Some were excited about the new stores and services it might bring in. Others were mourning the loss of the forest and the natural beauty of that area just outside town. And there was the give-them-an-inch camp that saw the strip mall taking over the whole town within months of its completion.

Lisa hung up the phone and offered to leave a message for Andrews.

"No, that's okay. I'll try to reach him later. Hey, do you have any news on Gary Landess?" I knew I was pushing my luck, but I had to try.

"No, he's still back in holding. They're waiting to transfer him to Grand Rapids. His lawyer has been in and out all day demanding this, that, and the other." Her hair didn't move when she shook her head.

"Nothing new, then?"

"Well, you know they don't tell me much." She frowned. "But, I'm pretty sure they're treating it like it's all wrapped up."

12

I left the police station lost in thought and found myself a few minutes later in front of Stark's place. How convenient. It concerned me that I was practically haunting the Grill—I didn't want to be lumped in with the "regulars" who sat in the back booth and gossiped all afternoon—but these were desperate times. I needed to talk to Alex *now*.

It was after the lunchtime rush, so the dining room was mostly empty. I stepped inside. A young man with hair in his eyes was bussing tables in the slow and distracted fashion of the truly bored. He didn't notice me weave through the dining area and up to the kitchen door marked EMPLOYEES ONLY.

Just as I was about to push it open, it swung toward me and would have given me a black eye if I hadn't jumped back in time.

"Oh, sorry," said the Baxter-petting, Tish-arguing man.

"No problem. I was standing too close to the door," I said. My mind raced through every person I had ever known trying to figure out how I knew this guy. It was the eyes that got me.

"If you're looking for Alex, he's in the back." He hooked his thumb over his shoulder, smiled, and headed out the front door.

The busboy gave him a "Later, dude" which didn't help me at all.

I blinked and squinted at the bright lights of the kitchen. After the dim dining room, I was surprised the waitstaff didn't routinely run into each other through temporary blindness.

I found Alex in the walk-in fridge, taking inventory of his produce. He dictated his list to a young man with a buzz cut and tattooed arms.

"Clyde, hi. Did anyone see you come back here?" He looked past me over my shoulder.

Not the warmest welcome, but I understood. Joe Stark had a strict policy on visitors to the kitchen.

"I don't think so. The busboy is in some alternate universe and the dining room is empty."

"Stark just left, Alex," the assistant said.

"Oh, good." Alex took the top pages and handed the clipboard to his assistant. "Come on back to the office," Alex said to me.

"Hey, did you see a guy back here just before I came in? Shaved head? A little taller than me?"

"Yeah, that's Milo."

"Milo?"

"Milo Jones." Alex said the name slowly, as if he was speaking to a recalcitrant busboy. "He's the land developer in charge of the strip mall project out by the highway. He's also Joe's son, which apparently gives him the right to muck around in my kitchen."

"That's Milo Stark?" I could feel that my mouth was hanging open in an unattractive way, but I couldn't help it. No wonder he'd looked familiar. But, he'd changed a lot since I'd seen him last. For one thing, he used to have gorgeous dark curly hair.

"Milo *Jones*. I don't know why they have different last names. Joe introduced him as his son." Alex shrugged and sat at his desk, unbothered by the reappearance of Milo Stark.

"Don't you remember the Milo Stark scandal?" I said, and sat in the only other chair. "I was still in junior high when it happened. I guess it had all died down by the time you moved here in high school." I was mostly mumbling to myself—a habit Alex adored.

"What are you talking about?" He sighed, glowered at me, and set down his papers.

"Milo has been gone for a long time. I heard he joined the army. Then I heard he was dead. No one knew what happened to him." I was talking fast, feeling edgy as I remembered those days after Julia Wyatt went missing.

"Well, clearly, he's alive and well and planning on building a strip mall, when he isn't interfering in my kitchen. Why the mystery?"

"There was some trouble the summer after he graduated from high school. A girl went missing, and he was the last person seen with her." I forced myself to slow down. "Of course, everyone in town got involved. The psychics all weighed in on whether she was dead or alive and where she might be."

There had been tarot readings and animal consultations at my house. I had still been young enough that I hadn't turned my back on the feelings and messages I received. My mom and Vi had hounded me every morning for a dream report and watched me for any change in demeanor that could indicate I knew something. All I saw when I thought of Julia was bruises. I could hear her crying and saw the grayish-purple marks on her arms and legs, but nothing more. Grace had moved all the way to New York City by then, due to one of my dreams. My family was looking to me to solve the mystery of Julia's disappearance and establish myself as the true heir to my grandmother's talents.

"Wow, I can't believe I've never heard this. I thought Sara was the first murder in Crystal Haven."

"Well, technically that's true. Julia's body was never found, but her clothing was discovered in the woods. She and Milo dated for most of high school. He left town shortly after the investigation closed, and he hasn't been seen since, as far as I know."

"He certainly hasn't been acting like a fugitive from justice," Alex said. "He's been acting more like returning royalty if you ask me. He's been in and out of town all spring, working on this project. And has no qualms about rearranging my kitchen and giving helpful hints to the staff. He and Stark are at each other, though. Joe doesn't want the strip mall, so he's always fighting the zoning."

"There's not a lot of fatherly support?"

"You could say that."

"I saw Milo arguing with Tish today. What could Tish have to do with him? And Milo knew Baxter. He stopped to pet him outside the restaurant the other day."

"I couldn't tell you. I wouldn't be surprised if he argues with plenty of people in town."

I left Alex to his work and was halfway to my car when I remembered I had wanted to tell him about the digging and Sara's land.

I went home to get two things; a stack of targets and my gun.

Thoughts and suspicions swirled in my head. I had to go do the only thing guaranteed to clear my mind: shoot things.

I don't like hunting. But I discovered while in the police academy that I like guns. I like to shoot them and to hold them and the sound they make and the power that shoots up your arm when the bullet leaves the barrel. Even though my police career was possibly over due to a shooting incident, I still hadn't found a better way to think than in that moment before I pulled the trigger.

I grabbed my Browning .22, since it is my favorite target pistol. I left my Glock locked in its box. I had no intention of shooting it until I decided whether I was returning to Ann Arbor.

I stopped at the small cabin my father had built when my sister and I were young. We used to come out here and camp in the summer. Now my father used it chiefly to get away from my aunt. It was set on three acres of woodland that was about a half mile west of the hotly disputed land of the developer. I wondered what would happen to our place if Milo succeeded in building his strip mall.

I walked out to the poor tree that had always served as the hanger for the target and hung the first one of the day.

I walked away from the tree, turned, and took three deep breaths.

As I took aim through the sight, I felt the calm enter my body. When my hand was steady, I held my breath, pulled the trigger, and braced for the recoil. I felt it go up my arm into my shoulder. My mind was mercifully blank. I unloaded the clip into the tree and felt more at peace than I had since I found Sara's body lying motionless on her kitchen floor.

A quick examination of the target showed I was a little off my game, but at least the shots were all near the center.

I shredded four more targets until my arm got tired.

I felt calmer, but no nearer to a solution. I was past caring whether the answer came from my rusty psychic sense or from that intuitive flash of insight that I sometimes felt when working a case. My "gift" was not in the habit of helping out when I wanted answers. It was more likely to give me riddles and scary visions. I still had questions without answers and was unsure how to proceed. I was suspicious of Milo, Tish was acting strangely, and I didn't know whether Gary was capable of killing his ex-wife. And, after my mistake in the spring, I realized I no longer trusted my instincts.

I packed the gun and targets away. The rutted trail that led to my dad's cabin was barely passable in a car. The Jeep bounced along through the trees and I breathed a sigh of relief as I pulled out onto the highway. I glanced in my rearview mirror and thought I saw a bald man walk into the woods. But when I slowed and turned my head to look, he had disappeared.

13

❧❦

I arrived home to chaos. My mother's angry voice came from inside the house. Dad and Seth met me in the front yard. I asked what was going on inside.

"I was on the computer, I got distracted . . ." Seth began.

"It looks like a 10-80 in there. I'm going back to work."

Dad had every Wednesday afternoon off, so I knew that was a lie. He shook his head and mumbled something about the "usual insanity" before slamming his car door.

Seth looked to me for a translation.

"10-80 is a bomb explosion," I said.

Seth nodded. "That's about right. I'm really sorry," Seth said.

"What did you do?" I asked.

"Not me—Tuffy."

Seth and I took the steps two at a time and followed the shrieks toward the living room.

"Look at this room! It's ruined!" my mother said, her arms out to encompass the wreckage.

Tuffy was nowhere to be seen, but his handiwork was evident throughout the room. The throw pillows were scattered everywhere, some of them gutted, their fiberfill innards spilling onto the carpet. Fringe had been ripped from its ribbon and the strands were draped on the furniture like tinsel on an overly adorned Christmas tree.

"Now, Rose, you know he's distraught. You're scaring him. I won't be able to find out why he did this if you don't calm down," Vi said. She was approaching my mother while patting the space in front of her as if trying to calm the very air around her.

Unfortunately, my mother spotted Seth and me standing in the doorway.

"You two are responsible for this." She pointed a shaky finger at us. Seth stepped behind me.

"Mom, what happened?"

"Tuffy happened, that's what. Where have you been? You should see the bathroom. It's like a band of drunken teenagers got lost in there and tried to TP the entire room."

"Where's Tuffy now?" I asked, glancing around the room.

"Who knows? He disappeared as soon as I discovered what he'd done in here."

"You mean as soon as you started screaming," Vi said.

"Nana Rose, I'll clean it up. I should have locked Tuffy in my room," Seth said from over my shoulder.

That statement left me speechless for a moment.

"You will?" I asked.

Seth nodded.

"Let me go find Tuffy. I'm pretty sure I know where he is," Seth said, and headed toward the bathroom.

We traipsed after him.

The sea of white assaulted us as we peeked into the room.

"What the f—heck?" I said. I glanced at Seth.

He looked at me with flat eyes. "Really? F—heck?"

I shrugged.

Seth bent to one knee by the toilet and talked quietly. After a moment, a quivering ball of fur emerged from behind the toilet bowl and rushed into Seth's arms.

"Well, I'll help you clean up, Seth," Vi said. "Let's get Tuffy settled in my living room, and we can fix up this room and Rose's living room right quick."

The three of them scooted past my mother and disappeared down the hall.

My mother's face was returning to its normal shade of pale, which made me feel better.

I knew what would calm her down.

"Why don't we have some tea, Mom?"

"Okay." She nodded slowly. "Then I probably ought to help them clean up, too. They'll never do it right."

Over our cups of tea, my mother told me about Tuffy's strange behavior that afternoon. He'd begun barking at the wall in the living room, cocking his head and looking up, wagging his tail a little. She had gone to get Vi to show her. They had gotten involved in a conversation about the neighbor's cat and some gossip about their teenage daughter sneaking out at night. This made me grateful we'd never had a tattletale cat when I was growing up. By the time they went back out to find Tuffy, he had destroyed two rooms of the house.

"Vi says it must have been Sara visiting Tuffy. Dogs can see Spirit better than we can. Sometimes it scares them. But really, did he need to shred every pillow in the room?" She tucked a stray hair back into what was usually a smooth bun.

I felt a cold tingle run down my back when she mentioned Sara's ghost. I thought back to that morning when I had felt something strange and Seth had said Tuffy was scared. Sensing, seeing, or talking to ghosts was *not* one of my gifts, thank goodness. But I had felt something. . . .

"I don't know, Mom. He's a strange little dog. He's always acted afraid of me, every time he's seen me. The only person besides Sara I've ever seen him respond to is Seth."

"Well, at least we don't have that small pony of Tish's to deal with anymore."

"Mom, what's up with you and Tish?"

My mother suddenly took a great interest in her tea mug.

"There's nothing up with Tish. Same old, same old," she said. But her voice was tight, and she had a death grip on the mug.

"She hasn't been here to visit since I moved in. She used to practically live here. What happened with you two?" I tried to catch her eye, but she avoided my gaze.

"Oh, you know Tish. She can get herself all worked up over one thing or another." She waved her hand to indicate the many things Tish could get worked up about. "She'll come around."

"Yeah, but what *is* she worked up over?" I asked.

"This and that. It has to do with the city council and Sara." She stood and took her mug to the sink. "Nothing you would care about. Psychic stuff."

I hated this little game. She was trying to draw me in,

and the next thing I knew I would find myself in front of the council applying for a license. Well, I had learned a few things since I'd left home.

"Okay," I said.

As I walked out of the kitchen, I didn't have to turn around to know she was staring after me with her hands on her hips.

14

I had left Seth and Tuffy to deal with the disaster at the house and finished the dog-walking on my own. It was nice to be out on a warm and breezy day walking the streets of Crystal Haven. But even the calming effects of exercise and gentle breezes through the trees weren't enough to stop my brain from spinning with possibilities and suspicions. I headed to Diana's hoping to catch her before closing.

Moonward Magick was deserted. The Wednesday afternoon slump hit everyone, even the witches. Diana knew about my various battles with my mother and was always willing to listen. I found her in the back of the store, sorting through boxes of crystal balls and stands. She was muttering to herself and I waited, thinking she was casting some sort of selling spell. Then I heard "ordered three, not thirty" followed by a string of colorful profanity. I hoped it wasn't a spell, or the person who had messed up the order was in for some interesting anatomical rearrangements.

"Hey," I said, and tapped her shoulder.

"Aaah!" She dropped her packing list and spun around, eyes wild, her hand grasping for her necklace. This was an old and amusing trick. Diana was easily startled, but it never lost its charm.

"You know better than to do that," she said, clutching her amulet.

"I do, but it's really fun to watch," I said.

"You're lucky I didn't spin around and throw one of these at you." She gestured to the crystal balls.

"I came to hear the séance story, if you have time." I glanced around the empty store and raised my right eyebrow.

"Very funny. Okay, let me turn on the door buzzer. We can have some tea in the back, and you can tell me about your mother."

I sighed. She always knew what was really bothering me.

After we were settled to her satisfaction with organic black tea and homemade carrot cake, she started her story. The séance had been scheduled partly as a demonstration, and partly at the request of Melanie Hicks. Melanie was recently widowed and desperately wanted to contact her deceased husband. Sara needed more people to complete the circle and, as word spread, the spots had filled quickly.

"Obviously, Cecile and Joe Stark came," Diana said through a mouthful of cake. "I think she's addicted to psychics. Several of the readers in town will only see her once a year, but she has enough access that she's probably getting a reading every week."

I nodded agreement about Cecile's dependence on

psychic advice. Some people did come to rely on it for just about everything, unable to make the slightest decision on their own.

"There were six of us besides Sara, all sitting around the table." She had closed her eyes, and she spoke as if she was seeing the table again in her mind. "Melanie, Tish, Milo Jones, Joe Stark, Cecile Stark, then me, then Sara."

"Cecile must have dragged Joe. I didn't think he was into séances," I said.

Diana nodded. "I think she did. Milo seemed to be really interested, but Joe just looked uncomfortable. Anyway, the séance started, and it was incredible. Almost immediately the room became frigid."

"Had you been to one of Sara's séances before?"

"Yeah, once or twice, and she was really good, but I had never seen things happen that fast." She sipped her tea, and her eyes stared past me for a moment. "The dead husband started to give a message to Melanie. He was talking to her about her golf swing, of all things. I thought it was pretty silly to come back from the other side and waste your time talking about golf, but she seemed to think that was typical of him. Then, right in the middle of his message, Sara's voice changed, and *another* spirit seemed to come into the room. This one made everyone feel uncomfortable."

"Was it the sound of the voice, or something else?" I asked. I put my fork down and tried to catch her eye. But she looked down at her plate.

"I don't know how to describe it, but it seemed angry, and for the first time I was scared at a séance. Sara started saying, 'Where are you' and looking around the circle. She didn't sound friendly. Then she looked straight toward the end of the table, and said, 'No murder will go unpunished.' I couldn't tell if she was looking at Tish or Joe or Milo. They were all at that end of the table, and Sara was unfocused and still seemed to be looking for someone." Diana had been mashing her cake with her fork and suddenly seemed to notice what she was doing.

"What happened after that?" I was getting all the signals that I usually tried to ignore: buzzing ears, cold hands, tight chest. Something important had happened that night.

"Tish broke the circle." Diana shrugged. "She stood up and sort of stepped behind Milo and Joe. Sara looked at her, and said, 'I know what you did.' But I couldn't tell if she was talking to Tish. Tish was totally freaked out and backed up into the cabinet Sara has there in the dining room. A few of the display plates fell and shattered. That was the end of the séance. Sara came back from her trance and was disoriented for a minute, but she quickly recovered."

"Did she remember everything that happened?"

Diana shook her head. "I couldn't tell. She acted like she did, but she ushered everyone out pretty quickly. The rest of us were shaken up and didn't linger to discuss the séance the way we normally would. I just wanted to get home and get warm again." She rubbed her arms.

"Wow, it sounds like someone got a message. It's just not clear who." I'd lost my appetite and pushed the cake away.

"Well, they never really did clear Milo of that whole mess in high school."

"That's true. . . . Did the voice sound like a man or a woman?"

"You know how these things are. It's hard to tell." Diana lifted her shoulder and tilted her head.

"Tish has been acting really strangely. My mother says it has to do with the city council and Sara, but I saw her arguing with Milo over at the Reading Room this morning. Do you think she could have something to do with Sara's death?"

She finally raised her eyes to mine and took on her serious tone. "Clyde, Tish was more like a mother to you than your own mother. She was always there for you, for both of us, whenever we got in trouble. I just can't imagine her hurting anyone."

I put my hand up to ward off any further lecture. "You're right. I just don't know what's up with her, and I'm not convinced it was Gary who killed Sara."

"If they arrested him, it sounds like the police believe it was Gary."

"I know. Mac won't even talk about continuing to investigate. I haven't been able to talk to Tom."

"Well, Mac hasn't had the best luck with psychic intervention. . . ." She sipped her tea again and then focused on her smushed cake.

I chose to ignore the comment. We had been over this ground too many times. Diana knew Mac and I had clashed over my psychic abilities in the past. I was about to launch into a whine about my mother when the buzzer sounded.

Diana jumped up and peeked out into the store.

"I'll have to go deal with this. It's a whole group and they look a little lost."

"Okay, I should be getting home anyway."

After pushing my way out through the crowd, I walked toward the police station, where my car was parked. I checked my watch and tried to remember how much time was left on the meter. When not fighting crime, the Crystal Haven police aggressively ticketed all expired meters.

Rushing to rescue my car from a ticket, I almost ran right into Sara's daughter Alison, who stood outside the police station wiping her eyes with a wad of tissue and breathing heavily. We had met about a month before when I first started walking Tuffy. She didn't see me coming, and I didn't see her until I was almost on top of her.

"Alison! I'm so sorry. I didn't see you there." I grabbed her shoulders to keep her from stumbling.

"Oh, hi," she sniffed. "I met you at my mom's right? Are you a client?"

"No, I took care of Tuffy for her." I stuck out my hand. "Clyde Fortune." She briefly gave me a damp, limp hand. Must have learned that from her father.

She nodded. "I remember. You're the brave one taking care of him." She gave me a watery smile.

"Are you okay?"

"No." She took a shaky breath. "I just found out that it was my statement that got my father arrested." Tears began leaking out of her eyes again.

"What statement?"

"I don't know if I should be talking about this." She glanced back at the police station. "But you were a friend of my mother's, weren't you?"

"Yes, I think so. I didn't know her well, but we were friendly and my mother was very close to her."

"Oh, right, Rose's daughter!" She rummaged in her pocket for more tissues. "My mother adored her." This statement brought on a new round of tears.

She scrubbed her eyes, smearing mascara onto her cheeks.

"I'm sorry," she said after cleaning up her makeup using a small mirror she produced from her bag. "What were you saying?"

I reminded her about the statement.

"Oh, yeah. I'd given my father an alibi for the morning of my mother's . . . death." More tears but not as many.

"And then you changed your statement?"

She nodded while she looked for more tissues.

"I know he didn't hurt her, but after I talked to Tish, I just couldn't lie anymore."

"Tish? What does she have to do with this?"

Alison seemed to be gaining control of the tears. She took a deep shuddering breath. "She stopped at my apartment to tell me how sorry she was about my mother, but also to say she had been in contact with her and that she said I should always be truthful." Alison's eyes were wide and sincere.

"Tish told you your mother wanted you to be honest? So you came to the police station and changed your statement, removing your father's alibi?"

She nodded. "I just wanted to protect him. I know he wasn't at my mother's house that morning, but I couldn't lie anymore and say he was with me." She gestured with her wad of tissues. "Her death has to have something to do with whoever was tormenting her on the Internet."

I was completely lost and must have looked it.

Alison took a couple of bracing breaths. "There was someone who was threatening my mother through her website with comments on her blog. Whoever it was accused her of putting on a show to cover her lack of talent. They said she should stop doing séances or face the consequences. At first she just shrugged it off, but I know it started to bother her. That's who they should be looking for; my father didn't do anything." This led to another round of sniffles and eye-dabbing.

"What happened when you changed your statement?" I feared my question would set her off again, but I had to find out how much trouble Tish had caused.

"My dad is scared. He won't reveal his alibi, and since we lied, they think he did it and that I was protecting him. He's facing murder charges, and they're deciding whether to charge me as an accessory—to my own mother's murder!" She began sobbing in earnest, and all I could do was gently pat her shoulder and murmur soothing lies about how it would all work out.

That night, Seth and I stood near the back porch steps and played fetch with Tuffy. It had been a tough day for all of us. Tuffy was no longer welcome in the house without an escort. He may or may not have been visited by his dead owner. Sara had accused someone of murder at her last séance, only we didn't know who. Tish was acting strangely, and my mother was keeping something from me. Seth was sulky and I didn't know if that was normal teenage behavior or some other thing to worry about, and Milo (Stark) Jones was back in town.

"What do you think will happen to Tuffy?" Seth interrupted my morose thoughts with his own brand of doom and gloom.

"I don't know. Gary can't take him right now, and it doesn't sound like Alison will want him. I'm not really up on the custody rules with dogs. Maybe they'll interview him and let him decide." I tried for a smile, but Seth seemed to take this suggestion seriously.

"I hope he picks me. I really like him." Seth kicked at the grass. "I've never had a dog."

"We'll have to wait and see what happens, Seth. I wouldn't get my hopes up if I were you."

"I don't think Gary did it. But I also don't think Tuffy would want to live with him."

"Why do you say that?"

"I don't know." He continued to study the ground.

"Well, Tuffy didn't seem that happy to see him, I'll give you that. But he was never happy to see anyone, except Sara and you."

"Vi says it was probably Gary, but she never liked Gary and she lets it color what she thinks," he said to his shoe.

"She does have strong opinions. . . ."

"Well, you can't let your opinions influence what the animals are trying to tell you."

I turned to look at him in the fading light. His face was turned away from me, watching Tuffy follow the scent of a rabbit or squirrel, which was hours old but still entertaining.

"Who do you think did it, Seth?"

He shrugged. "But whoever it was scared Tuffy to death."

15

I found myself on Thursday morning waiting for Mac in a coffee shop. I couldn't believe how much had changed in just three days. I picked apart my scone and slowly sipped my coffee. The Daily Grind, owned by Alex's partner, Josh, had the best coffee in town and the best scones in my known universe. It was small, with a half dozen tables in dark wood to match the counter, and two highly coveted couches. The room held the blended aroma of fresh-brewed coffee, cinnamon, and sugar. Mac was almost never late. I checked my watch, sighed, smiled at Josh. I had asked him once if I could live there—just use a sleeping bag in the back office—but he'd started in on health codes and whatnot. The only reason I had procured a table was because it wasn't a weekend. The locals avoided the coffee shop on Saturday and Sunday as it became a take-out-only type of place by necessity, with a line snaking out the door and spilling into the street.

Finally, I saw Mac round the corner down the street. I tidied the area to make it seem like I had just sat down, and looked at Josh with one finger to my lips. He shook his head and shrugged.

"Hey, sorry I'm late. I got held up at the station and couldn't get away," Mac said as he limped into the café.

"No problem. I just got here myself." I waved off his apology. I heard a distinct snort from behind the counter but didn't risk sending a glare that way.

Mac left his cane at the table and went to the counter to order. When he'd settled with his food, he smiled and rubbed his hands together. Mac loved coffee and, apparently, scones.

"I wouldn't have guessed you were a scone kind of guy."

"I'm not, but the ones they have here are in another category." He proceeded to add four packs of sugar and cream to his coffee.

"Well, I'm glad you had time to meet me today." I looked away from what he was doing to his drink.

"I'm always happy to see you, Clyde, particularly now that you aren't part of an active investigation." He bit into his scone and tried to smile around it.

"That's sort of what I wanted to talk to you about." I broke off another piece of cranberry scone but didn't eat it.

Mac's smile vanished.

"You want to talk about Sara's murder?"

"Well, yes. What did you think I wanted to talk about?"

"I . . . wasn't sure, but I didn't think it would be about a case that was closed." Mac sat up straight and began clearing his half-eaten pastry away, brushing the crumbs into a napkin. Now that things were all business, I supposed he didn't want to be distracted. "What do you have to say?"

I steeled myself and thought of my promise to my mother. "I don't think Gary did it." I thought this was better than saying the pendulum didn't think Gary did it.

Mac held up his hand like a stop sign.

"I know how you feel about this, Clyde. But you don't have all the facts. How would you feel if someone was poking around in one of your investigations?"

"I'm not poking around. Did you know that Tish put Alison up to changing her story about Gary's alibi?"

Mac grew still. "No, I didn't know that." His eyes were hard to read, and he wouldn't meet my gaze. "Do you think Alison is lying?"

"No, I think she's telling the truth now." I could hear my voice going up an octave but was powerless to stop the whine that was creeping in. "But it concerns me that Tish got her to change her statement by claiming it's what Sara wanted."

"She told us she'd had a change of heart. In either case, her father doesn't have an alibi, and he lied about it in the first place. It makes him look pretty good for the murder. Most homicides—"

"—are committed by someone close to the victim. I know." I tried not to sound completely frustrated. "Are you even considering other suspects at this point?"

"I really can't talk about this with you. You're a witness. You could be called to testify." He sat back in his chair and crossed his arms. I knew from long experience that he was wrapping this up, and I'd better make my case quickly.

I swallowed, and then dove in. "Have you heard about Sara's last . . . séance?"

I didn't quite flinch, but I was mentally preparing for the onslaught of either laughter or lecture. Mac was the world's biggest nonbeliever—even the mention of psychics or spirits usually caused him to turn an unattractive shade of purple. His mother had been widowed young and had spent the rest of her life and much of her income on mediums in an attempt to contact Mac's father. It was an ongoing argument between them. He did not have an open mind on the subject. But I thought the *accusation* of murder, whether from a spirit or not, could have put Sara in danger and Mac needed to know about it.

"The one where a 'spirit' accused everyone there of being a murderer?" He sighed and rubbed his forehead as if an aneurism was coming on. "Yeah, I heard about it."

"Well? Are you looking into that at all?"

"Listen," Mac said. He leaned forward as if he was going to tell me a secret, but something over my shoulder distracted him. I turned. Tish and Joe Stark were across the street, clearly arguing. Tish said something to Joe and turned to walk away. He grabbed her arm, and they struggled for a moment. I wouldn't have wanted to be on the receiving end of the look she gave him before she stormed off toward the Reading Room. Joe smoothed his hair back, checked up and down the street, and walked in the opposite direction.

"Something's up, Mac. You should go talk to him."

"It's none of our business. Whatever they were talking about, it's over now. If I stopped every person in town that had an argument, I wouldn't have time to do my job."

"Maybe your job would be easier if you followed up on a few arguments."

"Really." His voice was flat. "This is how you're going to play it?"

I picked up my cup, but it was empty. "You can't overlook the séance just because it involves psychics."

"I'm not overlooking it. I just don't have anything to go on yet." His mouth was a tight line. "However, if Sara did accuse someone who then killed her, that person is still out there. I don't want you mucking around and getting yourself into trouble."

"I can take care of myself." I knew I was starting to sound like a rebellious teenager and hated that we had slipped into this old way of relating.

"I know that. But people are afraid of you. They think you know things. Just try to stay under the radar on this. I don't want you getting hurt." I was torn between feeling happy that he was concerned about me and annoyed that he was treating me like some sort of helpless damsel.

"Mac, I—" His steel blue gaze stopped me. He was capable of extreme stubbornness, and pushing him further would only lead to both of us stalking off into our respective corners. I started again. "Okay, I get it."

"Good, that's settled." He smiled, but I knew he didn't buy it. "I'm glad you wanted to meet me anyway." He looked for his snack, but he had balled it all up into a napkin. "I hoped we could talk. I'm sorry about the way I acted the other day at the station."

"No worries. Like you said, 'ancient history.' " I echoed his slice through the air. I was still irritated that he wouldn't listen and hated this ability of his to change the subject and pretend nothing was wrong.

"Don't do this, Clyde. I'm trying to—"

"To what? To make yourself feel better for disappearing?" The words were out of my mouth before my brain had time to edit. I did not want to talk about this.

He tilted his head and took a breath. "I'm trying to say

I'm sorry. And I didn't disappear; you knew where to find me." I wasn't sure what he was talking about. The way I remembered it, he fled across the state because he couldn't deal with my premonitions. Technically, I knew where he'd gone, but he hadn't encouraged me to follow. I had joined the force in Ann Arbor to get away from the psychics and to forget Mac.

"And you made it pretty clear you didn't want to be found." I realized my voice had gotten loud when I saw that everyone in the café had stopped what they were doing to better listen in on our conversation.

Mac looked surprised, but then leaned forward and lowered his voice. "I'd like for us to be friends. Can we get together for dinner or something and talk?"

"You mean like a *date*?" I was purposely trying to annoy.

He sat back and narrowed his eyes, as if trying to decide his next move in a chess game. I had expected a blustery denial, or an irritated "forget it."

"Sure. A date. Tonight? I'll pick you up."

I felt my eyebrows rise in reaction. I nodded, not knowing how else to respond. I feigned interest in my scone again, trying to regroup and figure out how this had happened. Mac stood and nodded at the crowd still watching us and walked out the door, hardly using his cane.

I grimaced at Josh and turned to look out the window at Mac's retreating back.

This was the last thing I had expected. I was convinced Mac and I were done. We'd been together for almost a year when he left. I had thought he was *the one*. But he couldn't deal with a girlfriend who predicted death, and that was the end of it. When he realized that I had known Dean Roberts would die and hadn't told him, he was furious. Forget the fact that he claimed not to believe in premonitions. No matter how I tried to explain that I was never sure of these things and that I hadn't found a way to prevent anything from happening, he had stopped listening. Dean had been the police chief and like a father to Mac; his heart attack had been devastating to everyone, but Mac took it especially hard. I wasn't sure what was going to happen next, but the butterflies in my stomach were doing loop-de-loops, and I could feel my mouth stretched in a grin at the thought of going out with Mac.

I drove home to get Seth for dog rounds and was surprised to see Tish's car in the driveway. Violet opened the door before I had a chance to grab the knob and, with a crimson-tipped finger to her lips, dragged me off to her apartment.

"What's with the cloak-and-dagger stuff?" I said once she had closed the door.

Baxter came over to sniff my pockets and drool on my jeans.

"Tish just got here," she whispered, and looked over her shoulder, even though we were alone in her sitting room. "She said she needed Rose to do a reading. They wouldn't let me sit in. She claimed Baxter needed some attention." Her glance in his direction indicated she thought this was a lie. "Something's up, I can feel it."

"So why did you drag *me* back here? Where's Seth?"

Vi paced in front of me.

"Seth is upstairs with Tuffy. You're going to help me figure out what's going on."

"What are you talking about?" I pinched the bridge of

my nose to stop myself from watching her aggressive strides up and down the room.

"Baxter's been telling me about the level of stress he's been under at Tish's house. He can't take the pressure anymore. We have to help."

I glanced at Baxter. He flopped to the floor and sighed.

"I think he's hungry," I said.

She stared at him for a moment and shook her head.

"We have to find out what's happening in that reading."

"Can't you ask my mom when they're done?" I was edging toward the door to escape further involvement.

"No. She's got this client-confidentiality thing." Vi made finger quotes in the air. "You'd think she was a lawyer or doctor or something. At least my clients don't care who I talk to."

I wondered how she knew that but didn't go into it.

She continued on her back-and-forth journey. Baxter followed her with his eyes.

"There's no choice. You're going to have to use the crawl space." She stopped in front of me.

"Oh come on, Vi." I put my hand up to fend off her suggestion. "I haven't been up there in years. I won't fit." Plus, I was pretty sure there were spiders.

"It's the only way to hear what they're saying."

There was a crawl space above my mother's parlor. It was mostly used for storage and only accessible through the front hall coat closet. At one time it was probably part of the attic until the various additions and remodelings changed it to a small loft-like space. Grace and I used to go up there to hunt for Christmas gifts, and we discovered that the acoustics were very good from Mom's office. For a while we had my mother convinced we were extremely talented psychics as we recited readings she had given. It was a dark day when she discovered that not only had we been spying on her, but we also were not as talented as she had believed. Grace still held a grudge that she had lost her driving privileges for the summer while I was only denied the beach for a week. The fact that I was eight and she was seventeen at the time didn't matter. She claimed she was really being punished for not having better psychic talents.

"This is crazy," I said, but I was already heading back toward the front door and the closet. I wanted to know what Tish was so desperate to ask the cards, too. And maybe I could find out what had come between her and my mother.

We quietly set out the step stool and I hoisted myself up onto the rickety ladder that dropped down out of the ceiling. Vi's *shh*ing was loud enough to bring the neighbors over to investigate, but the parlor door remained closed. I shimmied through the opening. Vi stayed below as lookout.

Once in the crawl space, I held a small flashlight and carefully made my way toward the parlor area. There had been a time when I could walk upright in the space, but not anymore.

Finally, I got into a good position and could hear voices clearly. Tish was talking.

"I've just been so nervous since she died. I don't know what to do."

I heard the *rrrip!* of shuffled cards. This was clearly not the same deck my mother had used with me. That deck hadn't made a sound in twenty years. Mom felt very strongly about the transfer of energy to objects like cards. For some reason, she was using her teaching deck with Tish, which made me even more curious about Tish's situation and their relationship. My mother was protecting her favorite cards from Tish, and I didn't know why.

"Why would you be nervous, Tish? You hardly knew Sara."

The shuffling stopped.

"I know, but I feel like I didn't treat her very well, you know? Maybe she'll get back at me somehow."

"That's ridiculous and you know it." I could imagine my mother shaking her head in that *tsk-tsk* way she usually reserved for me.

"I'm really sorry about the trouble I caused her. Honestly, I was just jealous."

"Jealous? Of what?"

One of the chairs creaked.

"Of her, of what she could do. Of all the time you spent together."

"But, I was her teacher. . . ."

"I know. I just feel like I've lost my abilities recently. Have you ever given a reading that isn't from the cards, but you know it's true anyway?"

The cards riffled again.

"I don't know what you mean."

"Well, did you ever know something about a client and then do a reading to reflect that knowledge? To tell them something they don't know, but should know, even if the cards don't show it?" Tish said.

"No . . . I don't think that's ever happened. Why are you asking? Have people been saying my card readings aren't accurate?" Mom was likely sitting up straight, ready to defend her honor.

"Oh no. Nothing like that. I just wondered. It's such a gift we have. Sometimes it's a burden, too."

I played the narrow beam of my flashlight over the small room. A thick layer of dust coated boxes, old blankets, and a child-size teapot that I knew had a chipped spout. My nose tickled and my eyes watered—I quickly buried my face in my elbow to quiet the sneeze.

The room below got very quiet.

"Did you hear something?" Tish asked.

"I don't think so." I imagined Mom cocking her head like Tuffy, listening. "That's probably enough shuffling. Do you have a specific question for the cards?"

"Just general guidance would be good. I need to know whether to act on something or not."

I could hear the flick of cards on the table as my mother set them out.

Someone gasped and the table below rattled.

"Don't worry about that card. It just means change. This is not as bad as it looks," my mother said.

"I can read cards, too, Rose. Danger, threats, and death." Tish's voice rose with each word.

"Sit down, Tish." I panicked for a moment, imagining Tish walking out into the hall and finding Vi guarding the closet.

I heard the chair squeak as Tish lowered herself onto it, and then things got quiet. Mom must have been studying the cards.

My ears strained to hear, and at last she took a breath and said, "Let's look at this layout as a whole. The cards have to be read as a group or they don't make as much sense."

I wished I had a peephole to look at them myself. My back cramped from standing hunched over. The dust tickled my nose and throat. All I needed was a coughing attack and they would know I was just above them.

"Okay," my mother said. I could tell by that one word that she was steeling herself to give some bad news. "These two in the center indicate how you are feeling and how you are acting. The first one shows a person contemplating the past and former accomplishments. Crossed by the Knight of Cups, it shows you are turning inward."

I closed my eyes and imagined the Knight on his white horse bearing a golden goblet. The horse's head is bent and is not looking where it is going.

"That makes sense. I have been doing a lot of thinking lately," Tish said.

"The next two indicate that you have a large burden that has possibly been taken on a little at a time. Along with the Nine of Swords, recent grief or sorrow, it looks as if you've been going through a rough time."

The Nine of Swords is one of the saddest cards in the deck. A man sits on a bed, head in hands. The nine swords float above his head. I remembered flipping through my mom's deck as a child and that card always made me feel terrible, like there was no hope of happiness. It had shown up a lot in the months after my grandmother died, when I would sit in my room and do my own readings. One of the other cards may have been the Ten of Wands—a man struggles to carry ten large sticks. His back is hunched, and he looks at the ground as he trudges along.

Tish sniffled, and her chair squeaked again.

"These two cards show a possible outcome. It looks like there will be defeat of the plans you have made, and the Queen reversed in the near future shows that you will feel cut off from an important source of communication and will not trust in your skills."

"This is worse than I thought," Tish said.

"Let's see what the rest have to tell us. The Moon in the 'self' position usually indicates a person who is becoming more psychic and who will allow this new energy into her life. I think the reversed Queen is warning you to continue to trust your instincts."

"Okay."

"The reversed King of Pentacles shows there is someone in your life right now who will do anything to get what he wants. Death in the 'hopes and fears' position shows that you are afraid of some major change or decision."

"If it's in that position that isn't good, is it?"

"It means that your fears are very strong, you're afraid of some major change, and you are fighting it. The Tower in the 'outcome' position shows a big upheaval will result from all of this."

I almost choked on the rapid intake of dust when I heard that The Tower was part of the layout. I hated that card. Just looking at it gave me the creeps, and it had caused nightmares as a child. The picture alone was terrifying, a tall tower struck by lightning with people falling from the top. When I learned about fire safety in school, I was haunted by the image of people leaping from a burning building. The sky was black and fire shot out of the windows. Poor Tish. Something big had been going on with her, and the worst was yet to come.

"It's not good, is it?"

"The cards aren't good or bad." This was my mother's standard spiel to people who have a terrible-looking spread of cards. "They just point you in the right direction and help you make choices. These cards are saying you've made some bad choices recently, but maybe you can fix your situation. You have to trust yourself and your talents."

Mom didn't like to give bad news and was unwilling to accept that her precious cards would ever put her in a position of having to do so.

"Well, thanks for seeing me. I know things haven't been great between us for a while. You'll never know how much I regret the way I treated Sara over her certificate. I'm sorry it came between us."

I heard my mother sniffle.

"You just let me know if I can do anything to help," Mom said.

They were wrapping things up. I had to get out of the attic.

I turned and headed for the trapdoor, but swung my head into a low-lying beam first. After my vision cleared, I continued and nearly fell out of the door onto the step stool. I was starting to fold it up when the closet door hit me in the back as it swung closed, shutting out the light.

"What are you doing out here, Vi?" I heard my mother through the door.

"Oh, nothing. Just on my way to the kitchen to get Baxter a dog biscuit."

"I thought you kept those in your rooms." My mother's voice betrayed her skepticism.

"Where's Baxter?" Tish asked.

"In my apartment. Why don't you two go get him while I get his treat?" Vi said.

Suddenly the closet door flew open. My mother stood there, hands on hips, glaring.

"I thought so. You were quieter when you were little. Hear any good readings lately, Clytemnestra?" she asked.

"Clyde? What are you doing in the closet?" Tish asked.

"She's just helping me store some winter coats," Vi said. She tried to shut the door.

"She's 'just' spying on us." My mother rounded on Vi, and grabbed my wrist at the same time.

"You two should be ashamed of yourselves. Acting like children!" my mother said.

"Why would you do that, Clyde?" Tish said in the smallest voice I had ever heard.

16

Tish and Baxter had stormed out. Even the dog managed a glare over his shoulder as he left. I tried to downplay the whole episode to Seth, but he was too clever for that. This was due partly to my mother's reiterating her disappointment in my behavior and partly to Vi's persistent questions about what I had heard.

Seth and I finally left the house to visit our clients for the day. Tuffy joined us.

"So it never ends, huh?" Seth asked. He clicked his seat belt and settled Tuffy on his lap.

"What?"

"Parents dragging you down."

"I guess it depends on the parents." I hit the gas too hard and sprayed gravel as we pulled out of the driveway.

Tuffy sighed loudly and looked from me to Seth and back again. I made a mental note to schedule a grooming appointment for him. He was starting to resemble a mistreated Barbie doll with ratted hair and a lopsided ponytail.

For the next hour, I wrangled the boy and the dogs and argued with myself over what I should do. I felt horrible. I usually avoided Vi's plots, but I had been so curious myself that I'd gone along with it. Now Tish was mad and hurt and I still didn't know much more than I knew this morning. She had a secret, she was confused about what to do, and now she had animal psychics and ex-cops spying on her. Great.

That evening, I waited on the porch for Mac. I didn't want to go through the whole chatting-with-the-family thing and figured he would be just as happy to avoid Vi's questions. Of course, they weren't subtle about the fact that they were watching from behind the curtains.

When he pulled up in his pickup truck, I hopped off the porch and went to meet him.

"Seems like old times," he said as I buckled the seat belt. "You never could wait to get out of there."

"It's better now, but only a little."

We chose safe topics of conversation on our way out of town. He told me about his time in Saginaw and the drug bust that had gone bad. He'd taken a bullet in his leg and was stuck with a cane until his strength improved. He wasn't sure how long he would stay with the Ottawa County Sheriff's Department but didn't want to return to Saginaw. I kept quiet about my own troubles in Ann Arbor, saying only that I had six weeks left of my leave of absence. No talk of murder, séances, or psychics. As soon as we passed the city limits and headed north, I knew where he was taking me for dinner.

Grand Haven was not far, and the Lighthouse Restaurant sat right on the beach. The food was good, but the view was the big attraction. I hadn't been there since Mac and I broke up.

It was obvious that things had changed when we pulled into the parking lot. The weather-beaten sign had been replaced with a carved wooden plaque, and the lot had been repaved and painted with marked parking spaces. As we approached the front door, I saw that the bright multicolored deck umbrellas had been changed for black shades and tables with real tablecloths. Mac and I exchanged a bewildered glance.

Inside, the upscale transformation was even more apparent. We stood by the hostess station and I began to worry my jeans and short-sleeve blouse would be turned away. But this was still Michigan in the summer, and the hostess didn't give us a second look as she led us to a table for two.

We caught up on the past eight years over a bottle of wine and surf and turf. Mac was funnier than I remembered and more relaxed. The wine mellowed us both, and we had veered into remember-when territory. I reminded him of the time we were driving out near Greer's Woods and Etta James's "At Last" came on the oldies station. Mac had pulled off to the side of the road, turned up the music, and pulled me out of the car. We slow-danced in the woods with only the headlights and the moon to guide us. Mac reminded me of the time we had almost started a brawl in a Grand Rapids pool hall. It was the most I had laughed in a very long time.

We reached for the wine bottle at the same time, and when his hand covered mine I caught my breath.

"Well, I never thought I'd see this."

I turned to see Charla Roberts grinning and standing at our table. I jumped up to give her a hug and knocked my wineglass over in the process. Mac dealt with the mess and then offered Charla a chair.

"Oh, I don't want to interrupt," Charla said. "I'm having dinner with Dean Junior and saw you from across the room."

"It's great to see you, Charla," I said. I secretly wished she'd waited a few more minutes. "I'm in town for the summer—we'll have to get together."

"I've heard all about you and your summer plans. Tom Andrews talks about you all the time." She cocked her thumb at Mac. "This one is a bit more secretive."

Mac cleared his throat and tried to gain control of the conversation.

"I don't have any secrets, Charla. I'm an open book." He held his hands out to demonstrate.

Charla glanced at him. "Yes, I can see that." She turned to me. "I can't tell you how happy I am to see you two together. Before Dean died, he told me how glad he was that you had found each other."

She didn't notice the shift in the atmosphere at the table. At the mention of Dean Roberts, Mac stiffened and his eyes lost their sparkle.

"We're just old friends out to dinner, Charla," Mac said.

"Okay, have your secrets." She smiled at me. "I'll leave you *old friends* to your wine." Charla made her way back across the restaurant.

The drive home was quiet, and there was no more reminiscing. We were lost in our own thoughts. I was ruminating about Tish and the debacle that afternoon, as well as trying to figure out where Mac and I had gone so wrong eight years ago. Mac was presumably remembering his reasons for leaving Crystal Haven. I was glad we had done this, even if nothing had changed. At least now I wouldn't feel uncomfortable when we met. I knew where I stood.

"Thanks, Mac," I said when he pulled up to the house. "I had a really nice time."

I reached for the door handle and started to get out of the truck. Mac grabbed my other hand and held it.

"Let's do this again, okay?" His eyes were intense, and I realized I had misinterpreted the situation—again.

My stomach flipped. My hands shook as I pulled the door latch. I nodded and went into the house.

17

When I woke, still grinning, on Friday morning,
I decided the only thing to do was track Tish down as quickly
as possible and apologize. Even though after the apology I
intended to grill her for information on why she went to Sara's
daughter and what was going on with my mother, I still felt
much better about myself.

After the morning doggy rounds, we parked in town and
gave Tuffy a drink. I told Seth to wait by the car while I
checked the Reading Room for Tish. Friday wasn't her usual
day, but she might be found there seeing walk-ins.

Several people blasted out the door just as I reached for
it. They hurried past, mumbling "excuse me" and continued
down the street. It took only a moment to realize what the
fuss was about. Tish's voice was loud and clear, and an angry
male voice tried to shout over it. I stepped cautiously inside,
and Harriet flapped over to me, her cardigan sleeves straining to stay tied at her neck.

"Clytemnestra, do something! I think they're going to tear the place apart."

"What's going on?"

Gary gestured wildly, strands of his thinning hair standing on end. Tish pointed a shaky finger at him. Phrases like "none of your business" and "liar" filled the air.

"Gary came in a few minutes ago. He accused Tish of getting him arrested."

"How did he get out of jail?" The two were so wrapped up in their argument that they hadn't noticed me.

I waited for Harriet to reply, but a gruff voice surprised me. "Gary finally gave us his alibi, and we didn't have enough evidence to hold him," Mac said from the door. "You have a knack for finding trouble, Clyde."

"Oh, Detective McKenzie. Thank goodness you're here," said Harriet. Her adoring glance made it clear *some* people in town were glad Mac was back.

Gary and Tish had stopped arguing long enough to notice Mac at the door. Mac stomped over to them, his cane telegraphing his annoyance with aggressive thumps, and offered a choice of calming down versus taking the whole argument to the police station. I decided this was a good time to retreat. I wasn't going to get any information out of Tish with her aura in an uproar. Maybe I could find out how Gary got out of jail while Mac was busy breaking up the fight.

"Hey, did Detective McKenzie find you?" Seth asked when I got to the car.

"Well, I saw him. Was he looking for me?"

"I think so. He stopped to pet Tuffy and asked where you were. I told him I thought you went into the Reading Room to talk to Tish. Sorry if it was supposed to be a secret." Seth hung his head.

"No, it's fine. Tish was . . . busy. Mac had some other things to do, so I didn't really get to talk to him. Why don't I bring you and Tuffy back home for lunch?"

I drove back to town after dropping Seth off at home. Tom was not at the police station, and Mac had gotten to Lisa. Despite my attempts at drawing out the story, she remained tight-lipped on the subject of Gary and how he had gotten out of jail. She was willing to tell me that Tom had gone a few blocks down the street to investigate a report of vagrancy at Millie's Book Nook.

Headed that way, I hoped Tom would be finished before I got there. Millie's was the "regular" bookstore in town. Besides Diana's store, there was one other, but it only sold psychic and spiritualist titles. Millie's sold all of the new releases in fiction and nonfiction and boasted a great selection of mysteries and biographies. Millie was at least ninety years old and was in a constant feud with her "good for nothing" third husband, Howard. They had been married for thirty years. He was only eighty, and according to Millie he didn't pull his weight around the store. Millie had been my first employer—paying me to come after school and stock the shelves with new books. Most of my earnings were funneled directly back to the store to feed my fiction habit.

A small crowd had gathered on the sidewalk. I caught a glimpse of Tom in the middle of the throng. Knowing I would regret it, I walked right up to the small, wiry nonagenarian who was pushing Tom backward with the sheer force of her pointing finger.

"Now, Mrs. Fessler, Howard is not a vagrant. He says he fell asleep while doing inventory," Tom said. He held his hands up as if she were pointing a gun and not a crooked digit at him.

"I want him arrested." She poked Tom with her finger. He mouthed the word "ow" and rubbed his chest. Tom tried to take a step back and almost lost his footing on the steps of the store. While he struggled to keep his balance, Millie continued. "He's a lazy fool, and now he's sleeping on the job. If I found anyone else sleeping in my reading area, you'd come and cart them off to the lockup." She glanced at the crowd, assessing the need for arrests.

Howard stood in the doorway, his few wisps of white hair askew. He blinked at the crowd through his glasses and scowled at Millie.

This had the potential to go on for hours, or at least until Millie got tired. I decided to rescue Tom.

"Hi, Mrs. Fessler." I tapped Millie on the shoulder.

She swung around, finger at the ready. Her frown broke into a huge grin when she saw me.

"Well, Clytemnestra. How are you?" She clutched my hand in hers.

"I'm fine. What seems to be the trouble here?"

"It's Howard, sleeping on the job again. He never used to do that when you were here with us. I hear you're a policeman now."

"I—yes, I am."

"What do you call yourself now? Cletus? Clover?"

"Clyde, Mrs. Fessler. It's always been Clyde." I smiled down at her. She didn't top five feet, even with her chunky orthopedic shoes.

"That was my first husband's name. He was a mechanic. Nice man, but he had no stamina, if you know what I mean." She nudged me with her bony elbow.

"You've mentioned him before." I didn't want to wander memory lane with Millie.

"Is this your new boyfriend?" She hooked a thumb in Tom's direction.

Red blotches rose to his cheeks. I was momentarily speechless.

"You always had a thing for policemen," she said.

"No! We're . . . friends. Mrs. Fessler, maybe you and Howard could go back inside and work this out."

She looked up at Howard, who was still standing in the door. He smiled at her as if she was the most beautiful woman on the planet.

"Oh, fine. I'll give him one more chance." She waved her hand at the crowd to get them to move out of her way.

She went inside with Howard, and most of the bystanders followed them. I'd often wondered if she staged these little one-act plays when business got slow.

"I need to talk to you," I said when Tom and I were alone.

"Yeah, I need to talk to you, too." He smoothed his uniform and brushed off his hat.

We scanned the street, looking for a place to meet where we wouldn't be seen by Mac or by anyone who might tell Mac. Then I remembered the Memorial Garden.

"Meet me in the garden in three minutes," I said, and walked away without looking back.

The garden took up a corner lot right in the middle of the commercial section of town. The restaurant that had stood there for half a century burned one September evening twenty years earlier, and the owner's widow had decided to plant a garden rather than rebuild. She took the insurance money off to Chicago and returned once a year to visit the site.

I used to go there every day in the summer, wandering the pathways while eating my ice cream or talking to Diana or Alex about some teenage crisis. The gates were closed at night, and only the bravest of the teenage crowd hopped the fence to enter. It was said to be haunted by the man who had died in the fire.

I entered through the gate and breathed in the scent of roses, lavender, and lilacs. A small bench sat at the back, hidden from street view.

I didn't have to wait long before I saw Tom come through the gate and look quickly around. I stood on the bench and waved, and he made his way over to me.

"Thanks for helping out with Millie back there," Tom said.

"No problem. We go way back."

"I have some interesting news." He sat next to me on the bench and glanced around to be sure we couldn't be seen. "Gary is out of jail."

I told him about seeing Gary and Tish fighting at the Reading Room.

"This is not good." Tom shook his head.

"How did Gary get out? Mac said he had an alibi?"

Tom nodded.

"He didn't want to tell us at first, which is why he got his daughter to lie for him. He was at an illegal poker game in Grand Rapids. I had heard rumors when he and Sara divorced, but he confirmed them today. He's in debt to several bookies and one very bad loan shark. He was at the poker game trying to 'earn' enough to pay the debt."

"Wow. That must be why he was anxious to sell his land. Sara wouldn't sell her share, and that put him in a bind."

"I suppose." Tom shrugged. "All I know is the lawyer managed to find a couple of the guys who were there, and they alibied Gary after we said we wouldn't press charges about the poker game."

"Mac must be looking at other suspects." I thought about how many times I would make Mac admit he was wrong.

Tom shook his head. "Mac still thinks Gary did it. He says he has an even better motive now that we know he needed the money from the land deal. Plus he doesn't trust the guys who gave the alibi."

Maybe the simplest answer *was* the best. Gary could have gotten desperate for the money and fought with Sara. That solution didn't feel right, but I was trying to stay out of this. Tom wanted me involved, Mom and Vi wanted me involved, and I just wanted it to be over so I could get on with my summer. After last night, the summer was looking more interesting.

"Listen, Tom. I think Tish knows something. She's been acting really strange since Sara died."

"We talked to her already because she was at the séance."

"You interviewed the people from the séance?"

"Well, not all of them yet, but we're working on it. Why wouldn't she have told us what she knew?" His naïve question made me chuckle. I covered it with a cough.

"I don't know, but I'm going to try to find out. I think she knows who killed Sara." I didn't mention I was starting to suspect Tish herself.

The bushes rustled next to us. I stood up quickly and saw Cecile kneeling on the other side. I realized our mistake—we couldn't be seen, but we also couldn't see out. And we could be heard.

"Can I help you?" I said.

"Oh, Clyde. Hello. I was looking for my glasses. I dropped them around here somewhere and just can't find them."

Tom stood up and peeked over the shrub. "Do you want some help, Mrs. Stark?"

"No!" She stood up quickly. "No, I'm not sure I dropped them here. I'm just returning to places where I might have lost them. Thanks, bye."

She hurried off, weaving along the path toward the gate.

She had been very quiet, and I had no idea how long she'd been there. Sensing eavesdroppers would be a useful talent.

"Do you think she heard us?" Tom asked, reading my thoughts.

"I don't know. I hope not."

"She was at the séance, too. Mac said she didn't add much to the séance story when he interviewed her."

"Did she mention that Tish left her house really early on the day Sara died?"

"Not that I know of, but I haven't seen Mac's report yet."

I watched Cecile's head bob out through the gate and down the street.

"Clyde, you don't think Tish could have killed Sara, do you?"

A cold chill crept down my spine with his question.

"No. She may not have liked Sara, but Tish isn't a murderer. I'm sure of it."

As I walked out of the garden with Tom, I tried to convince myself that I was right.

18

After finishing the afternoon's work, I went to
Tish's house. Seth had left several messages on my phone to
say he was waiting for me to pick him up to continue our
rounds for the day. But I had other things to do.

Tish's Tahoe sat close to the front walk. Baxter barked
somewhere deep inside the house. A few kids played basket-
ball down the street, but otherwise the neighborhood was
quiet. Taking the porch steps two at a time, I raised my hand
to knock when I saw the sign: READING IN PROGRESS,
PLEASE WAIT.

My hand dropped to my side. I felt prickly and cold even
on that muggy summer day. Shivering and rubbing my arms
to warm up, I peeked in the front window. That was odd—
Tish usually sat with clients in her front room, but it was
empty. I checked my watch.

I knocked on the front door. There was no answer, so I
knocked again and tried the knob with a growing feeling of

concern. She had to be in there. Then I got a very bad feeling.

I took the key from under the mat. As I slid the key into the lock, I heard a loud *pop!* like a car backfiring. Instinct kicked in and I dropped to the floor of the porch. There were no cars on the street. I had heard that sound before. A gun had been fired inside the house.

From my vantage point on the porch, I spotted a forgotten spade among the bushes. Makeshift weapon in hand, I finally turned the knob after fumbling with the lock. With only a gardening tool as a weapon I slipped inside. It went against every bit of training I possessed. Baxter was barking more vigorously, and I wondered where he could be.

Keeping to the periphery of the front room, I inched toward the dining room—no one there. I kept the spade cocked like a baseball bat. Softly creeping around the edge of the door, I made my way toward the kitchen. The back door slammed. Three strides took me to the kitchen doorway. Tish was on the floor. A dark red stain had soaked her shirt and spread across her chest. I stifled a cry, scanned the room, and checked the backyard, but saw no one. Baxter's barking had become a keening howl, and I realized he was locked in the basement.

Tish lay on her back. Her legs made quotation marks on the floor. One of her high-heel mules had slipped off and sat not far from her bare, unprotected foot. I saw the slight movement of her chest. Tish's face was white and her eyes fluttered briefly as I said her name. Her right hand scrabbled at her chest, her left arm lay tucked under her back. She tried to talk but only wheezed.

I let the spade drop to my side and focused on breathing. I replayed other shooting injuries I had seen, including the boy from last spring. The room began to feel hot, and I leaned against the wall for a moment until the spinning sensation stopped. I had to pull myself together. I dropped the spade and knelt next to Tish on the floor.

"It's Clyde, Tish. I'm calling for help." Her hand sat motionless in mine as I pulled out my cell phone and called 911. I gave the address, hung up, and turned to her again. Her eyes were partly open.

I squeezed her hand. "Tish, who did this?"

She opened her eyes and stared past me. Her fingers pushed slightly against my palm. Baxter's howling filled the room. Her lips began to move, and I leaned closer in order to hear.

"Take Baxter . . . his bed." She struggled with these few words and then coughed. A trickle of red spilled from the corner of her mouth.

"Tish!" I shook her shoulder. "Tish, don't try to talk. Just hang on."

I ran through my first aid training. I knew I had to keep pressure on the wound, but I also knew that gunshot wounds to the chest caused all sorts of internal damage. I remembered one muggy August afternoon during training when they'd talked us through first aid for GSW to the chest. Something about covering the wound so the lung could expand. What was it?

Her eyes opened once more, but they were unfocused. Then I remembered. I needed to cover the entry wound with plastic to allow her to breathe. I got up and rummaged in her kitchen drawers for plastic wrap. I grabbed tape out of her box of first aid stuff.

"You're going to be fine," I lied.

I knelt next to her and opened her shirt. I fought the tide of nausea that came over me. How would she ever survive this? Tripling the plastic, I placed it over the hole in her chest and taped it down on three sides. I was pretty sure the next instruction had been to get the person to a hospital as soon as possible. Not knowing what else to do for her, I held her hand and told her reassuring things I didn't believe. At some point, I knew she couldn't hear me anymore.

The next several minutes were a blur. I kept checking Tish's pulse, but it was fading. Her breathing was shallow and rapid. I didn't think my plastic-wrap trick was helping. I felt my throat tighten and my eyes grew hot. Fighting a rising sense of panic, I shuffled through my mental catalog of first aid maneuvers that I had learned everywhere from Girl Scouts to the police academy. But I couldn't think of anything else to do. Mostly I forced myself to ignore that this was Tish, one of my best friends in the world.

Finally, the EMTs arrived, but they were too late. They tried to stabilize her blood pressure with fluids, and they put in a breathing tube. She'd lost a lot of blood—I had most of it all over me. My hands were crusted and stiff with blood; the knees of my jeans were sticky and damp where it had soaked through the fabric. A sharp metallic taste stuck in the back of my throat. The EMTs pronounced her dead after ten minutes of trying to resuscitate.

The EMTs sent me to the living room to wait for the police to arrive. It was disorienting after all the blood in the kitchen to see a place untouched by tragedy.

The cozy room reminded me of all the time spent there as a teenager. I used to think it was her decorating that made me feel at home. It was warm and unfussy—unlike my mother's overly fringed and accessorized rooms. But as I sat there and thought about Tish, I realized it wasn't her stuff that made it cozy. It was her. A great listener, never jumping in with advice or comments unless I asked, she had always been there for me.

I had repaid all that by suspecting her of murder—spying on her and sneaking around town, prying into her life because I had forgotten who she was. There was a roaring in my ears and a wave of nausea forced me to focus on breathing slowly and staying in control. It was the one part of my police training I could rely on. In the midst of a crisis, I had learned to push all emotion into a small box to be dealt with later. I wished now that I had stormed in the minute I got to her house and scared off the person who had done this. Or that I had been able to foresee what was coming. Why could I sense some things that were about to happen and not others? My "gift" for seeing future events seemed limited and shallow if I couldn't stop bad things from happening to the people I loved.

Baxter had quit howling just before the paramedics arrived, as if he knew Tish was already gone. I'd forgotten all about him until one of the EMTs dragged him into the room by his collar. Baxter stopped short a few feet from me, sat down, and moaned.

"Come here, boy, it's okay," I said.

He didn't budge.

"Uh, ma'am? He might be able to smell the blood," the paramedic said, gesturing toward me with his head.

In a daze, I had forgotten about the blood. I'd tracked some of it into the living room, and I felt the stiff and sticky glove of blood on my hands.

"I'll go wash it off," I told him. "Just hold on to him until I get back."

A good five minutes of soap and steamy water seemed to do little. I felt I'd never get my hands clean. I looked in the mirror and saw the terror in my own eyes. I had wiped blood across my forehead at some point. Another wave of sickness assaulted me, and I splashed cold water on my face to calm down.

Baxter's low bark from the front of the house broke into my thoughts, and I went to rescue the EMT.

Mac stood in the front doorway. Just a glance at his eyes, which were warm and soft and not the usual stern ice, melted all my resolve to get through this without crying. Suddenly my cheeks felt wet, and Mac was there, holding me. I tried to remember why I had been mad at him for so long, and couldn't.

Eventually, I pulled myself away from Mac and wiped my eyes. The paramedic stood in the doorway, averting his gaze. Mac asked me to wait in the living room and limped to the kitchen to begin the long process of investigating the scene. The rest of the county crime-scene crew was due to arrive within the hour.

My thoughts bounced from Tish to Sara and how their deaths could be related. I had actually been suspicious of Tish, but obviously that was way off. That left me with Gary, or Sara's mysterious website stalker, or Milo. When I realized how little I knew, I thought of Tish and how much I would miss her.

In our shared sorrow over the loss of Tish, Baxter and I leaned against each other and waited.

We didn't have to wait long. After surveying the kitchen and hearing the report from the EMTs, Mac sat with us and began the questioning immediately. What was I doing there? Why did I come over? What had I heard exactly? Did I see anyone?

Feeling about as useful as Baxter, I told him the story of the past hour. I hadn't seen anyone. I heard the gunshot. Yet again, the only one who could identify the murderer was a dog. Aunt Vi was going to be insufferable.

"Was she still conscious when you found her?" Mac asked.

"She was, but just barely. She told me to take Baxter and said something about his bed." I rubbed Baxter's ears, wondering what I was going to do with him now.

"Her last words were about the dog?" Mac scrubbed his face with his hands.

"I know it would have been more convenient if she'd named her killer, but all she said was 'take Baxter and his bed,' or something like that," I said.

"I don't know what that means," Mac said, hands outstretched to include Baxter in his disbelief.

"She was barely there, Mac. I don't know that she knew what she was saying," I said. I felt my throat tighten as I remembered her struggling to breathe and force out those few words. Her last words had been about Baxter. Had she known? Would she have said something more useful if she'd known she only had a few words left? I looked away from Mac and blinked back the tears threatening to well up again.

"Okay." Mac put his hand over mine. He stole a glance at his watch. I knew he had a lot of work to do. "Can you drive yourself home?"

"Yeah, I'm fine." I attempted a smile to show how fine I was. I could tell by the way he searched my face that he didn't believe me.

"Let's meet tomorrow morning and go over your statement."

Just the plan to see him again made me feel better, and I nodded.

"Can I take Baxter with me?" I sniffled, and rubbed my nose with the wad of tissues Mac had quietly handed me.

"Yeah, that'll be fine. It sounds like she wanted you to have him."

I packed up Baxter's things, including his dog bed, which he had never used when staying at my mom's, and took him out to the car.

Mac walked out with us and helped me load Baxter into the backseat. His method involved lifting all one hundred thirty pounds of dog and tossing him in. It worked better than *my* system of pushing, pulling, and ending up in the dirt.

"Clyde, be careful." He put his hand on my shoulder and leaned against the open window. "Whoever killed Tish is probably the one who killed Sara. I can't believe that after years of no homicides, we could have two unrelated murders in the span of a few days. Just lay low and let us do our job."

"Right. Okay," I said. I stared forward through the windshield so he wouldn't see the new determination in my eyes.

As Baxter and I pulled out, I waved to Mac, who turned and went back into the house.

"Don't worry, Baxter. I'm going to find out who did this," I said.

Baxter rested his wet chin on my shoulder and moaned.

19

We were met by a loud babble of voices at the door. There were arms hugging us and questions being asked and it took me a moment to realize who was in my house. My father had been listening to the police band again. He said if my mother can spy on the town with her readings, he should be able to back her up with the police reports. He'd heard the call about Tish's death on the radio. My aunt and mother had assumed the rest when I didn't arrive to pick up Seth. They had called Alex, who had called Diana, and I arrived home in the middle of a wake.

Baxter looked exhausted and lay down in the center of the chaos, which was where Tuffy found him. They curled up together as if they understood that they shared a similar tragedy.

Everyone spoke at once as they gathered around.

"Are you okay?"

"Is it true?"

"I was so worried."

"I just knew it!"

I could hardly identify who said what, except for the last statement, of course, which could only be Vi. I tried as best I could to reassure them I was okay. This was difficult, considering the amount of blood on my clothes. What I really wanted was a long shower, a whiskey, and bed. I settled for a short shower.

I left them all hovering over Baxter. Vi was on all fours trying to get some information out of him. He looked like he could use a break as well. I thought I saw him cast a wistful look at the stairs as I climbed toward the bathroom, but he was quickly swallowed by the crowd.

I stripped off my jeans and T-shirt and threw them in the trash. There was no way I would ever want to wear them again, even if the blood did wash out. I turned the water on as hot as I could stand and got in the shower. I washed quickly and then stood in the searing spray, trying not to think or to feel anything at all. The heat couldn't stop the trembling that started up as soon as I relaxed. My whole body shook, and the tears came—some for Tish, some for Sara, some I had been saving for Jadyn, the boy I'd shot in the spring. The police psychologist had said I should let my emotions out more. But it only left me exhausted and red-eyed.

After the shower, I tried to calm my eyes down with cold water but had only minimal success. I would just have to face the mob downstairs looking like I was suffering a severe allergy attack.

They were all in the dining room because my mother insisted on feeding people when a tragedy occurred. A pot of chili sat on the table, but no one was eating. Seth looked scared and young and sat with both dogs on the floor. Alex and Diana were at one end of the table, Mom and Vi at the other. My father was manning the neutral middle territory.

"Here she is!" My mother gestured toward the door as if I were entering royalty.

I gave a small wave to the gang and sat across from my father. They had broken into the whiskey, and I helped myself to a small glass.

"Tell us everything. Don't leave anything out," Aunt Vi said.

I took a deep breath. "I went over to Tish's to talk to her. I felt bad about what happened yesterday." I gave Vi an icy glare she pretended not to notice. "She had her sign up saying to wait. I waited for a few minutes, but I didn't feel right. . . ."

"What do you mean?" Mom leaned forward. "Did you sense something?"

"I don't know that I sensed anything. I just felt cold and not-right. I knocked, and when she didn't answer I got the key and unlocked the door."

"Oh, Clyde, you could have been hurt, too!" Diana said, and grabbed my hand.

I glanced quickly her way but didn't want the shaking and crying to start up again, so I gently pulled my hand away and continued.

"As soon as the key was in the lock, I heard a gunshot. By the time I unlocked the front door, the back door slammed, and I went in and found Tish."

"Why would you just go in after a 10-72?" Dad said. His eyes were red and wet. He must have had a scary afternoon, wondering if I was safe.

"I didn't just barge in. I went in quietly. I was worried about Tish, and after I heard the door slam, I figured there was no one in the house." Listening to my own story, I realized how ridiculous it sounded. No trained police officer would ever enter a scene like that without a real weapon and some sort of backup. But at that moment I wasn't a police officer. I was just Tish's friend, and I wanted to help her.

"Did you see anything at all?" Alex asked. His eyes were red, his face haggard.

"No. Whoever did this was gone before I got to the kitchen. I didn't see a car or anyone running away. . . ."

"They could have been hiding in the back," Seth said from the floor.

A cold chill skittered down my spine as I realized he was right. I hadn't searched the yard or locked the door while focused on Tish. All my training had disappeared when faced with Tish's attack. I put my head down on my arms.

"Well, we need to organize a memorial service for her," my mother said with a shaky voice.

"She doesn't have any family." Vi shook her head.

"I'll really miss her," said Diana. She sniffed and dabbed at her eyes.

Sniffles and muffled coughs made their way around the table. Baxter moaned. I was focused on who might have done this. My mother could worry about the memorial; I wanted the murderer caught and punished. Gary was a very real possibility. He was out of jail, had just been fighting with her, and because she had talked Alison into reneging on her alibi, Tish was partly responsible for his arrest in the first place. Maybe she'd known something she hadn't yet told the police.

Maybe she'd talked Alison into changing her statement because she'd known Gary had done it and he knew she suspected him.

"I'll bet it was Milo Stark," Vi said.

"What?" Alex said, as Mom nodded and Diana raised her eyebrows.

"Now, don't start that again, Violet." My father poured himself another shot of whiskey.

"He's the best suspect. He killed that girl years ago, left town in a shower of scandal, then returned and within a month—two more murders!" She pounded the table to make her point. "I'd like to find out where he's been living and see what *their* murder rate has been."

"What is she talking about?" Seth asked, looking from me to Diana to Mom.

I glanced at Diana to gain some courage, and then began the story of Milo Stark/Jones. As a senior in high school he had dated Julia Wyatt. She was beautiful, a cheerleader, on the debate team, straight A's, the whole package. Her family was not psychic, and they ran the hotel in town and owned the marina. This lack of psychic ability put them on a lower social rung, according to Vi, but Milo's family was also not psychic. They owned the restaurant. Everyone expected Milo and Julia to end up married, but, just before graduation, Julia disappeared. Some of her clothes were found in the woods near the highway. The clothes had bloodstains, and Milo was the main suspect in a possible murder. Her body was never found. Without a body the authorities couldn't arrest him, but the town did a good job of trying and convicting him anyway. Just about every psychic in town had a crack at locating her body, but no one was successful and she hadn't been seen since. Her father had been distraught and had ranted about the incompetence of the police force right up until he'd died a year ago. It was Crystal Haven's terrible unsolved mystery.

"Humph," said Vi when I finished.

"What does that mean?" I said, turning toward her.

"It means you still think Milo is innocent," she said, her eyebrows accusing.

"I think there has to be evidence before concluding he's guilty," I said.

"Well, I can tell you, even though no one could locate the body, there were plenty of people who thought she was dead and that he had killed her." Vi waggled her finger at all of us.

"Now, Vi, let's not get worked up over Milo," my mother said. "That was a long time ago. No one has ever contacted Julia in life or in Spirit." She patted Vi's hand into submission.

"Something is wrong with that Milo," Vi grumbled. "I'm telling you, he's never been right. Takes after his mother. I'm sure Joe regrets ever taking on the whole mess after Mike died."

I sensed my parents go very still.

"What? Mike who?" Alex asked. Diana and I shrugged and looked to Vi.

Vi kept her gaze on the table, but said, "Mike Jones was Milo's biological father. Joe Stark adopted him. Cecile was pregnant with Milo when she married Joe, which was right after Mike died."

My father was glaring at Vi across the table. She looked up, possibly sensing the waves of irritation directed at her.

"What?" she said. "Everyone knows." She put her arms out to encompass the room.

"*Now* they do. Cecile and Joe made it clear they wanted it to remain quiet for the boy's sake," Dad said.

"Well clearly 'the boy' found out, or he wouldn't have changed his name," Vi said.

My mother started nervously dishing up chili. She had a tendency to flit about when my father and Vi argued.

"Frank, Vi, please. It all happened a long time ago. Let's just leave it alone, okay?" she said.

"How did Mike Jones die?" I ignored my mother's pained look.

"Hunting," said my father.

"What do you mean, 'hunting'?"

"He and Joe were out hunting, and he got hit by a stray bullet." My father had become interested in the pattern on the tablecloth.

"They never found out who shot him, the gun was never found, and the hunter never came forward. Cecile was devastated." My mother wiped a tear and glanced at Vi, who had become very still.

I had a sudden feeling that there was much more to this story than they were telling. The fact that I had never heard it before was curious in itself, but Vi now looked paler than when she heard Tish had died.

"I think I'll go lie down for a little while," Vi said, and stood quickly. Her hands shook as she pushed the chair back under the table.

We all watched her go, and it felt as if the room itself held its breath for a few moments after she left.

"Okay, spill it," I said, glaring at my mother and then my father.

"What are you talking about?" My mother had assumed a confused expression that I knew from long experience was fake.

"What's up with Vi?"

"There's nothing 'up.' She's just been under a lot of strain trying to get information out of the only witnesses to the murders of two of our closest friends." She passed out the chili-filled bowls and didn't look at me. "I would think even you would understand that, Clyde."

I focused my glare on my father.

He glanced at Mom, who refused to look up, and then back at me. Cringing away from my pointed stare, he sighed heavily.

"Vi and Mike were a couple. They were supposed to be married, and then Cecile came along and, well, that was it. Violet never met another guy like Mike." My father hung his head.

"Vi has been carrying a torch for a dead guy all these years?" I said, looking from one parent to the other.

"Shhh! She'll hear you. And I don't appreciate your tone, Clytemnestra," my mother said. "It was a tragedy the way he died. I felt terrible for Cecile, but it changed your aunt as well. There was a lot of bad feeling between Mike and Vi back then. Vi never had a chance to work through it."

"What happened?" Diana asked.

My mother looked at Seth, who was listening intently. She and my father exchanged a look.

"Joe Stark and Mike Jones were business partners. They

owned the restaurant together, but Mike had a larger stake." Mom hesitated and glanced at Seth but continued. "Vi claimed Cecile was a gold digger. Her father owned the auto repair shop on the outside of town, and she always felt she could do better. She wanted to be respected here in Crystal Haven even if she didn't have any psychic abilities. When things fell apart with Vi and Mike, Cecile ended up pregnant. Cecile and Mike got married. It wasn't long after that he was dead."

"Wow, I never knew any of this," Alex said.

"It was a long time ago. But sometimes, for Vi, I think it's still happening," my mother said. She crossed her arms and gestured at us to eat.

After my mother's revelations, and a few bites of dinner, the group scattered. Dad went off to listen to his police scanner, and Seth shuffled to his room with the dogs. Mom took her cards and the pendulum to Vi's apartment. Alex and Diana had their own plans and unfortunately they involved me. It reminded me of when my grandmother had died. After the first shock of the death had passed, each person had his or her own way of coping.

"C'mon, Clyde. You need this," Diana said as she took my hand and dragged me out of my chair.

Alex helped her push me toward the stairs, and I noticed he snagged the whiskey bottle on his way. At least they had their priorities straight.

Diana led the way up to my room. She and Alex had spent a lot of time there in high school discussing music, movies, parents, and our future plans. Her large tote bag bulged and clanked as she took each step. I had a lot of experience with that Mary Poppins bag, and not all of it was good. I looked to Alex for help but all he did was shrug and hold up the bottle.

My room hadn't changed much since high school. I'd left everything behind when I moved to Ann Arbor. The color scheme was sky blue and dark brown, very trendy at the time. The bedspread was a swirly floral thing in brown and blue that I had loved when mom brought it home. Nancy Drew and Agatha Christie still dominated the bookcase. My shelves were cluttered with the combination of my current life and my previous one. My holster shared space with stuffed animals. Softball trophies had been pushed aside to accommodate my laptop and printer. The desk faced the large window that looked over the backyard and was cluttered with phone chargers, dog treats, and extra leashes. Alex and I sat on the bed while Diana set up her items on the desk.

"I should have done this after you found Sara's body, but now the situation is out of control. We need to do a few different rituals, but they're all simple. Don't worry." She fished around in the bag and pulled out a small glass jar, a package of needles, a package of razor blades, a paper bag, and a drinking glass.

I had seen this setup before.

"I don't want to do this one," I said as she put the glass in the bag and smashed it with the base of a trophy from the desk.

"What are you doing, Diana?" Alex wiped his mouth and passed the bottle to me.

"I'm making a very strong protective spell for Clyde if she'll stop whining and just do what I say." She dumped the broken shards, the needles, and the razor blades into the glass jar.

"No, forget it. That's disgusting." I held up my hand to ward off her offering of the jar filled with sharp objects.

"It works, Clyde. You've been close to murder twice in the last couple of days. You need protection, and this is one of the simplest spells I know that you can do for yourself."

"Then let's do a complicated one."

"What does she have to do, put her hand in there?" Alex asked, taking the jar and peering inside.

"She wants me to fill it with urine," I said.

Alex made a face and shoved it back at Diana.

"Wiccans are sick!" he said.

Diana rolled her eyes at both of us.

"Okay, fine. But this protection lasts at least a year, maybe longer. As long as no one digs it up, you're good."

"You have to bury it?"

"Yes, you say the spell and you bury it and then you are protected, but you need the urine of the person you are trying to protect, and that person is not cooperating."

"Okay, moving on. What else did you bring?" I said.

Diana took a moment to glare at both of us.

"I expected this. We can do a short spell to try to control the situation and then another one to help clear your mind and focus on solving Tish's murder."

Alex started giggling. He had no tolerance for alcohol, and was not always on board with Diana's magickal approach to life.

"Shut up, Ferguson," Diana said.

Diana groped in her bag and pulled out a brown candle,

a piece of paper, and a small bottle of oil. She wrote on the paper, and then turned to us.

"The current situation is that Sara and Tish have been killed. What should we ask for as an outcome?"

"That we figure out who did it?" I asked.

"Yeah, but we have to be really specific. Do we just want the person caught, or do you want to be the one who figures it out, or do you want the police to catch them?"

"Oh, come on. If that worked, I'd be burning brown candles every day asking to win the lottery," Alex said.

Diana sighed. "You can't ask for something like that. And you need to know the spell."

"I don't really care how the murderer is caught, as long as they pay for what they did," I said.

"Okay. I'll write that we want the murderer brought to justice."

She wrote on the paper, slipped it under the candle, put a few drops of oil near the wick, and then began to talk quietly to it. Alex leaned forward to try to hear what she was saying, but other than the lilting cadence, we couldn't make out the words. Diana lit the candle and said, "So mote it be."

Alex leaned over and whispered to me. "What's a mote?" He typically avoided Diana's spell-casting if he could.

"It's like saying 'must' or 'may,' but it's very old."

"That's it then? Can we all have a drink now?" Alex asked.

"I think we should do one more thing—a banishing spell. I used it after my parents died, and it helped a lot." Diana thrust her hand back into her bag.

"What do we do?" I sighed, resigned to a night of Wicca and whiskey.

Diana pulled a small velvet bag out of her tote and tipped it onto my palm. A black stone landed in my hand. She set a bowl on my bedside table and poured water into it, then stirred in some sea salt.

"Hold the stone in your right hand and close your eyes. Visualize your grief for Tish moving into the stone." Diana's voice was quiet and soothing. Even Alex was paying attention.

I held the stone and felt it begin to warm up in my hand. I imagined it taking on all the pain I felt today after Tish died and added all the sadness I had been carrying around for Sara and Jadyn. When I was done, the stone felt quite warm. She handed me a piece of paper and indicated that I should read it.

"Banishing stone, take my grief as your own. Banishing stone, set me free, so mote it be," I read.

She pointed to the bowl and I dropped the stone into the water.

"Okay, stir it three times. Then we can take it outside and you have to throw it as far as you can away from the house."

The stone was still warm when I took it out of the water, and I started to feel like maybe just the ritual of throwing my sorrow away would help. We trooped quietly through the house and out the back door. I threw it as hard as I had ever thrown anything. The stone arced high in the air and caught a glint of moonlight as it flew. I never heard it land.

20

The woods feel damp and close. My chest is tight and I gasp for breath but keep moving. The darkness makes the familiar woods threatening. Twigs and roots grab at my feet and legs. My hand flies up to block the branches as they slap past my face and shoulders. I am holding a leash and it is pulling me forward, but I know I will be too late.

My feet crunch over the fallen leaves and suddenly I am in a small clearing. All I can hear is my heart pounding in my ears. I stop to catch my breath. It comes ragged and harsh. I see Baxter up ahead as moonlight bursts into the clearing. Mac is there, shouting something. I run toward his outstretched arms, his eyes warm and inviting. I feel, rather than hear, an explosion. Mac looks surprised just before I fall. When I stand up again, Mac is gone and my hands are covered in blood. Baxter starts to howl and, as I wake up screaming, "Nooo!" I realize I am the one howling.

My room felt like an alien place as I awoke. I looked

around for any lurking threat, but it was all just as I had left it. My laptop sat closed on the desk. Diana's bottle of sharp objects sat next to it, patiently waiting for me to change my mind about the protective spell. The curtains were drawn, but sunlight leaked through the cracks. The dream left me feeling disoriented and confused. My T-shirt was damp and my heart was thumping, but I began to calm down once I realized I was home and safe. That had been one of "those" dreams. The kind I wished to banish; a dream that warned of disasters to come. I went through it again in my mind—Mac, the blood, and me running toward him through the woods. It could only mean one thing: being with me would put Mac in danger. Even though I had never had success in altering the outcome of these dreams, I thought that, if I avoided Mac, I could keep him safe. I would have to figure out a way to maintain my distance.

I stumbled downstairs in search of coffee, glad that it was Saturday and I didn't have any responsibilities. My brain was still foggy from the dream and probably from all the whiskey Alex had supplied. Mom greeted me by tapping her watch and giving me the look I used to get when I was late for the school bus.

"We have to leave in fifteen minutes," she said.

"Leave?" I rubbed my forehead, trying to remember what we could possibly have to do this early in the morning.

She sighed. Then I noticed the black dress, pearls, and high heels. My mother only wears high heels to weddings and funerals. The funeral!

"I can be ready in ten." I poured a cup and raced back up the stairs.

She followed me out of the kitchen. "Make it quick. I'm not waiting for you."

Twenty minutes later, Mom, Dad, Vi, and I piled into Dad's 1980 Buick Regal. It was held together by rust and a prayer, but he refused to consider a new car. This one had "history." Seth stayed behind with the dogs.

The packed parking lot gave testimony to either Sara's popularity or the lure of violent death. Most of the town milled about on the church steps and courtyard. Diana and Alex stood off to the side under an oak tree. I hugged Mom and told her I'd see her after the service. I didn't want to sit with my family. Vi whispered loudly about everyone around her when she was in public, and my mother was sure to sob through the whole thing—she was already welling up. As for Dad, I felt a little guilty about leaving him to fend for himself with the sisters, but not bad enough to stay.

Organ music began as I reached Alex and Diana. We barely had time to say hello before the crowd swept us into the church. While my family took seats toward the front, I gestured at Diana to grab a seat at the back, on the aisle. I like a quick escape route, and I wanted to observe the crowd. Gary sat in front with his daughters, Harriet Munson took a pew with several psychics I recognized from the Reading Room, and I spotted Milo Jones alone halfway back on the right. The Starks arrived late and scooted into the last pew on the far side of the church. I recognized most of the people gathered to say good-bye to Sara. It was likely her murderer was sitting in one of the pews pretending to mourn.

Just as we got settled, everyone around us stood to sing "Amazing Grace." I rolled my eyes thinking of how Grace had convinced me as a child that the song had been written about her. Once we were seated again, Reverend Frew began his eulogy. My eyes prickled and my throat felt tight as he described Sara's daughters, friends, and clients, who had loved her and who had lost Sara too soon. I couldn't sit sobbing in church like my mother. We had been trained in the police academy to hide emotion and keep our feelings to ourselves. I would never pull that off if I had to sit there and hear stories about Sara right on the heels of Tish's death. I tried not to listen to the words but just let the sound of the reverend's voice wash over me. Big mistake.

Reverend Frew had also performed my grandmother's service fifteen years earlier. I had hardly been to church in all that time, so the sound of his voice, the smell of the flowers, and the sounds of people sniffling brought back my grandmother's funeral in vivid detail. My chest tightened, and I felt tears forming behind my eyes. I breathed slowly and focused on the ceiling, willing myself to gain control. Spiritualists believe that the dearly departed are merely moving to a different place. That the dead are still with us. But I knew I had never seen or spoken to my grandmother since her death.

The summer before she'd died of cancer, she'd promised to teach me how to filter the impressions that bombarded me throughout any given day. She said she could help me understand my dreams and that I probably was having "good news" dreams but was not aware of them, because they were much less intense than the "bad news" dreams. I had been thrilled with the idea of learning how to control the images and feelings that came to me uninvited.

Then she got sick and, before I knew it, before I had a chance to accept that she might not be in my life forever, she was gone. All she left was a small handwritten journal of her advice for me. I'd flipped through it briefly after her death, looking for quick answers, as only a fifteen-year-old can do. Frustrated by her advice to meditate and keep a record of my "precognitive experiences" to better hone my talent, I latched on to the one or two sentences that would free me the quickest: "Ignore your guides and they will eventually become quiet, waiting for you to seek them" and "Discounting feelings in favor of 'facts' will lead to unreliable and diluted information."

I had done both. I ignored all input that wasn't based on the normal five senses, and I never followed up on any "feelings." Only a few messages came through after that. I dreamed of Diana's parents dying and never told anyone, in a superstitious hope that by remaining silent I could stop it from happening. Dean Roberts had been the last straw. After Mac left for Saginaw, I told my mother I was done trying to develop any psychic ability, and our long feud began. This past May, I finally followed a hunch, and screwed up so badly that I ran home to Crystal Haven.

I must have spaced out during the eulogy, because my thoughts were interrupted by loud organ music. I didn't recognize the song, but the organist was dragging out the notes to lend a dirge-like cadence to the piece. The coffin made its way down the aisle and out the front door, carried by Gary and several men I didn't recognize. My mother had said some of Sara's lawyer friends would be in attendance.

"Let's get out of here," said Diana. She clutched a damp tissue and dabbed at her eyes.

We slipped out along the side aisle, avoiding the reception line, where Sara's daughters, Alison and Isabel, looked like they were holding each other up. I didn't want to force them to make small talk with me and skipped the line. We stood blinking in the sunshine before the organist could begin his next song.

Alex beat us out of the church but got caught in conversation with Joe Stark. Joe's hair was slicked back and touched the collar of his dark, immaculate suit. He watched Alex walk away and said something to Cecile, who looked in my direction and quickly glanced away.

"What was that about?" I asked Alex when he caught up to us.

"Stark wants me back at the restaurant 'pronto,' " he said. "He thinks there will be a big crowd gathering after the funeral."

"He doesn't seem very happy today," Diana said, shielding her eyes to better spot Stark among the crowd.

"He's never happy," Alex said. "He spends most of his time counting his sales receipts and grumbling about the bills."

I was about to respond when I felt a tap on my shoulder. I turned to see Mac leaning on his cane; he gave me a half smile.

"Hi." He nodded to Diana and Alex. "Are you up to meeting with me to talk about Tish? I forgot when we made our plans yesterday that the funeral was today."

"Yeah, I can meet with you." I grabbed Diana's arm as she tried to edge away. "In about an hour, Daily Grind?"

"Sure, good." He hesitated with his hand up, and I thought he was going to hug me, but he let his arm drop and turned away.

"What's up with him?" Diana said. "He was nice."

I nodded as I watched him weave through the crowd.

I waited again at The Daily Grind. I sipped my coffee and glowered at the clear blue sky as I replayed last night's dream. I should never have let Diana do those spells. I knew from experience that her spell work tended to bring on the dreams. I'd never told her, and certainly had never mentioned it to my mother, but something about Diana's rituals got my dream-mind working.

For Mac's own safety, I had to stay away from him. I'd have to pick a fight or come up with some excuse to keep my distance. It wouldn't be any different than the past eight years, but it made me sad. I wished once again that I had been given no "gift" at all. I often wondered if my grandmother knew about her own impending death.

"Clyde . . . hello." Mac waved his hand in front of my eyes, interrupting my thoughts.

"Hey, Mac. Sorry." I shook my head to clear it.

"I waved to you from outside, said hello when I came in, got my coffee . . . you were off somewhere else." He smiled and sat down.

"Sorry, rough night."

"I'm sure. I'm sorry about Tish. I know you were close." He coughed and focused on dumping cream into his coffee cup.

We talked quietly about Tish, and I went over the timeline with him again.

Josh walked over with the coffeepot.

"Want a warm-up, Clyde?"

I nodded and pushed the cup toward him.

He started to pour and stopped.

"Man, things are not going his way," he said, looking out the window.

Mac and I looked across the street to see Milo striding away from Cecile. She caught up to him and grabbed his arm, but he shook her hand off hard enough that she stumbled as he continued up the street.

"What's that all about?" I looked up at Josh.

"Dunno, but he and Joe were getting into it yesterday." Josh shook his head and finished pouring the coffee.

"What do you mean?" I said.

"Same thing. Milo came barreling out of the Grill, Joe right behind him, but he turned on Joe and pushed him against the wall. I don't know what they said, but it didn't look friendly."

"Well, Joe isn't supporting Milo's bid to develop that land out along the highway. Maybe they're having some father-son disagreements about Milo's plans," Mac said.

Josh shrugged and walked over to the counter to help the next customer.

I leaned forward to avoid being heard by nearby coffee drinkers. "Do you know Milo isn't really Joe's son?"

Mac looked up from his coffee, holding my gaze for a moment.

"Yeah. I know. I didn't think that was common knowledge, though."

"How did you find out?"

"I worked the Julia Wyatt case." He glanced out the window. "It came up then."

"Don't you think he could have something to do with what's been going on around here?"

"No. I don't." His eyes jerked back to me and had taken on that steely color I didn't like.

"Why are you being so stubborn about this?"

"Stubborn? I'm doing my job. I'm working with real facts, not—"

"Not what?" I lifted my right eyebrow. Combined with the different-colored eyes, I thought it was very compelling. This might be my best chance for a fight. A way to put some distance between us.

"Not . . . hunches." He glanced down again.

I stood quickly and knocked the chair over. I hesitated, feeling like maybe I had overplayed it.

"Wait, Clyde. I didn't mean it that way." Mac stood and blocked my planned stomp out of the café. He took my arm and tried to steer me back to the chair.

"What way did you mean it?" I kept my voice low because the other customers were not even pretending to be minding their own business.

"I meant that this case is not your problem. It's my job to find the killer. Just . . . let me do my job and stay out of it."

"Oh well, now that you put it *that* way . . ." I jerked my arm out of his grasp and brushed past him out the door. I didn't have to fake being mad this time.

I stormed up the street until I remembered I'd parked in the other direction. Faking a fight wasn't necessary to keep my distance—I could just have a conversation with Mac about the case and it would happen by itself. I kept walking rather than go past the café again and run into him. Who did he think he was, telling me to stay out of it? Tish was my friend. My feet seemed to be taking me around the block, which was a good idea. I came up to my car from the other side. By the time I got there, I knew what I needed to do.

I **pulled into** our driveway and was pleased to see both Alex's blue Honda and Diana's green VW bug. I hoped everyone would be on board with my plan.

I found them all in the dining room. They had the pendulum out again, but it didn't seem to be going well. Alex was gripping the chain, his knuckles white. Vi hovered, obviously fighting her urge to just grab it from him. Mom and Diana watched for any signs of movement. Dad read the newspaper at the far end of the table.

"Oh, there you are!" said Vi. I had only seen her briefly on the way to the funeral, but something was different about her. She seemed older to me today—her hair was in a tangled braid, the lines near her mouth were more prominent.

The rest of the group turned to the door, and Alex set the pendulum down with a look of relief. My mother's eyes were puffy and her nose red from crying. Diana's skin was blotchy, and she had mascara smeared under her eyes. Even Dad looked haggard, and I could tell he wasn't reading the paper as much as staring at it.

"Hi. Where's Seth?"

Diana pointed down; my mother glanced heavenward for strength.

"I'm under here." Seth's voice floated out from under the tablecloth.

I bent to look and was met by three sets of eyes.

"Aren't you a little big to be playing 'fort'?" I asked.

"I'm not playing. Tuffy's all worked up about something, and he doesn't want to come out."

I glanced at Vi, who raised her eyebrows and shrugged. I sat next to Diana, across from Alex.

The doorbell rang.

My mother rushed out.

"That's probably Tom Andrews," I said. "I called him on my way home."

"Oooh," Seth said with a schoolyard singsong, "it's your boyfriend."

I tried to kick him under the table but missed and caught Alex instead.

"Why is he here?" Vi asked, ignoring the antics.

"I think we need to be more proactive about this," I said.

"Proactive about what?" asked Alex. He was rubbing his leg and glaring at me.

"This situation. Two people have been killed, and we don't know why. I think Milo Jones has something to do with it."

"I'm in. That guy bugs the cra—"

I shot a look at Alex.

"—ackers out of me," said Alex.

"Crackers? Really?" Seth's voice asked from below.

"I knew it!" said Vi, oblivious to the giggling of Seth and Alex.

My mother and Tom came into the room, and everyone took a seat except Seth, who stayed under the table.

I looked at my motley crew and drew in a big breath. All eyes were on me, and I hesitated at the absurdity of my plan. I almost called it off, but I owed Tish my best effort. I had to find out who had killed her. Since the police were watching Gary, we needed to watch Milo.

"Okay, why do you think Milo is involved?" Diana asked.

"I saw him arguing with Tish just before she was killed." I held up fingers counting off my suspicions. "He's been arguing with his parents, and I know that Sara was holding up his land-development plans. She didn't want to sell her parcel of the land she and Gary split during the divorce. Without it, he couldn't develop the area the way he wanted."

"That doesn't sound right," Diana said. "Do you really think he would kill Sara and then Tish over some strip mall?"

"I don't know what he would do." I shrugged. "I don't know what he's up to. All I know is that he's back in town and two people are dead."

Vi nodded vigorously; my mother wrinkled her forehead. Dad set his paper down.

"I guess Sara could have been looking at Milo during the séance . . . ," Diana said.

"That's just it." I held my hands out, palms up. "We don't know what happened at the séance exactly, but it may have spooked him. Maybe he thought she was accusing him; maybe he thought she knew something," I said.

"What about Gary?" Tom asked.

"The police department has him covered. I doubt he'll have any secrets left when Mac gets through with him."

"Okay, what do we do?" Diana said.

"We'll set up a rotating schedule of surveillance," I said.

Heads nodded. My family doesn't wallow; they like action.

"I'll take the first shift!" said Vi. She stood to leave.

"Vi, where are you going?" asked my mother.

"I'm off to keep an eye on Milo. We're going to watch him and catch him in the act, right?" Vi looked better already.

"Uh, the act of what?" said Alex.

"We don't know what he's up to," I said. "We need to keep an eye on him in a *subtle* way." I glanced at my aunt.

"I think we need to do more than that," said Alex. "We need to entice him to act again."

"You mean you want to tempt him?" asked Tom.

"Oh, that sounds dangerous," said my mother. "Maybe we should leave this to the police."

"The police aren't doing anything, Rose," said Vi. "They don't think Milo's guilty. That's what Clyde's telling us."

Everyone looked to Tom to confirm.

He hung his head. "It's true. Mac doesn't think it's Milo. He's keeping an eye on Gary." He folded his hands on the table and didn't look up.

"We could pretend Clyde knows something." Seth's muffled voice came from under the table. "Everyone in town thinks she's psychic; they'll all believe it if we say she knows who did it."

We looked at each other, considering. Seth had a point. But undercover work was dangerous, even for a highly trained police division. I'd certainly never entertained the possibility with only a rookie officer and this sort of ragtag group as backup.

"Clyde, no. Don't put yourself in danger like this," Diana pleaded.

"Let's start by following him and reporting back on his activities." I put my hand over Diana's to reassure her. "Let's see what he's up to. He's certainly been arguing with enough people in town."

I heard Baxter groan from under the table, either out of boredom or disgust at our lack of action, I wasn't sure.

"Do you think we need to use disguises? I have hats and sunglasses we could use," Vi said. She started to get up.

"I'm sure no one needs disguises," I said.

Vi slumped in her chair.

"I'll keep an eye on him when he's at the restaurant mucking around in my kitchen," Alex said.

"I can take a shift when I'm off duty," Tom said.

"I'll alert the cats to be on the lookout," said Vi.

"That's a good idea, Vi." My mother nodded while talking, as if agreeing with herself. "They're really helpful when it comes to this type of thing."

"That's *if* they want to be helpful," Vi said. She peered around the table to be sure no one was expecting much from the cats.

"We'll figure out a schedule that makes sense for everyone, and we'll try to make it look natural. No one has to sneak around looking like spies." I held Aunt Vi's gaze for a moment. "That will only bring more attention to what we're doing."

"What should I do? I should do something," Mom said.

Vi patted her hand.

"We'll all get to do something. It's going to take a lot of people to keep track of Milo without him noticing," I said.

"What should we do if he spots one of us? Do we have a code-word distress signal? I think we should have one of those," Vi said.

My father put his head in his hands, and I noticed he was taking slow breaths.

"No. No distress signal. He's not likely to be a threat to any of us."

"Except you, if he's heard you suspect him." Diana's eyes were bright with irritation.

"Okay, let's just take this a step at a time. For now, we will simply follow him and see what he's doing around town." I started passing out sheets of paper. "Write your phone number and pass the sheets around."

Dad got up and mumbled something about maps; he hurried off to his den.

"So we'll text each other as the suspect moves around town?" said Tom.

"Your father doesn't text, Clyde. He thinks texting is when he slips me a note while I'm talking on the phone," said Mom.

"Texting is very unreliable," said Vi. "You never seem to get my texts, Clyde."

Oh boy. I took a deep breath.

"We'll set up a phone tree; those who can't manage to deal with a text will get a phone call if possible."

"Texting *is* much quieter," Vi said. "I saw a movie once where a guy sent a text with the phone in his pocket. That's a skill that could come in handy." She pulled out her phone and studied it.

Dad returned and gestured at everyone to clear the table. He spread out his ordinance maps of the area. Dad used the maps while listening to the police band; he could track the officer's movements and stay in the comfort of his own easy chair.

He placed an X on the hotel where Milo was staying. He then began a complicated zoning of the areas around it using glasses and saltshakers to indicate each of us and where our "territory" would be located.

Vi kept moving pieces when Dad was busy in another zone. She seemed to be trying to take over a larger area than was originally allotted to her pepper mill.

"Who takes the first shift?" Alex asked.

"Seth and I are the most mobile. We'll find him and keep an eye out and, if he goes somewhere we can't follow, we'll call one of you to let you know he's heading your way."

"Well, he never comes to the house, so what should Rose and I do?" Vi said. Her mouth pulled downward as she noticed her pepper mill was back in the smallest zone on the map.

"You can come into town if you want and keep track of him while he's there and then hand him off when you have clients scheduled," said Tom.

"All right, I guess that will work," said Dad. He stood back to study the map.

"Frank can listen on his scanner to get an idea of where the police are and whether they're following Gary," Mom said. "I can stay here by the phone in case anyone needs to get a message through."

"Good idea, Mrs. Fortune," said Tom. "It's good to have a backup plan."

We were going to need a lot more than that, I thought.

21

Operation Catch Milo had been in effect for just
under twenty-four hours. It felt like twenty-four days. Vi had
figured out how to text. My phone vibrated every few minutes
with updates of her status, whether she was "on duty" or not.
She had embraced the texting lingo and even invented her
own words. It was easier to decipher a string of vanity license
plates on game day in Ann Arbor. *url8, ivlsthim, wrru?*
("You're late, I've lost him, where are you?") Typically by the
time I'd deciphered the message, she had given up and texted
a real message to Seth. She and Seth were also practicing
texting "blind." It wasn't going well.

Seth and I walked the canine gang through town while
watching for Milo. Because it was Sunday, I'd called some
of my clients and offered a free walk just so we would have
a cover story. Vi and one of her cat spies had lookout duty
at the park, which faced the hotel where Milo was staying.
Mom had a lot to say on the subject of a son who stays in a

hotel instead of with his parents "regardless of his age." I was seriously regretting this whole thing.

My phone buzzed for the fourth time in five minutes, and I pulled it out of my back pocket with my free hand. *subject on move*, it read. Vi must have found the vowels on her keypad. I was about to turn it off when my other arm jerked forward and someone shouted.

"Get off! Down! Sit!"

All seven dogs sat. Even Baxter and Tuffy sat, and they were up the street with Seth.

I looked up to see who had worked this miracle, and saw Mac. I tried to calculate how long it would take to get rid of him.

"How did you do that?" I asked.

"Do what?"

"Get them to sit like that?"

"I said, 'Sit.'" Mac shrugged. "Don't you know it's not safe to walk and text?"

Seth's thumbs flew over his mini keyboard. Probably sending out that distress signal I had said we wouldn't need.

According to the plan, we should have been walking toward the park to pick up Milo's trail from Vi. Unfortunately, we were stymied by a chatty Mac, who stood in our path asking about the dogs.

I tried to answer him quickly and step past him, but the dogs were rooted to the spot, watching Mac as if he were their long-lost alpha. He glanced down at them and shook his head.

"How do you keep track of them all?"

"It's not that hard once you get to know them. They each have their own personality, just like people," I said.

Seth bounced on his toes, clearly hoping this conversation would wrap up soon.

"Am I keeping you two from something important?"

"No," I said.

"Yes," Seth said.

Mac looked at us, his head tilted, questioning.

"We just need to get these guys to the park to finish their walk," I said, and handed a few leashes to Seth, hoping he could escape and get to the park quickly. "They start to get antsy if their routine is messed up."

"Oh, well, don't let me stop you." Mac backed away to let us pass.

We started off toward the park, and Mac fell in beside me. My expression must have been less than welcoming.

"Is it okay if I tag along?"

"Sure, fine," I said, and tried not to look at Seth, who was jerking his head as if he had a tic.

"How's the case going?" I said.

"It's not. There's very little evidence and no witnesses. You know the longer a case goes unsolved, the more likely it will stay unsolved."

"Are you expanding your list of suspects?"

"You mean to include Milo Jones? No."

"Mac, be reasonable. It can't be a coincidence that two people died right after he returned to town." I hesitated as I realized I was agreeing with Vi's assessment of the situation, and that was never a good thing. "Plus, he was never cleared of the Julia Wyatt disappearance. I don't know why you won't even look at him." I had stopped to make my point while Seth walked on ahead.

"I know it wasn't him, Clyde."

"How do you know?"

"Let's just say I have a feeling."

"Oh, you're hilarious. Psychic humor from the biggest skeptic in town."

I glanced forward just in time to see Milo approach. He and Mac nodded a greeting, and Milo navigated his way past the dogs.

Out of the corner of my eye, I saw Vi hurry over to Seth, gesturing up the street after Milo. When she spotted Mac, she turned and zipped back across the street to the park, which might have worked if she hadn't darted in front of two cars and caused all that honking.

"What's Vi doing here?" said Mac.

"Vi? I don't see Vi," I said, and turned to look behind us.

"She's right over there behind that tree. I think she's peeking at us. Does this have something to do with all these dogs?"

"No, I don't think so. Maybe she's just out for a walk. She likes to stay in shape."

I tried to get Mac's attention back to me and the dogs, but he was drawn to Vi, hiding behind a skinny maple tree in the park.

Mac started across the street toward Vi just as Tom rounded the corner of the hotel. He was moving too quickly to turn around at first sight of Mac. Unfortunately he tried anyway, and his attempt at looking natural while turning in mid-sprint and then slamming full force into a parking meter caught us all off guard.

Tom was bent over and wheezing by the time Mac and I got to him.

"Andrews, what are you doing?" Mac said. He raised his voice to be heard over Tom's labored breathing.

Seth ran over to us with his five dogs. My four acted as if they hadn't seen the other group in years. Between the wheezing and the exuberant dog greetings, a crowd had gathered. Seth continued texting with his free hand and made such a show of it that Mac noticed and grabbed the phone from him.

"What's going on around here?"

I reached for the phone and for a moment our hands were entwined but not in the nice, stroll-along-the-beach way. This was a fight-for-possession kind of entwining.

"This is an illegal search and seizure!" I said.

"Give me a break, Clyde. I'm not going to arrest him. I *would* like to know who he's texting so furiously in the middle of this chaos." He glanced across the street. "Vi seems to be focused on her phone as well. Does she know how to text? Or is she still sending messages through the cats in town?"

I was still attached to the four biggest dogs by their leashes, which were wrapped in my left hand. As Andrews struggled to regain an upright posture, they noticed him and lunged in his direction. I was pulled along and lost my grip on the phone.

Seth was forced to follow by the pulling of his pack, and we watched in horror as Mac glanced at the small metal device divulging all our secrets. His expression went from bemused to stormy as he scrolled through the text conversation between Seth and Vi.

As we stood watching Mac, I noticed my mother's orange

smart car turn the corner about a block away. It drove slowly past the park and then stopped at the curb. Vi darted out from behind the tree just as Mac turned to call her over to our little gathering.

"Ms. Greer! I need to talk to you!" He started toward Vi.

Vi hopped in the passenger side. My mother must have hit the gas pretty hard, because the car took off, its tires squealing. I didn't know her car could accelerate that fast.

Tom had regained control of his breathing and stood upright, but his face turned an unpleasant shade of green when Mac turned and headed back in our direction.

Mac used his patented stare-down technique on us. I knew what he was doing and carefully avoided eye contact. Seth held up okay, as well. He studied his shoes and waited for the adults to make the first move. I could tell Tom was weakening.

"Mac, I don't know what you think is going on here, but you have no right to keep Seth's phone," I said.

He silently handed it to Seth.

This was going to be tougher than I thought.

"Andrews, what do you have to do with this?" Mac said.

"I don't . . . I didn't. Nothing, sir."

Mac focused his full attention on Tom and, I have to say, it was impressive. Tom was stronger than I thought. He stuck with his story, which put Mac in a tough spot. No one had done anything wrong, but he knew from the phone that we had been watching someone, and he was smart enough to realize that the someone was probably Milo.

Seth's phone buzzed. We all looked at it. Seth pressed a button on the side and slipped it into his pocket. He bent and patted the dogs, who had also become strangely quiet during this stare-down.

"Okay, you three need to really hear me on this." Mac looked at each of us. "Stay away from Milo."

"We weren't—"

"You aren't a good liar, Clyde. Don't even try."

"You two are not to pursue this investigation." He pointed at Seth and me. "Andrews, I would pull you off this case right now if I had the manpower to cover your absence."

"Yes, sir."

"I understand you want to know who killed Tish. But whoever did it is dangerous. I don't want more people hurt."

"Okay," I said, as sincerely as I could.

Seth glanced at me to see if I was really giving in.

"Okay," Seth said.

"Someone needs to get a message to Thelma and Louise. Tell them to quit following Milo." He turned and looked at me. "And tell your mother I'm not against giving her a reckless driving ticket if she keeps leaving tire marks on the street." Mac bent down, gave a pat to Baxter, and limped up the street.

Monday afternoon, my psychic/psycho gang gathered in my mother's dining room again. Vi had taken to calling it "headquarters." Seth and I had just returned from morning dog rounds. It had been a long week since discovering Sara's body, and we all looked worn out. Only Alex was missing, as he was finishing with the lunch crowd. Tuffy joined us at the table; he was on Seth's lap. Baxter rested his head on the table near Vi. She was knitting something long and orange and kept shrugging him off her arm when he leaned too close.

"I saw Milo buy bacon," she said.

"Maybe he likes bacon," said Dad.

"My cats saw him take a shovel and put it in his car," she said.

"Really? A shovel?" I said. I looked up from the book Diana was showing me. There were more spells and talismans she wanted to try.

"Well, they didn't call it that. But that's what they described. They said they could tell he was up to something and he put 'a large dirt-thrower' in his car."

"I've been checking the cards, and it's clear that Milo is involved in all of this somehow," Mom said.

"Tommy, you said someone's been digging out in the woods, right?" Vi turned her attention to Tom, who shrank into his chair.

He nodded.

"Why would Milo carry around a shovel unless he's the one digging up the forest floor?" She set her knitting in her lap and put her hands out as if this was the most logical conclusion in the world.

"Milo has no reason to dig in the woods, Vi," Dad said.

"How do you know? He's probably looking for the body of his ex-girlfriend." She began furiously knitting again. "He needs to find it and move it before all the digging starts for the construction."

A hush fell over the table as we considered this possibility. Even though most of it was based on cat reports and hearsay, it *was* a possibility.

"So you're saying Milo's an idiot?" Seth asked.

Diana snorted, and Dad chuckled.

Vi's face turned a dangerous red. "Do you have a better idea, Mr. Smarty-pants?"

"It just seems to me that if I had buried a body out in the woods I would have a general idea of where it would be." Seth didn't look up from his iPod as his thumbs waged war on zombies or aliens on the tiny screen. "Plus, I wouldn't return to town with a building project guaranteed to dig up that body."

Seth had scored a point but at great cost; he would have realized this if he had looked at Vi while he was talking. Vi didn't like to have her theories squelched. Part of my brain considered her idea; Milo had something going on besides the strip mall project.

"Tom, what can you tell us?" I hoped he would have something good to divert Vi's attention.

He'd been watching my mother's cards as if she were performing magic tricks. "Things are not very good at the station," Tom said. "We don't have much to go on, and Mac is getting irritated."

"I'm sure we didn't help much yesterday," I said.

"He hasn't mentioned it again, actually. I thought he'd bring it up every chance he got, but he's been all business. Everyone's checking and double-checking the evidence. Mac spent some time in the archives, but I don't know what he was looking for. He sent us back out to canvas the neighborhoods for witnesses. That's what I'm supposed to be doing right now."

"Well, you have two witnesses right here, so technically you *are* doing your job," Vi said, and gestured to the dogs.

"Too bad they're both sticking to the same bacon story. And none of you seem interested that Milo was buying bacon." She narrowed her eyes at the dogs and rested her chin on her hand, which dragged her mouth into more of a frown than usual. Her knitting had tangled, and she let it slip to the floor.

Seth reached over and patted Baxter's head; he shot Vi a look and held Tuffy tighter.

"All we have right now is that both Sara and Tish were shot with a small-caliber revolver," Tom said. He consulted his ever-present notebook. "The ballistics test says it's the same gun, so whoever shot Sara didn't think he needed to get rid of it."

"That's interesting," said Diana. "It takes a certain amount of arrogance to kill someone and then assume you're never going to be a suspect."

"There was no sign of a break-in at either address. We're assuming the killer knew both victims," Tom read from his notes. "The only other thing we're looking into is the threats that were coming through Sara's website."

"What threats? She never told me about any threats," Mom said. She looked around the table to see if she was the only one in the dark.

"Gary told us about it. Apparently, in the past month or so she'd been getting threatening comments on the blog at her website," Tom said.

"What kind of comments?" Mom said.

"Mostly it had to do with her work as a psychic. Gary said she thought it was another psychic in town trying to scare her off," Tom said.

"Alison mentioned it the other day," I said. "It started with comments about her being a fraud and needing lots of 'theater' at her séances. Then the tone became more threatening. They said that if she kept doing her séances she would regret it."

"According to Gary, Sara thought it was Tish." Tom flipped through his notes again. "Tish said she didn't know anything about it. She never went to Sara's site, according to her computer-search history."

"You know you can delete browsing history," Seth said. His voice indicated he didn't think Tom could even turn on a computer.

"I *know*." Tom glowered at Seth. "We have a computer guy in Grand Rapids looking at both machines for us. So far, there's no link."

"I heard there was some issue with Gary and Sara over this land deal," Diana said.

"Yeah, he came clean on that one." Tom nodded.

He explained Sara and Gary's fight over the land and their divorce settlement.

"I remember her telling me about that," said Mom. "She wanted to build there someday but was waiting to see what would happen with Milo's strip mall plan. She didn't want to live next to a business area, but she also didn't want to sell and help him in his quest for more space."

"All right. Gary needed money and had land he couldn't sell because Sara wouldn't sell hers." Dad ticked the points off on his fingers. "Milo really wanted both plots of land, and Sara stood in the way. She was getting threats from someone about her séances, and had recently come up against Tish when applying for her certificate," Dad said. He looked at his fingers and shook his head.

"Don't forget the séance she did just before she died. She

basically accused someone in that room of being a murderer," Diana said.

"There's only one thing to do," said Vi, looking around the table.

I didn't want to know what she had in mind, but she was unstoppable.

"We're having our own séance," she said, and crossed her arms.

"Wicked!" Seth said. His grin spread, and his eyes snapped with excitement.

22

Vi claimed that a séance would be most effective in a place where Sara felt comfortable. She was quickly backed by Mom and Diana. We were going to break into Sara's house. We waited for Alex to finish at work, because he didn't want to miss out.

It was after nine o'clock when Seth and I approached Sara's house through the woods. I felt a bit like a SWAT team member except that what we were doing was against the law, and my backup team consisted of tarot readers, Wiccans, pet psychics, and a dentist. I didn't want to think about what would happen if we got caught. Certainly I wouldn't have to make a decision about Ann Arbor; that would be the least of my problems. Even though Sara didn't have any neighbors close by, Tom had given strict instructions to leave cars parked several streets away and to come through the back to avoid having any neighbors or drive-by traffic notice us. He was our lookout.

We arrived in groups of twos and threes. The rest of the crew had gone ahead of us.

Seth tensed as we neared the back door, and I put a hand on his shoulder.

"Do you think they've cleaned up in there?" he whispered.

I shrugged. "I hope so, but I don't know."

"You go first," he said. He hung back and pushed me toward the house.

I hesitated at the door, took a deep breath, and then swung it open. There was no sign of the violence that had occurred a week earlier. I breathed out slowly and sent a quick thank-you to whoever had cleaned up, and signaled Seth to follow.

Mom was in the kitchen and rushed to meet us at the door. I hadn't described Sara's body lying on the floor to Mom, so she didn't have the same aversion to the room as Seth and I did.

"You have to stop her, Clyde."

"Who? What are you talking about?" I pried her hands off my arms.

"It's your aunt. It's not bad enough that we're in the same house where Sara died, now she's going through her things." Mom took a shuddering breath. "She's in there 'tossing' Sara's office. She claims Tuffy told her Sara spent a lot of time there in the past few weeks." She pointed through the kitchen to the small office beyond.

Diana stood on the other side of the desk from Vi and Alex and cast worried glances our way. Vi had opened every desk drawer and rummaged through it.

"Here's something!" she said, and waved a sheet of paper. She handed it to Alex.

"Vi, what are you doing?" I said. I had hurried in to stand next to Diana.

"I'm searching the scene of the crime for clues." She continued to search when Alex said that her find was just a flyer for window cleaning. There was a phone number on the back that Vi thought we should track down.

"It's probably the Pizza Shack number. The police already did this," I said.

She looked at me doubtfully.

"Well, they didn't do a very good job. It doesn't look like they touched the desk."

"They probably left it the way they found it, which is more than I can say for you," Mom said from the doorway. She took a step forward and then stopped, clutching her protective amulet.

"Oh, please. They either didn't look or they just opened and closed the drawers hoping something would jump up and down screaming, 'I'm evidence!'" Vi punctuated this statement by making the flyer jump up and down.

Seth giggled. Diana smiled. Alex flipped through the bottom file drawer.

"Here, let me do that." I started around the desk.

Alex held up his hand to stop me. "Look at this. Sara had copies of old newspaper clippings stuffed here under 'Taxes 2007.' "

He pulled out the copies and we all leaned forward to look. Vi cleared her throat as we read the headline: "Hunter's Death in Greer's Woods Ruled an Accident."

"What's she doing with these?" Vi looked up, her eyes bright and wet.

I took the file and inspected the articles. One stack covered the shooting death of Mike Jones from the time it was reported until the time they closed the case. A second group followed the case of Julia Wyatt and the search for her body, including finding her clothing in Greer's Woods.

"I think we should turn this over to the police," I said.

"We can't do that. We're not supposed to be here," Diana said.

"Can't we just tell Officer Andrews to search the place again?" said Seth. "And tell him how to find the office, and how to open the desk, and where to look—"

"That's enough, Seth. He's not that bad," Mom said.

"He's not that good, either," Seth breathed into my ear.

"I can't remove evidence, but I'd like to get a copy of these," I said. I put them back in their original order. "I'll have to get Tom to copy them for me."

Seth had gone to Vi's side of the desk and opened a panel.

"You could just copy them now," he said. He did something inside the panel and then we heard clicks and beeps.

I handed him the papers and motioned everyone else into the dining room. Dad arrived just as we were setting up.

We'd decided Diana would run the séance, since she had the most experience. She wasn't a medium, but she knew what to do. Vi hoped that the combined "psychic talent" of the group would carry us along in our ignorance. It was getting dark outside. We pulled the curtains and left the lights off so no one would get curious. I wished we had stuck to the pendulum and tarot cards. Séances creep me out.

Seth came into the room with the copies and stood too

close. His hand shook when he handed me the sheaf of papers.

"Okay, we need to sit around the table here. I brought some candles," Diana said. "Rose, did you bring some food?"

"Sara always liked my banana bread. I brought some of that." My mother placed a small basket on the table.

"Is a ghost going to eat that food?" Seth asked.

"No, we just put it there to attract her spirit," Diana said. "We light the candles for warmth and light, which is also attractive to the spirits."

"Let's get the show on the road here. I don't want to get caught in Sara's house like this," Dad said. I almost hugged him.

We sat, and Diana lit the three candles.

Vi's eyes glittered across the table toward me, the candles lighting her face with an eerie glow. I felt a familiar chill settle along my spine. I really hate séances.

"Everyone focus your energy and your thoughts on Sara. We all need to be thinking of her to get her to communicate with us." Diana's voice was quiet and soothing; I wished I were sitting next to her.

I had Seth, whose eyes had grown to what looked like twice their normal size, on one side, and Alex, who had his eyes shut tight just like he always did in scary movies, on the other. These two were not the ones I'd want backing me up in a dark alley. Dad looked worried next to Mom, then came Diana and Vi.

Everyone seemed nervous except Diana and Vi. They acted like they were about to attend a party.

"Put your hands on the table and lightly hold your

neighbor's hand. The circle will be broken if you let go, and the spirit will leave."

I saw Mom give Dad's hand a squeeze; she glanced at him, and he seemed to relax. I got no reassuring squeezes from Alex and Seth, but I did hold on to Seth a little tighter than necessary. He looked a bit unsettled, and I didn't want the circle broken by nervous vomiting.

Diana closed her eyes, and said, "Our dearest Sara, we bring you gifts from life. Commune with us, Sara."

The few séances I had attended in the past had been disappointing. We had never been successful, and as the silence stretched it looked like this would be another bust.

Someone sniffed. Alex cleared his throat. The silence became heavy, then uncomfortable as we waited. Nothing happened. The flickering candles cast long, jumping shadows on the walls. I heard the unfamiliar noises of Sara's house all around us. The refrigerator's quiet groan in the next room, the pops and clicks of a house settling in for the night, the high-pitched whine in my ears that I only noticed when it was really quiet, all became louder and more sinister as we sat in expectation. Diana repeated her request, and we waited. Still nothing.

Alex shifted in his seat, and I glanced at him; he got ready to say something when Vi spoke.

"There is murder here." She stared at a spot above my head, and it was all I could do not to turn around and see if there was something there, but I didn't want to break the circle.

Diana looked surprised and turned to Vi.

"Sara? Are you with us?" Diana asked.

"No, not Sara. She has crossed over," said Vi.

Vi continued to stare without blinking, just over my head.

"A murderer is unpunished. You must use your talent before another dies," Vi said.

"Who are you? What can you tell us about the murders?" Diana asked.

Something brushed my cheek, and I fought the urge to scrub at it. At the same time, Alex sneezed and broke the circle. The candle in front of Vi went out, and she slumped in her chair.

Everyone else jumped out of their seats and rushed to her side. She looked around and blinked. I was the only one still seated. I ran the last few seconds through my mind—I thought I had seen her blow out the candle.

"Vi, are you okay?" said Mom.

"Who do you think that was?" said Seth.

"This is very strange," said Diana. "Vi, has this ever happened to you before?"

"I don't know. . . ." Vi put her hand to her head. "I just sort of spaced out for a second, and then I guess I broke the circle. Sorry, everyone."

"You don't remember what you said?" Seth asked.

"I didn't say anything." Vi frowned at him.

I caught her eye and raised an eyebrow. She cocked her head and looked surprised, like she didn't know what I might mean.

"Well, we're not likely to have any more 'manifestations' tonight," said Dad. "Let's pack it in."

Everyone talked at once as Diana blew out the other candles and stowed them away. I tucked the packet of articles in my bag. There were quiet exclamations of "fascinating" and "unusual." I stayed out of the conversations and tried to make sense of what had happened. The discussions finally died out, and we left in groups of twos and threes, sneaking through the backyard to where the cars were parked.

Seth chattered away in my ear the whole way home. He was no longer green; he was geeked.

I wondered if everyone had been fooled by Vi's performance.

I wait on the stone bridge in the woods near Message Circle. The sun is bright overhead, but the leaves filter the light, which is soft and gentle. I can hear the small stream trickling along under the bridge. I am happy and I am waiting for Mac.

I see him come through the woods, along the path. He's not using his cane, and his stride is long and purposeful. He speeds up when he sees me. In a breath or two he is at my side, and then I am in his arms and we kiss, and I lose track of where we are. I feel dizzy and my head is spinning. When the kiss ends, I turn and we are no longer in the woods, we are in the front of a church and all our friends are there. I am wearing a dress and he is wearing a tux and smiling, smiling.

A slamming door invaded my sleep. It took me a moment to recognize that I was in my parents' house and not my Ann Arbor apartment. I began the day by cursing myself for coming back to Crystal Haven.

I had come to think of it as the wedding dream. It was the dream that had changed everything. The first few times I had the dream, it started with Grace's wedding. I could see Paul clearly, and I knew the wedding was in New York City. I was devastated when Grace took this information and packed up to move to New York. Even though she was jealous of my "talent" and called me "psycho sister," she believed as much as my mother in the prescience of my dreams. But I missed her the way only a younger sibling can miss an adored big sister. After Grace met Paul, the dream changed and focused on the part where Mac and I were together. The beginning was different each time, but it always ended the same. It visited every year or so and left me feeling sad and confused. Sad that I had once believed it to be true, and confused that it persisted even after all this time.

I was still thinking about Mac and the way his face had fallen when he realized I had known about Dean, while I sipped my coffee in Mom's kitchen that morning.

I took a deep breath. I felt cooped up in this house with my dreams and memories. I decided to go out to Message Circle and think things through. Before I was old enough to have a gun, walking through the woods and sitting at Message Circle had been my therapy.

I took a fast shower, yanked my hair into a ponytail, threw on my jeans and a T-shirt, and grabbed my car keys. I planned to spend some time in Greer's Woods and be back in time to go on dog rounds with Seth.

Twenty minutes later, I stood on the bridge from my dream. I had taken the long way from the parking lot just to see it again and dispel the feeling from the dream. It was overcast, so the light was different. I heard the birds call to each other and the squirrels chatter, which drowned out the sounds of the stream. Then I saw Mac coming down the path, but he was using his cane. He made his way carefully up the bridge to meet me in the center.

"Clyde." He gave a quick nod.

No embrace, no kiss.

"Mac. What are you doing out here?"

"I was on my way to your house to talk to you and saw you drive away."

"You followed me?"

"It's not like I'm stalking you. I just wanted to talk," he said.

I waved my cell phone at him.

"You know I hate the telephone."

He leaned his cane against the gray stone wall of the bridge and crossed his arms. I could tell by the tight line of his mouth that I wasn't going to like what he was about to say.

He took a deep breath. "I don't know what you think you're doing, but it has to stop. I know you think I'm being unreasonable. I know you think I'm not considering all the possibilities." Mac held up his hand when I started to respond. "Let me finish. I need to consider not only how to solve these murders but also how to keep innocent people safe."

I broke into his lecture to defend myself. "I want to keep innocent people safe, too. I think Tish was innocent. Certainly she didn't deserve to be murdered. It's bad enough that Sara was killed, but whoever did it is now attacking others." I stopped, realizing I had just made his case for him.

Mac smiled. It was the slow smile I had loved long ago.

"Then you understand why I am asking—no, begging—you to step away from this case?"

"I understand." I looked away from him at the murky stream below.

"I don't think you do." He grabbed my shoulder and forced me to look at him. "I don't know if it was you or one of your gang of amateur spies that did it, and it doesn't matter."

My heart raced in panic at the thought that he'd found out we had broken into Sara's house to have a séance.

"I don't know what you're talking about." I shrugged my shoulder free.

"Lisa Harkness told me this morning that everyone in town thinks you know who killed Sara and Tish. Apparently, the story goes, now that you're back you'll be 'assisting' the police in the investigation using your psychic powers." He threw his hands in the air and walked a few steps away.

"I didn't start that rumor, Mac. I didn't have anything to do with it." But I thought I knew who had. Either Lisa had misinterpreted my meetings with Andrews, or Vi had been working her own angle on the case. It would have been nice to know I was being set up as bait.

"I don't want you hurt." Mac turned back to me and lowered his voice. "When I think of you walking into Tish's house, unarmed, with a murderer probably only a few seconds away . . . I just want to shake you for being so stupid." He grabbed my arm and shook it to demonstrate and threaten.

I flinched a bit at his intensity.

"I said I understand."

"I know what you said. I also know that you won't stop until this is solved. I don't know why you're mad at me, but don't let it cloud your judgment." His eyes had gotten dark, and I couldn't look away. "I need you to consider one thing—your friends and family are involved now. You might think you can protect yourself, but can you protect all of them?"

"Got it, Mac. I'll back off." I took a step away from him and rubbed my arm. "I'll get the rest of them to back off."

"I'm going to hold you to this." His eyes were the steely gray of Lake Michigan before a storm.

"Just get to work." I turned away from him and listened while he clomped up the trail the way he had come.

23

I walked the rest of the way to Message Circle after Mac left. There had been no kissing. Maybe my dreams were not as predictive as I thought, although that one had felt like it was telling me something.

Message Circle was formed in the 1940s, when so many people flocked to town for messages about loved ones that it became easier to do group readings. Grandma always felt that vibrations were high in this section of the woods. Whether it was from a cache of crystals buried there or some other confluence of energy, messages came frequently and in bulk.

By the time I came along, Message Circle had become more of a "free taste" kind of service. The mediums and psychics would do short, free readings for anyone in the audience, and these inevitably led to paying sessions. I couldn't remember what the summer hours were, but I was pleased to find it deserted.

I sat on the boulder centerpiece of the circle and waited. I had never personally received a message here—only the ones that Tish or one of the other readers had passed along during the daily circles. One had been from my grandfather, telling me to keep an eye on my grandmother. That was the year before she died. The rest were from unidentified sources, telling me that they sensed great talent. I always suspected my mother had planted those readings. The place was deserted now and peaceful.

I had come here often after my grandmother died, hoping for something, anything from her. Wishing she were still alive to tell me what to do with the dreams and visions, but mostly wishing she had passed on the secret to blocking them.

Later, I decided to do the opposite of whatever her book told me to do. Once I did that, only the occasional dream, like the wedding dream, or the one about Diana's parents, ever stuck with me. For the past few years in Ann Arbor, I had been free of them entirely. I wasn't happy that they seemed to be coming back.

I listened to the birds and squirrels for a while until the coffee I'd gulped earlier began to burn in my otherwise empty stomach. I remembered Mom's banana bread sitting on the counter at home and decided that today was not going to be my first-message day.

I had grabbed my bag and stood to go when I heard a clicking in the distance. It didn't sound like any bird or squirrel I had ever heard. It sounded mechanical. Then it stopped. I shook my head, thinking I was hearing things, but as I started to walk I heard it again. *Click-click-click.*

I couldn't see anything in the woods. It stopped again.

"Hello? Is someone there?" I said to the woods.

No answer, no clicking.

If this was my message, I had no idea what it meant. My stomach growled. I shook off the feeling that someone was out there in the woods. I'd spent hours—days—of my life wandering among these trees and knew it was easy to get spooked by weird sounds.

I took the path toward the parking lot, and either the clicking had stopped or my shoes on the path drowned out the sound, although I felt my ears straining to catch it.

In my Jeep I took a deep breath and realized I had been speed-walking. I turned on the car, rolled the windows down, and pulled out onto Singapore Highway. It ran parallel to the coast of Lake Michigan about a mile in from the water. It was my favorite road to drive because it curved through the trees, but it didn't have a ridiculously low speed limit.

I was enjoying the wind in my hair and trying not to think about Mac, when I came upon the one sharp turn in the road. I tapped the brake to take the turn but nothing happened. I pressed hard on the brake as my Jeep sped toward the curve. The pedal went straight to the floor. I downshifted into second gear, but I was going too fast, and my tires hit the gravel shoulder. It was too late to straighten the wheel, and suddenly the Jeep was rolling and I couldn't tell which way was up. Something slammed into my left shoulder and it exploded in pain. There was a loud screeching, grinding noise and then silence.

I waited a moment, trying to get my bearings. I'd only rolled once, down into the slope at the side of the road, but now my Jeep was lying on its side, driver's side down. Fortunately, the windows were open, so there was no broken glass near me. The windshield was cracked, the engine was still running, and I reached out with a shaky hand to shut it off. I unlatched my seat belt and looked for my bag. My entire left arm throbbed, and when I tried to move it the pain shot up my arm into my shoulder. Blood soaked through my shirt. I needed to call for help. But I couldn't see my bag.

"Hey, are you okay?" a voice shouted from outside.

"I think so. I need help getting out. Do you have a phone?"

I heard crunching footsteps and looked up to see Milo peering into my car. I saw my reflection in his sunglasses and realized that the man I most suspected of killing two women had me trapped.

"Are you hurt?"

"I think it's just my arm. Will you call for help?"

"Let me get you out of there. Can you stand up?" He extended his hand through the passenger window.

With Milo guiding me and then lifting me out of the wreckage, I was finally free of the car. As soon as I could, I backed away from him, and looked around for anything I could use as a weapon if needed.

"What happened? Did you swerve to avoid hitting something?" he asked, handing me my bag, which he had also rescued.

"No, my brakes didn't work, and I was probably going too fast when I hit the turn." I put the bag on my right shoulder.

"I didn't see it happen; you were in the ditch already when I came along." He glanced inside the Jeep.

"I practically stood on the brake, and it went right to the floor. Nothing. It was like I didn't have any brakes." I rummaged in my bag with my right hand and found my phone.

I felt my shoulders relax just knowing I could contact the rest of the world.

He walked around to the other side of the Jeep and took off his sunglasses to look at the undercarriage.

"Someone's messed with your brake line." He pointed with his glasses.

"What?" Forgetting my suspicions, I went around the car to see what he was looking at.

There it was—a hole in the brake line; just big enough to slowly drain the fluid. I thought back over the morning. The car had been fine on my way out to the woods. No other vehicles had been in the lot when I got there or when I left. How long had I been sitting at Message Circle?

"What have you been up to?" Milo shielded his eyes from the sun.

"What do you mean?" I took a step back. I hoped to get the car between us again.

"Someone just tried to kill you."

24

I didn't want Mac to find out about this, but I watched as Milo pulled out his phone and called the police.

My heart had kept up a steady, rapid beat, and my hands shook from the adrenaline. My fight-or-flight response was in overdrive, and I didn't know which I was going to need to do. I put some more distance between us and hoped that someone, anyone, would drive along the road.

"I'm sure they'll send someone soon. Thanks for the rescue and all," I said. I thought my voice sounded thin, but all I could hear clearly was the blood rushing in my ears and my self-defense instructor telling me to go for the eyes.

"You're welcome. Do you want to wait in my car?"

"No, you must have lots of things to do." I backed up some more and scanned the area for anything I could use to defend myself. "You don't have to wait with me."

Milo narrowed his eyes.

"Are you afraid of me?" He stepped closer.

"No, of course not." I clutched my phone and stood my ground. "Why would I be afraid?"

"I don't know. But you're holding your bag like it's a weapon, and you jump away when I get within three feet of you."

"You're imagining things," I said, and forced myself to smile.

"You *are* afraid. Why?"

"Well, the last time I saw you, the whole town suspected you of murder."

His eyebrows twitched up, as if he hadn't expected an honest answer. He had nice eyes and couldn't quite hold the tough-guy glare.

"Is that why you've been following me with your sidekick and that pack of dogs?"

"He's not my sidekick, he's my nephew, and no one's been following you." I adopted my own squinty expression.

He smiled. "Okay. But you aren't very subtle. And the old lady you have working for you is not great at hiding."

I sighed. I knew Vi would be terrible at this. "That's my aunt Vi. She thinks she's a spy."

"You've probably discovered I'm not that interesting," he said.

"Why did you come back here? No one's seen you in sixteen years. Some people still think you killed Julia." I shifted my bag to my left hand, forgetting about my arm for the moment and wincing.

"I've got some unfinished business. Hey, let me take a look at that." Milo gestured to my arm.

"I'm sure it's nothing," I said, glancing at my blood-soaked sleeve.

"I know; you're a tough police officer and all."

I looked up and held his gaze.

He shrugged. "You're not the only one who listens to gossip."

He stepped closer, gently took my left hand, and turned it to examine my arm. And then I knew. Mac was right. As Milo held my hand, I knew that he hadn't killed Tish or Sara or Julia.

Sometimes during a police investigation, I would sense innocence from touching a suspect—it felt light and happy, like root beer bubbles popping against my nose. The other feeling was dark and deep in my stomach, like something awful trying to claw its way out. It didn't happen very often, but I couldn't misinterpret it. Milo was one of the good guys.

My shoulder ached and my arm burned high up under my sleeve. I felt a tug and heard a rip.

"Sorry. This shirt was a goner anyway." Milo tossed the ripped fabric into the Jeep. "You must have landed on something sharp. It tore your shirt, and you've got a pretty good gash here."

I looked down to see a three-inch, oozing cut along my upper arm. I started to touch it, and Milo grabbed my hand.

"Your hand is filthy from climbing out of the car. Come sit *by* my car. I have a first aid kit."

He led me to his tan Honda sedan, and I leaned against the hood while he got his supplies.

"How's the strip mall development going?"

"It's not, so far. I haven't quite worked out the zoning issues, and I need to buy some more land." He found some sort of stinging stuff to drip on the cut. My eyes watered.

"I'm sorry your return to Crystal Haven has been unsuccessful," I said through gritted teeth.

"Oh, I haven't given up hope yet." He wrapped gauze around my arm and tied it gently.

I was feeling more secure now. Cars zipped past every few minutes. Some slowed and the drivers asked if we needed help. Milo waved them along.

Finally, a squad car pulled onto the shoulder and threw gravel as it skidded to a stop. My pulse pounded in my ears when Mac jumped out of the car.

"Clyde, are you okay?" He'd left his cane in the car in his haste, and he stumbled on the uneven ground. Even with everything else going on, a warm feeling flared in my chest when I saw how worried Mac was.

"I'm fine, I think." I moved my arm a bit, saw the gauze turn red, and decided to keep it still. Mac saw it, too, and when I looked in his eyes I saw anger and something else. Something like fear, but it was gone in an instant. He nodded at me and turned to Milo.

"Milo, thanks for stopping to help." Mac shook his hand.

"Let me show you what we found." He led Mac down the incline to where my Jeep lay on its side.

The two of them gestured and bent to look closer. Mac rubbed his jaw, glanced at me, and quickly looked away. Milo shook his head and pointed up the road. I turned my back on them. No longer afraid, my face felt hot with anger. Someone had cut my brake line. They could have killed me. What if Seth had been with me? My promise to Mac faded as I resolved to find the person who had done this.

Mac insisted on stopping at the Urgent Care Clinic. By the time I got home, everyone knew about the accident. A few of the passing drivers had felt the need to call my mother. And, of course, Dad had heard the call go out on the police radio. Mom hurried out of the house to meet us as Mac and I pulled up the driveway.

"Oh, Clyde! Are you okay? What happened? I heard you rolled your car." She was already opening the door, and Mac was forced to slam on the brake. "You always drive too fast along that road. I've told you before. . . ."

Mac held up his hand.

"It wasn't her fault, Mrs. Fortune. There was something wrong with her brakes, and she couldn't slow down to take the turn."

"I've been telling her to get a new car for a long time, Mac. That thing is an *antique,* is what it is. Now I hope you'll listen and get rid of it, Clyde." I refrained from mentioning Dad's Buick.

"Mom, can I go in the house, please?"

Her eyes welled up as she took a good look at me. My arm was mummified in white gauze and I was covered in dirt. I probably hadn't pulled all the leaves and twigs out of my hair. The blood on my shirt didn't help matters. I must have looked even worse than I felt.

"I'll make you some coffee and something to eat." She flapped her hands in the direction of the house and followed behind me. "Mac, do you want to join us?" She turned back after starting up the front steps.

Mac looked at me for a moment, and I sensed his hesitation.

"Mac has a lot of work to do, Mom."

He nodded once and looked away.

"Mrs. Fortune, Clyde is supposed to rest today. She's had stitches in her arm and the doctor couldn't rule out a concussion." He had the nerve to wink at me.

I glared at him and turned to go into the house. He knew that telling my mother I had orders from a doctor was the best way to keep me out of his hair for a while.

"You go right to the couch and lie down," Mom said, fussing. "I'll bring you something to eat."

Dad squeezed my good shoulder and said he was late for the office. He rushed off after making me promise to stay home. Seth, Vi, and Mom peppered me with questions about the accident, and I tried to answer in between bites of sandwich. Vi said Seth had mentioned he'd felt weird this morning, and then the calls came in about my car. Vi and Mom were convinced Seth had had his first vision. I thought he'd had too many candy bars.

I was not allowed to do anything after the lie Mac told my mother about the concussion. The doctor had said my arm would hurt where the stitches were and that I should take it easy, but that was it. He didn't say I was an invalid. Mom chose to believe Mac's version. She scurried in and out of the room, providing more food and drink.

"I think we should go back out to Message Circle and see if anyone saw anything," said Vi.

"No one was there, Vi." I watched her pace through the living room.

"If there's a reading going on, someone might know something, plus there are plenty of animals in those woods. I might get a description of whoever was messing with your car."

I choked on my coffee. "Are you going to start interrogating squirrels?"

Vi leveled her gaze at me. "Squirrels are notoriously unreliable. They can never make up their minds."

Seth's eyes widened as he watched this exchange.

"No, I'm going to see if there are any deer or rabbits around." She nodded to herself, having solved that dilemma.

"You know, this might not have happened at all if everyone had kept their mouths shut," I said, and narrowed my eyes at Vi.

"What are you saying?" Vi asked.

"Mac told me there's a rumor going around that I'm helping the police. That I'm working as a psychic."

My mother bustled back into the room and stopped short when she saw Vi and me in a standoff.

Vi's finger came out, and she pointed at me. "She's accusing me of . . . spreading rumors!" She looked to my mother for backup. Vi prided herself on her ability to keep secrets, even though she shared almost everything she learned with my mother. She considered that "information gathering" and "processing."

Mom looked confused, and Seth filled her in while Vi and I continued our staring contest.

"Oh no. Is that why you had the accident?" Mom's eyes were big, and she clutched the tray she was holding as if it were a life raft.

Vi and I swiveled our gazes to look at her.

"I talked to Jillian yesterday." Mom set the tray on the coffee table. "She asked how I had gotten you to finally use your talents. I told her that's not what you were doing, but she didn't believe me. I'm so sorry. I think she started that rumor when you were helping Tom."

Vi sat back and crossed her arms, giving me a self-satisfied smile.

"I'm sorry, Vi. I should have known you would never . . . gossip."

She nodded. "Da—arn right," she said and glanced at Seth.

He shook his head and pulled Tuffy onto his lap.

After we finished eating, I was subjected to another tarot reading with dire predictions. They brought out the pendulum again, and it was adamant that Milo was not the killer. I was inclined to believe it at this point, but Mom and Vi decided they needed to go buy a new one. They also announced they would take care of the dogs for me, since Seth knew the routine, and the three of them set off, leaving me alone.

I didn't mind. It gave me time to think, something I couldn't usually do in my mother's house with all the activity, psychic and otherwise. I was furious at the thought of someone tampering with my brakes. I hadn't thought to ask Milo where he'd been coming from when he saw me in the ditch. Maybe he saw someone leave the parking lot.

I had no idea where Gary had been this morning. I assumed Mac would be looking into that, although he'd refused to discuss it when we were at the clinic.

The crew had left me in the living room with enough food for a wake, a Thermos of coffee, and my laptop. I was under strict orders to remain on the couch until they returned. Since my Jeep was in a ditch, I was stuck. I hoped it was fixable. It was fifteen years old, but I didn't want to replace it. Apparently, excessive attachment to cars was genetic.

I felt fine, and my arm hardly hurt. I used the time to visit some of the websites of mediums and psychics in town. I also researched whatever I could find on Gary. Someone had killed my friends, and now they were after me. Maybe there was a person in town I hadn't even considered who had a grudge against Sara and Tish and now me.

After an hour on the computer, I had learned the following: there were hundreds of psychic websites, it wasn't hard to cut a brake line, and Gary actually looked better now than twenty years ago when he sported a mullet and a mustache. A quick search of psychics took me to sites where people promised all sorts of mystic knowledge for $1.99 a minute—precisely the people I thought of when I refused to join Mom's "psychic empire." I finally found blogs and websites of people in town by searching for specific names. I noticed Sara had been updating her site a few times a week until about a month ago, when things tapered off to once a week or less. The comment section of her site had been locked. I tried to find some of the comments Alison had mentioned, but it looked like Sara had removed them. She must have been trying to discourage the threats. Or maybe she just lost interest in the anonymous masses once they started getting nasty.

Scarier than the psychics were the instructional videos on how to cut a brake line, accompanied by the disclaimer that you shouldn't try this at home because you could hurt someone.

I pulled out the file of newspaper clippings that Seth had copied from Sara's desk. A quick perusal confirmed what I had thought the night of the séance. Sara had collected old news articles from Crystal Haven's twice-weekly newspaper and even some from the *Grand Rapids Press*. One thick set covered Julia Wyatt's disappearance; the other was a thin pile describing Mike Jones's fatal hunting accident.

I read through the stack, remembering the summer Julia had disappeared. Everyone had gotten involved after they found her clothes in Greer's Woods. Huge search parties formed and spread out through the woods, hoping to find her alive, but fearing they would find her dead.

July 10, 1997

JULIA WYATT STILL MISSING

Authorities suspect foul play in the disappearance of a recent high school graduate from Crystal Haven.

Forty-five-year-old James Wyatt reported his daughter missing on the morning of June 22. Mr. Wyatt reportedly awoke on the morning in question to find his daughter gone. Phone calls to her friends and place of work yielded no leads. He could not provide information on whether any of her belongings were absent. Police began a search immediately, but it was not until June 24 that some of her personal items were found in Greer's Woods.

Authorities report that there were signs of a struggle and fear for Julia's safety. No further leads have materialized.

If you have any information regarding Julia Wyatt's disappearance or her current whereabouts, please call the Ottawa County Sheriff's Department at 1-800-555-6239.

The news reports failed to capture the sense of terror that gripped the area after Julia went missing, but I remembered. The town mourned the loss of its young golden couple. A Julia memorial erupted in the woods as her friends and neighbors left flowers and stuffed animals where her clothes had been found. With fresh worries about safety, parents drove their kids everywhere. The streets were empty by evening, as the children were brought inside. I was only fourteen at the time, and my parents had essentially locked me in the house for most of the summer. The pervasive apprehension was such that I didn't even mind. Rumors of Julia sightings filtered back to Crystal Haven from as far away as Chicago, but gradually the search was abandoned and the town returned to normal. Milo left at the end of August. We knew because Tish told us she saw him packing up his rusty old Datsun. Once school started in the fall, Julia Wyatt became a faint echo for most of us. Her father insisted right up until his death that she was still alive.

The articles about Mike Jones were more interesting to me, since I had never heard that story prior to Friday night. The reports were thin and lacking the sensationalism of Julia's case, although the journalist was much more dramatic than my parents had been. She described the frantic 911 call from a panicked Joe Stark, who had run through the woods and driven to a nearby gas station. Cecile, the young and pregnant widow, was depicted as a strong, but tragic figure. The shooting had been ruled an accident. Sara had clipped a business news article to this pile as well. It described the planned sale of Mike and Joe's restaurant to a Grand Rapids investor. According to my dad, Joe Stark and Mike Jones started the restaurant together in the early '70s. Joe had changed the name to Stark's Place after he married Cecile and they became co-owners. In the margin, Sara had scrawled: *Never sold? Check Milo's birthday.*

The beginning of an idea started to form just as my phone rang from somewhere under the couch. I fumbled with my computer and sent a sharp slice of pain through my shoulder as I tried to extricate myself from the couch and feel underneath for the phone. Baxter chose that moment to be helpful, and his large head blocked out any light that might have leaked under the sofa. It was a blind grope through slobbery upholstery that finally claimed the phone, but not before it had stopped ringing.

I listened to the voice message: "Ms. Fortune—Rupert Worthington here. I hope to meet with you tomorrow after the funeral. As Ms. Twining's lawyer, I have some matters to discuss. Call me if this is not convenient, otherwise I will see you right after the services. Good day."

I patted Baxter's head, wondering where he would be spending his days after Tish's will was read.

25

I was having an uncomfortable déjà vu on Wednesday morning as the organ music began and the church settled to listen to Reverend Frew. If the last memorial service had brought memories of my grandmother's funeral, this one brought out the despair after her death.

It didn't help that Tish had loved lilies. The sickly sweet smell filled the stifling church. The congregation fanned themselves with funeral programs and spread the scent all the way to the back, where I was seated. I had sent my family up front again, claiming that my arm hurt and I might need to step out. In reality, I wanted a good vantage point to watch the attendees, certain that one of the mourners had killed my friend.

I spotted Seth between Vi and Mom. Dad was next to Mom, his arm across her shaking shoulders. A few rows back I saw the gelled, dark hair of Joe sitting next to Cecile's spiky blonde highlights. Gary sat two rows ahead of me, red-faced and sweaty. I tamped down a surge of anger at seeing him. He'd shouted at Tish and called her names just an hour before she was killed. Even if he wasn't the killer, he had made her last moments of life unpleasant. I couldn't find Milo in the crowd. And somewhere, I was sure, was the person who had threatened Sara through her website. Alex and Diana were next to me. Diana strangled my hand in her own.

Reverend Frew was fading in his conviction that Tish was in a better place. He'd been much more convincing with Sara, but maybe my own black mood colored his words.

I closed my eyes for a moment and must have drifted off. I saw my grandmother's face, smiling at me, nodding. She held something up for me to see. It was a book, but I couldn't make out the title. Holding it out, she gestured that I should take it. She clearly wanted me to do something with it, but I didn't know what. Then she vanished, and I heard Tish's voice saying, "Take Baxter." The congregation's singing startled me out of the reverie, and I stood to join them.

I thought I knew what my grandmother was saying. She wanted me to read her journal and look for ways to *increase* the likelihood of psychic insights, not block them. I wasn't thrilled at the prospect but, for Tish, I would try.

Afterward, I waited outside for Alex and Diana. It was a bright, warm day. There was just enough of a breeze to rustle the leaves. I caught myself smiling at the fresh scent of cut grass before the thought that Tish would never enjoy another day like this stopped me cold. My chest squeezed. I couldn't breathe for a moment as the loss washed over me.

I scanned the crowd and spotted Alex talking to Josh.

They looked dazed in the bright sun. I had my hand up to shield my eyes, and when I turned to look for Diana, I almost elbowed Cecile Stark right in the face. She jumped back and looked at me accusingly.

"Cecile, I'm sorry. I didn't see you there." I was saying that a lot to Mrs. Stark.

"It's okay, Clyde. I'm sure you're distracted." She was stunning today in a tight black sheath dress probably meant for someone twenty years younger, and a black straw sun hat. Her eyes were clear, her makeup perfect. She looked like she was attending a stylish wedding, rather than the funeral of her neighbor.

"Have you seen Mr. Worthington?" I asked.

"No, not today. It seems I've seen everyone else, though." She took a deep breath and blurted out, "I heard you're helping the police with their investigation—that you know who killed Tish and Sara and are helping to make a case."

My mouth dropped open against my will.

"What? Who told you that?"

"Everyone knows, Clyde." She put her hand on my arm and squeezed. A sharp pain in my stomach caused a wave of nausea. It must have been the heat and the lilies. "There's no reason to be shy. Jillian is telling everyone that you've come back to take over the family business, and your first big feat will be to find whoever did this." Her smile was all teeth and didn't reach her eyes.

"That's not true." I shook my head as I started a mental list of all the things I would say to Jillian.

"Oh, then you don't know who did it?"

"No." I removed my arm from her grip and rubbed it where her nails had dug in.

"Hmm. Well, that's probably for the best. It seems to me someone is trying to keep people quiet. Tish and Sara were the best psychics in town. Maybe they knew something they shouldn't have. Maybe being psychic is dangerous."

"Am I interrupting?" Diana glanced at my arm and then at Cecile.

"No, no. Just saying how much I'll miss having Tish as a neighbor," Cecile said as she fluttered her fingers and moved off into the crowd.

"What was that all about?" Diana's eyes were red; her mascara had smeared, so she had the look of her goth days.

"Just Cecile being her usual strange self," I said as I watched her move through the crowd to make her way back to Joe. I remembered Tish telling me that Cecile had taken classes on and off for years to improve her intuition, and they never helped. It was hard to live in Crystal Haven with no discernable psychic ability; there was a subtle line between those who could and those who couldn't. Tish used to say that Cecile just tried too hard.

"It was a nice service, don't you think?" Diana stepped into my line of sight.

"Yeah, Tish would have liked it."

Alex had spotted us and walked over in time to hear the small talk. "Listen, when I die, I don't want a funeral. Just have a big party and get drunk. You promise?"

"I don't plan on dealing with that anytime soon, Ferguson," I said.

"Well, we could have a practice run right now. I could use a drink after that. Josh has to go back to work, but I'm off today." He put an arm around each of us and turned us away from the church.

"I need to meet with Rupert Worthington, Tish's lawyer," I said.

"What, right now?" Diana stopped.

"He wanted to meet me here. Maybe Tish had plans for Baxter. I don't know what Seth will do if we have to ship that dog off somewhere."

"Surely not. Who would take him?" Alex said. "*You* don't even want him, do you?"

I started to answer when I spotted Rupert weaving his way through the crowd that had spilled onto the front steps of the church. He was red-faced and moist when he stopped in front of us, his shirttail had escaped from his pants, his suit jacket carried that "rolled in a suitcase" aura.

"Hello, Ms. Fortune. Do you feel up to meeting for a few minutes?"

"You aren't going to take the dog away, are you?" Alex stepped between us. Who knew everyone was so attached to the big slobbering lug?

"No, I have no intention of doing anything with Baxter. He's quite a . . . handful."

"Meet you back at the house?" Diana asked.

"Can we go to your place, Alex? I don't want to face the circus just yet."

"Sure, see you in a little while." He gave Rupert a glare for good measure, and he and Diana went to find his car in the lot.

Looking around Rupert's office, I wondered how he got any work done. Files were piled everywhere in the cramped space. He had a beat-up wooden desk arranged facing away

246

from the small window. A metal filing cabinet loomed in the corner and held a dying jade plant, its leaves wrinkled and drooping.

"Who else is coming?"

"No one. You're the only person I need to see." He glanced up from riffling through the papers on his desk. I didn't hold out much hope he would find what he was looking for.

"Aren't you in charge of her will?" I reached out quickly to save a tottering pile from crashing to the floor.

"Ah, found it!" he said. He brandished a thick file and cleared a spot on his desk by making his other stacks taller.

"Here's the recent one. We just revised it." His eyes scanned the document. "I wonder if she knew . . ."

"Knew what?"

"About her own demise. She was very insistent that this will and testament be in place as soon as possible."

"Mr. Worthington, I don't know what you're talking about. I assume you're going to tell me I can keep Baxter?"

"Oh yes. You definitely can keep Baxter. You get everything, in fact." He set the paper down and spread his hands.

"What?" I leaned forward to see the document.

"Ms. Twining changed her will about a month ago. She left everything to you."

"What do you mean, 'everything'?"

"Her house, her car, her dog, bank accounts . . . everything." He smiled. "She does have one condition." He held up a finger. "You must live in the house for one year before you sell it. After that, you may do as you wish. If you don't abide by that condition, she has a clause here that allows the previous will to take effect."

"But why would she do that?" The guilt of the way things had been between us in the last days of her life settled around me.

"She didn't share that with me. She left you this letter." He handed a thin envelope across the desk. I took it and slid it into my bag. Whatever she had to say, I wanted to be alone when I read it.

"You said the will had been changed. To whom had she left her things before?"

"Well, that's really privileged information, but if you're worried that she'll have outraged relatives coming to contest it, don't. She had no family. She left most everything to various charities in the past." He flipped the file closed. "I heard you've just recently returned to Crystal Haven?"

"Yes, about a month ago." I nodded and continued to stare at the closed file.

"Mmm, Ms. Twining was very pleased about that." He opened a drawer and removed a set of keys.

"I don't plan to stay. What am I going to do with a house?"

"You'll have to decide whether you want to live in it or not."

He dropped the keys into my palm.

I walked from Worthington's office to the marina. I needed to clear my head and make a plan. Why had she left everything to me? What had she been thinking? She knew I wasn't staying in town.

The letter from Tish was folded and stuffed in my bag. I sat on a bench facing the water and pulled it out.

The envelope was light purple and had my name scribbled on it. On the back flap she had scrawled "I'm sorry." I ripped open the top and pulled out a piece of yellowed, folded notebook paper, and as I opened it, another, smaller purple note fell out onto my lap. But I wasn't paying attention to the purple note. The notebook paper wasn't from Tish; it was from Mac.

Dear Clyde,

I have to get away from Crystal Haven. I can't keep living my life based on messages and dreams. I don't think it's what you want, either. I'm not going to pressure you and I don't want to fight anymore. I'm going to Saginaw to take the job there. If you want to try a life together without all that mumbo-jumbo, meet me there.

Mac

There was no date, but I didn't need one. It wasn't his most romantic missive, but it would have changed everything. For weeks and then months after he left, I waited to hear from him. I had eventually accepted that our final argument about Dean Roberts had been Mac's last straw. He must have thought I had chosen Crystal Haven over him. Mac was not the kind of guy to track anyone down. He assumed I had made my choice and left it at that. But why did Tish have the letter?

The purple note explained everything. Tish wrote that she had promised Mac I would get the letter. He'd hidden it in our special tree at her house. Tish had taken the letter and "saved it for another day" because her guides told her it was not the right time for Mac and me. His aura was muddy; my aura was cloudy; all the signs said it wouldn't work.

I wished she were still alive so that I could scream at her. She'd never meddled in my life, and hardly gave an opinion unless it was dragged out of her. But, when she was entrusted with the most important letter of my life, she had not only read it, she'd kept it from me. The anger and sorrow at how different life would have been blended together into a dark mess in the pit of my stomach. I crumpled her note and stuffed it in my pocket, promising myself I would burn it later, maybe even let Diana do some sort of spell on it. This was something I would have expected from Vi, or my mother. Not Tish.

26

I snuck home, grabbed my Browning pistol, and headed out to Dad's cabin. I borrowed Mom's smart car, since mine was still in the shop. It was like driving a roller skate compared to my Jeep, and the bright orange exterior didn't help my desire for stealth. I texted Alex to say I would be delayed, and then shut off my phone. I needed to think.

The quiet before I pulled the trigger worked its magic. I lined up the target, sighting along my arm to the end of the barrel. Standing thirty feet away from the poor tree that served as target holder, feet apart, weight balanced, I held my breath and squeezed.

Still reeling from Tish's will and, more, from her letter, I tried to make sense of it all. Originally, I'd had no intention of staying in Crystal Haven. The summer was supposed to be a brief break from Ann Arbor and the mess I had left there. But now, I imagined what it would be like to leave Ann Arbor for good. I had entered the academy thinking I would help people, but the reality of the job was very different from my fantasy. There was less helping and more paperwork than I had imagined. The hierarchy grated on my independent nature, and I was frequently at odds with those further up the chain of command. And then Jadyn happened.

I had been so sure that night. My partner and I had answered a call for an attempted break-in. We'd chased the suspect through backyards and then to a cemetery. There had been no moon, and the graveyard had lain dim and sinister. When I heard a noise ahead of me and turned to see the tall, bulky suspect facing us, I *knew* he had a gun in his hand. I can't remember now if I saw it or *felt* it, but I was sure it was there. The guy was a threat. Standing in the dark among the headstones, I stopped listening to my normal senses and tuned in to something else entirely. Something I had spent many years trying to ignore.

But, the suspect didn't have a gun. He had a knife, in his pocket. I don't know what I thought was in his hand, but it wasn't there later when the other officers arrived with their lights and their questions. My intuition had betrayed me. My partner stood by me and claimed he had seen a gun as well, a trick of the light, perhaps. He risked his own job and probably lied, although every time I brought it up, he refused to talk about it. We had been in pursuit of a suspect who then turned on us with what I thought was a gun. Lethal force was warranted. That was the story we told, but the truth was, I *felt* the threat with senses that were rusty and apparently not very reliable.

I am an excellent shot. Police training doesn't include shooting to injure. If an officer fires her weapon, she should do so with lethal intent. But I shot his knee. Jadyn was only seventeen and he'd probably always need a cane.

Not only did I shoot a suspect that was not actively threatening, I had broken the unwritten rule. I should have aimed to kill. Now, to my colleagues on the force, I had become an unreliable back-up; too weak to be trusted in the heat of battle. But, I was thankful for that weakness. Thankful I hadn't killed him. Still, the experience left me filled with doubt. I doubted my actions and judgment. Most of all, I doubted my "gift." Like always, my psychic talent had caused nothing but grief.

I walked back from the tree after putting up another target. The first had been shredded. I held my breath and squeezed.

After four targets, I decided it was time to head to Alex's house and tell them the news about Tish's will. My arm throbbed where the cut had been stitched. I lined up for one final shot. Then I heard it again—that *click-click* sound. I looked around the clearing. Nothing. I lined up again and felt the recoil travel up my arm. I would be sore later.

"Whoa, so it's you making all this noise."

I spun around, gun still ready and aimed at the intruder.

Milo put his hands up, but his smile showed he wasn't afraid.

"Milo, what are you doing out here?" I put the safety on and released the clip.

He held a metal detector and a shovel. That was the clicking I'd heard; I knew it had sounded familiar.

"I like to come out and visit the building site, even if nothing's being built yet. It's only about half a mile that way." He pointed east.

"Are you searching for buried treasure as well?" I gestured at his equipment.

"This? Just having some fun. You never know what you might find."

"Well, you shouldn't sneak up on me like that." My heart raced, and I held my hand at my side to stop the shaking. I didn't know if it was fatigue or fear.

He shrugged. "I guess you didn't hear me coming with all the noise you were making." He took a few steps closer.

"No, I didn't hear you." I bent and quickly packed my things. I had to get out of there. Thinking about how wrong I had been about Jadyn started me thinking that I could be wrong about Milo.

"Are you alone out here?"

I stopped and looked up slowly, wishing I had left my gun loaded. Had he seen me release the clip, or could I bluff?

"Why do you ask?" I felt the reassuring bulk of the Browning in my hand.

"You should be careful." He nodded toward my hand. "Accidents can happen with guns."

I watched him head off into the woods, and then I jogged to the car, got in, and locked the door.

My hands were steady by the time I got to Alex's house. I told myself that Milo was harmless. It was just coincidence that he kept turning up in the woods when I was alone. He'd helped me when my car flipped over. I had never been wrong when the feeling resulted from physical touch. I even picked up things from objects sometimes. Something still nagged at me, though.

Alex and Josh lived in a cozy ranch-style house that sat back from the street, up on a small hill. They had landscaped it to the point that I felt I needed a wilderness guide to find the door. I think the front was a combination of stone and siding, but the ferns, bushes, and hanging plants obscured most of the facade.

I found Diana and Alex sitting in his small, welcoming living room. A bottle of Glenfiddich sat open on the table. Alex had broken into his favorite. They seemed to be fully involved in a game of "remember when" and drew me in immediately with the story of Tish convincing my mother that a U2 concert in Chicago was not only a good idea, it would be educational as well. She had volunteered to chaperone, but Alex, Diana, and I had to restrain her from throwing herself on the stage. She then freaked out a security guard with her psychic knowledge, so he let us backstage to meet the band. They were less impressed by her predictions, but she managed to snag a towel that Bono had used to mop his face. She claimed she'd never wash it. I guess that was mine now, too.

"I'll really miss her." Diana rubbed her nose and scrubbed her eyes viciously with a tissue.

I decided I needed some of that whiskey.

"What did the lawyer have to say?" Alex asked after pouring a shot into my glass.

"He read Tish's will."

"Was it just the two of you?" Diana asked.

"Yeah. She left everything to me. There was no need for

anyone else to be there." I took a sip and grimaced at the burn in my throat.

Alex whistled. "Whoa, Vi isn't going to like that. She probably thought she'd get rid of your parents if they got the house back."

"I know. I don't know what promises Tish made to my mother, but she did own the house. She had a right to do what she wanted with it."

"You don't want the house, do you?" Diana reached over to touch my hand.

I pulled away. "No, it's not that. She left a clause in the will. I have to live in the house for a year before selling it. If I don't, everything goes to charity."

"What about your job?" Alex asked.

I hadn't talked to either of them about my job and the way I had left it. They thought I was on "sabbatical." As if the police force gave sabbaticals. Even if I didn't return to the force, I had been planning on returning to Ann Arbor. I wasn't sure I could live in Crystal Haven full-time. I knew I couldn't live with my family for the long term, but maybe if I had my own place . . .

"I'm not sure I want to go back to my job," I said.

"It was that bad?" Diana's green eyes held mine, and I knew that she had figured out that there was trouble in Ann Arbor.

"Yeah, it was pretty bad." I downed the rest of the whiskey.

"What are you two talking about?" Alex looked from Diana to me.

I finally told them the whole story. It felt good, in the end, to let them know what I had been spending so much time avoiding.

"Is it still being investigated?" Alex asked.

"Yes. The kid I shot was definitely part of a gang. We don't know why he was breaking into that house, but he didn't have a gun when I shot him. There are a lot of people who want to see me lose my badge."

"Wow. I knew something was up with you, but I couldn't figure out what. I'm sorry, Clyde," Diana said.

"So, how are you going to break the news about Tish's house to your family?" Alex leaned forward in his armchair, setting his glass on the table.

"I don't know. I might have to do something drastic."

"Drastic?" Diana sat up straighter.

"I might have to call Grace."

27

Grace had not been back to Crystal Haven in years, but she was still an expert in parental and auntal manipulation. I called her for advice when I was really stuck. Our childhood had been fraught with jealousy on both sides, and our age difference had guaranteed Grace's aloof demeanor toward me. But the years had mellowed my jealousy, and I realized that I had something she'd never had: the focused attention of Mom. I could see how a little sister in the house who was held up as the next amazing family psychic might grate on a person. Plus, I had been a bossy pest.

She left town in her early twenties seeking her future in New York as I had described it from my dream. I was fourteen at the time. We'd settled into a cordial relationship that never quite lost the tone of big-sister tolerance of an annoying younger sibling.

But in this case, I needed Grace's take on how to handle

the family because things were going to get tricky when they found out that Tish had left everything to me and that I didn't want it. I went out to Alex's porch among the plants and dialed.

"Well, you have to decide what you want to do," Grace said, after I had explained the will and the requirements.

"I don't know what I want to do." I pulled a large cluster off a lilac bush and buried my nose in its petals.

"Clyde, just make a decision. Would it kill you to live in Crystal Haven for one year?"

"You won't even come back for a long weekend, and you want me to drop everything and move here?"

"What, exactly, will you be dropping? A one-bedroom apartment in Ann Arbor and a job you don't like?"

"It's not that I don't like my job . . . things just got complicated." I snapped the small flowers off the bunch one by one.

"Then why did you run home to Mom the minute things got tough?"

"That's not fair."

"The truth never is, kiddo."

"Fine. Tell me how to handle Mom and Vi." I tossed the remains of the lilacs into the yard.

"Well, I would spin the staying-in-town-for-a-year part of the deal. They thought they'd only get a month or so to work on getting you back into the business; now they have a year."

"Yeah, that's good. I could point out that I would take Baxter with me. Mom would like that."

"Plus, they aren't really losing anything. They haven't had

that house for years. Nothing is changed, except you'll be closer." I wondered how much her own part in losing the house contributed to her cavalier attitude.

"You know Vi. She'll make it a big deal."

"Not if you play it right."

"Okay." I sighed. She was less helpful than I had hoped. Maybe her distance from the family had blunted her recollection of the way we interacted and the way that Vi could turn any situation into a confrontation.

"Hey, Mac called." My stomach dropped.

I cleared my throat. "He did? Why?"

"He said you and 'a ragtag gang' were stalking private citizens and Seth was involved. He sort of hinted that he might be making arrests and that Seth didn't need that sort of blemish on his record."

"He threatened you?" I smiled as I said this, imagining *that* conversation. Mac must be really desperate if he had called Grace. He knew she tended to be protective of me. But by threatening Seth, he was risking his life.

"No, mostly he wanted me to threaten you. Consider yourself threatened. Just stay out of it. Anyway, it sounds like Mac has everything under control." I heard my niece, Sophie, shouting in the background. The phone was muffled, and then Grace came back on the line. "Plus, Mac said you were stalking Milo. I wouldn't mess with the Starks if I were you. They're creepy. Theirs was always the house we avoided on Halloween."

"It was?"

"Don't you remember? Just a sec." Grace covered the mouthpiece, but I could hear her shout, "Just a minute, Sophie!" She came back on the line. "Maybe you were too young. Tish always told me to steer clear of them. She had me scared to death when I was little. Then we moved, and I guess it wasn't an issue after that. But still, I never trusted them."

"I remember that Tish never liked them, but I thought it was because Cecile is such a busybody."

"Maybe. I have to go. Sophie's got an 'emergency' play-date situation."

"Yeah, okay."

"You aren't going to stay out of it, are you?"

"No."

"**Where have you** been?" Vi dropped her knitting and stood up.

"I was getting worried." Mom rushed toward me.

"I need to talk to you." Seth put his hand up like he was in class.

All of this greeted me the moment I entered the house. I hadn't realized how late it was. I'd missed the post-funeral reception and I was relieved, even if it meant hearing every detail later from my mother. Baxter hung back and didn't even check my pockets for treats. He could have been more stressed by the changes in his life than I realized.

Mom gave me a hug and told me again she was worried. Seth caught my eye and tilted his head toward the door—he wanted me to go outside with him.

"Where were you? With everything that's been going on, you could have left us a message," Vi said.

I found it harder to believe that they were truly worried as much as suspicious I had been investigating on my own. Dad would certainly have heard on his scanner if I had been in any further trouble.

"I had to meet with Mr. Worthington after the funeral, and then I went to Alex's place for a little while. I didn't know I needed to check in with everyone." I was feeling surly and a bit like a teenager again. I definitely needed my own place

"Oh. Well, we just figured we'd all come back here afterward. We have to make a plan for what to do next," Vi said. Mom nodded, and Seth flicked his eyes to the door again.

"Where's Dad?"

"He's reading the paper in the dining room. Why did you have to meet with Rupert? Does it have to do with your work situation?" My mom put on her concerned expression. This was a clever maneuver to find out what had happened in my work situation. If I needed a lawyer, she'd know *something*.

"Let's go sit down. I need to talk to everyone."

Seth slumped and shook his head.

We invaded Dad's quiet time. Tuffy and Baxter joined us—Tuffy on Seth's lap, and Baxter as far from me as he could get. I wondered if he blamed me for Tish's death. I wondered if he could still smell the blood. What was I going to do with him?

"Mr. Worthington asked me to meet with him in regard to Tish's will."

"Oh," Mom said, and began smoothing the fringe on the tablecloth.

"It seems that Tish left everything to me." Just like ripping off a Band-Aid—quick and painless.

"But I thought she—" Vi began. My mother quickly put a hand on her arm to interrupt.

There was a moment of silence as Vi and Mom exchanged a long look.

Dad broke the tension. "She left you the house and Baxter?"

"And some money. She had saved quite a bit."

Even the dogs seemed to hold their breath.

"What are you going to do with it? Sell it? That house was your parents', you know." Vi got her finger ready in case waggling was needed.

"Vi, it's okay . . . ," Mom began.

"No, it's not. You should have the house." Vi shot a glare in my direction.

"No, I'm not going to sell it. The terms of the will are unusual but very clear. I have to live in the house for at least a year before I can sell it. Otherwise, it goes to charity."

The ladies gasped at the same moment as if they were taking in the same breath.

"It wouldn't revert to Rose?" Vi said.

"I don't know what any previous will contained. I'm just telling you what I know. . . ."

"Then you'll be here in Crystal Haven for a year?" Mom couldn't cover the smile.

"What about your job? You worked hard for that." Dad was always the practical one.

"I think I can get a leave of absence," I said. Usually when you quit, you got to leave, but I didn't want to have that conversation right now. I decided to play my trump card. "Plus, I'll be able to take Baxter, and he won't have to live here."

Vi looked from Mom to Dad. "We should talk to Rupert. Or get our own lawyer. If you two want the house back, we should fight for it!" Vi stood as if she would go pull the lawyer out of the front closet.

Mom grabbed her hand and pulled her back into her seat. "We aren't going to take Clyde to court, Vi."

Vi glanced at me and looked away. "Right, of course not."

"It's not like we were *planning* on moving, Frank," Mom said to Dad.

He nodded and sighed. "Of course not. I just thought we might get our own place again someday. . . ." He didn't look at Vi.

"It's just a year, Dad. Who knows what will happen?" I said.

Dad smiled. "The good news is, we get to have you close by again." Dad put his hand on mine.

Vi clapped once and grinned. "I knew it! Didn't I tell you she'd be coming back to stay, Rose?"

"I don't remember, Vi. Did you?"

"Absolutely. I knew it." Vi looked around the table daring anyone to refute her claim.

While Mom and Vi discussed Tish's funeral, her will, and what it all might mean, Seth and I snuck outside.

He threw a tennis ball deep into the yard and both dogs ran after it, side by side, Tuffy at full tilt with his short legs blurring beneath him, Baxter in long, loping strides.

"Seth, what's up?" I said when he seemed to be taking an enormous interest in his shoelace.

"I have something to show you," he said.

Seth headed for the back of the yard, where my father had built a small tool shed. He looked toward the house before opening the door and reaching behind some sacks of mulch.

He pulled out what looked like a book wrapped in paper towels. I took it from him and unwrapped it. *My Diary* was printed in peeling gold foil on its dark green cover.

"Is this yours?" I asked. I hoped it wasn't, because the last thing I needed was to read a thirteen-year-old boy's diary.

He looked horrified for a moment.

"Of course not. I think it was Tish's."

The book felt warm in my hands, and I wiped my palm on my jeans.

"How did you get it?"

Seth looked away. He sighed. He squinted at the dogs, who were playing some tennis-ball game in the middle of the yard.

"Seth?"

"I found it in Baxter's bed," he said.

"What? How?"

"Please don't tell anyone, Clyde. Especially Vi, or Nana Rose . . . or my mother."

"Okay. What's going on?"

"I was trying to get Baxter to lie down. He paced around the house the whole time that people were here from the funeral. I brought him up to my room and tried to get him onto his bed. He refused to even go near it."

"So, you sat on it and felt the book?"

"No." He looked at the dogs again, then the house, then back to the diary I held in my hand.

"It was as clear as anything. He said the bed was too lumpy."

"Who said?"

"Baxter."

I felt my jaw drop.

"You think you heard Baxter talk? Oh, Seth." I reached out to put a hand on his shoulder, but he dodged away.

"I didn't hear him talk. I sort of *felt* what he was saying, in my head."

Seth was such a normal kid that I thought he had escaped. But then I thought of the way the two worst-behaved dogs I knew were obedience champions when he was around.

"When you checked the bed you found this book?" I tried to focus on the more concrete aspect of his story while I figured out how to deal with his Doctor Doolittle confession.

Seth nodded. "I felt something hard, so I cut open the seam and dug around inside. I found the book. I didn't read much of it; it seems like it's from when she was a kid."

I flipped the book open and looked at the date: 1975. Tish would have been around twelve at the time. Why would she hide a diary from when she was twelve?

"I don't know what to do, Clyde. I kind of like knowing what the dogs think, but I thought it was just a general sense. Today it was different. Today I heard real words in my head." His eyes were big.

"Vi has been able to get messages from animals for years. Maybe you should talk to her."

His head shook violently from side to side.

"No. I don't want them to know about it. I don't think Vi can really hear them; I think she just makes it all up based on a feeling she gets. I don't want my mom to know. She'll think I'm a freak."

I laughed. "Your mother grew up here. She won't think you're a freak. . . ." I stopped when I noticed his expression.

It was one of a wise teacher waiting for his stupid student to figure things out.

"Oh."

"Yeah. She always says she hopes Sophie and I get a 'useful' talent, if any at all."

"'Useful' being the one she has—predicting the stock market?"

"You have to admit it's better than talking to cats or telling people they'll find love during far-off travels."

I couldn't really argue with him. I had felt the same way growing up. The kids eventually realized I knew things about them they'd rather keep to themselves. No one feels comfortable around a person who knows when there will be a pop quiz, or who pulled the fire alarm in a deserted hallway.

"Have you had any more . . . messages? From Baxter?"

"No. Not as clear as that one. He's sad that Tish is gone, but he likes being here with Tuffy."

"Okay. Let me think about this. There must be a way to stop the messages. Do you want to stop communicating with them?"

Seth shrugged and watched the dogs. "No, I kind of like it. But, it's just so . . . freaky. What would you do?"

I sighed and put my hand on his back. "I'm still trying to figure that out."

I took the diary up to my room after sneaking past the dining room, where my parents and Vi were still rehashing the funeral and the will.

I wasn't sure what I expected, but there were no secret codes, no notes hidden under the liner papers, no invisible ink. After the shock of that letter from Mac, I had a new vision of Tish as a superspy. I was embarrassed to find myself holding pages up to the heat of a lightbulb to see if anything developed.

I flipped quickly through the entries, hoping for some highlighting or maybe another secret letter she had decided not to deliver. The diary covered the year Tish had turned twelve. It was painful reading. There had been crushes and bullies and mean girls and nice teachers. She wrote about my mother and how much she admired her. Was this why she hid it and told me where to find it? I already knew that Tish had idolized my mother when she was growing up. There were references to our house and how much she loved it. She wanted one "exactly like it" when she grew up. She got her wish on that one.

Tish and her mom had had their troubles. Most of it was due to her mother's drinking. I had grown up knowing that Tish didn't get along with her mother and that she had moved in with my parents for the last part of high school. I skimmed over the sections where a twelve-year-old Tish was trying to cover for her mother, trying to do the right thing to avoid her mother's anger.

In November, the entries changed. Tish wrote a long section about a babysitting night at our house. She'd been watching Grace, who was a baby at the time. Tish wrote that she could tell Grace had some psychic ability but that it wasn't what my mom had hoped for. Tish had just begun to feel that she might have some ability, a common enough fantasy at that age. She was living with a mother who was either not home or drunk. It would be wonderful to have a special "superpower." For Tish, the fantasy had come true. After years of work and training, she had developed a name for herself as a medium and psychic. But the girl writing this diary wasn't there yet. She'd apparently been in my parents' room that night, looking for my mom's tarot deck. Tish had the idea that the cards themselves were magical, and she wanted to try them out. There was a long section of justification for the snooping she had done. Then this:

> I don't know why I looked out the window. I wish I hadn't seen them at all. I wish I had stayed downstairs where I was supposed to be. It was so gross! They were kissing and they're so old. And she's married! No one will believe me. Now I wonder what happened to the gun. If I tell, she will for sure find out and then what will happen? But I have to tell don't I?

There was no special marking for this section, but when I started to read it, I knew this was why she had left me the book. But I didn't understand it. She'd obviously seen something that wasn't right, but who was she talking about?

According to the entries in December, she had gone to the police eventually and indeed they had not believed her. She was just the spooky girl with the drunk for a mother. They even brought in a social worker to determine whether it was likely Tish had been drinking that night. It wasn't surprising. The word of an imaginative twelve-year-old meant nothing.

I wasn't sure what had triggered the recent murders after all this time, but I was starting to think that Sara's séance had been much more disturbing for one of the guests than the others.

I decided to use my new set of keys.

I hesitated outside Tish's house. How long would I think of it that way? Glancing at the tree where Mac used to leave notes, I felt sadness settle over me. Tish had certainly caused some trouble with her penchant for "helping."

I went up the steps and ignored the police tape stretched across the door. *What's one more reason for Mac to be mad?* I stepped into the front hall and took a steadying breath. I imagined I could still smell blood, which was unlikely after five days and the thorough cleaning Rupert Worthington claimed to have arranged. Ignoring the flashes of memory and avoiding even a glance toward the kitchen, I went directly to the stairs. I took them two at a time and found myself on the landing outside what used to be my parents' bedroom.

Tish had put her own spin on things since she moved in, and her taste in comfortable, casual furnishings continued into the bedroom. It was decorated in neutral tones of brown and cream. She had a king-size bed between the two front-facing windows and a comfy-looking chair by the side-facing window. I suspected that this was the window she had been looking out of when she'd seen a married someone kissing a man who wasn't her husband.

What I couldn't quite get my head around was that Harriet Munson lived next door. I could not, even using all of my imaginative powers, see her having an affair. She was simply too rule-oriented. Ignoring the fact that she and her husband seemed to be one of the happiest couples in town—another shocker—I just couldn't imagine her doing anything so out of character.

I peeked through the window and tried to imagine what Tish had seen. But there was nothing to see. There was one small window on that side of Harriet's house, and I was at the wrong angle to see anything. Unless Harriet and her mystery man had been standing at the side of the house near our driveway, which would have made them perfectly visible from the street, Tish hadn't been looking this way.

I went to the other window and glanced out. This window faced the front, and I imagined would give a good view of the Stark's privacy fence. I was wrong again. I could see right into their backyard. I could also see into their kitchen. The driveway ran along the side of the house to the detached garage at the back.

My understanding of what Tish had seen shifted again. I pulled out my phone to call Tom.

28

The woods grew quiet as the sun disappeared. The sunlight that had been weakly filtering through the trees gave up and the moon took over. It was Thursday evening, eleven days after finding Sara. I reflected on how much had changed and hoped that soon we could all return to our version of normal. We had launched one more mission to follow Milo. The gang was certain he was up to "no good," as Vi would say. Since I now suspected someone else entirely, I had gone along with this to keep them safely watching the wrong person. Baxter's leash was taut in my hand as he strained to sniff the area around us. Seth and Tuffy crouched behind a tree about twenty feet away.

Vi and Mom had set up a vantage point along the road that led back into town; my dad was farther along Singapore Highway in case Milo headed south. He was testing out his new mobile police-band radio. Diana and Alex watched Message Circle. I had turned everything I knew over to Tom;

hopefully he was closing in on the murderer. The rest of us were wasting our time, but I felt reassured that everyone I cared about was currently watching Milo while the real killer was nowhere near these woods.

I saw Milo run his metal detector over the ground in the silver moonlight. The familiar *click-click* sound no longer seemed threatening. He stopped when the clicks got closer together, turned on a portable lantern, and began to dig.

I heard Baxter's heavy breathing at my side. I was surprised Milo hadn't noticed Baxter's loud panting. Seth glanced in my direction, and then I saw a blur of light brown as Tuffy took off into the woods.

Baxter pulled at the leash, and I had no choice but to be dragged along after him or lose him to the darkness. I gave up all pretense of quietly observing Milo and shouted at Seth to run. Milo dropped the shovel and bent to pick up the lantern. He shined it at the tree Seth had been hiding behind, but Seth was already up ahead chasing Tuffy.

I had no idea where Tuffy thought he was going. Wherever he was headed, it wasn't a silent approach. We made so much noise running, I was sure Milo must be following us as well. My phone vibrated in my pocket—a text. I didn't have time for Vi's update.

The branches that were too high for Baxter struck at my face, and I put my arm up to block them. The stitches pulled in my arm as I strained against the leash. I ran with my head down, tucked under my right arm, and hoped Baxter knew where he was going as he tugged me deeper into the woods. I saw a light up ahead in a small clearing and pulled on Baxter's leash to slow him down. Seth had stopped running as well, and we walked up to the edge of the clearing, breathing hard and staying behind the trees. My phone vibrated again; I reached into my pocket and shut it off. I felt the weight of my gun in the waistband at the small of my back and was glad I had brought it. I felt that I was back in that horrible dream from the night of Diana's spells. The woods, the moonlight in the clearing, the sense of being dragged through the trees: it all combined with the sound of my heart pounding in my ears. My legs felt boneless as I realized this was the place—the place from my dream, where Mac would be hurt.

Joe Stark was in the clearing with a lantern and a shovel. He had been digging for a while by the looks of the pile of dirt at his feet. He held Tuffy by the collar and tried not to get bit by the snarling, growling demon Tuffy had become. He picked Tuffy off the ground by his collar and got his arm around the dog to stop his struggling. Tuffy yipped and then continued growling.

The dog must have sensed we were nearby, because he stopped fighting with Stark and scanned the trees looking for us. Stark stood very still, his head cocked, listening.

"Hello? Who's there?" His face was in shadow, his long hair falling over his eyes.

I gestured to Seth to stay back in the trees, and I stepped forward into the clearing.

"Hi, Joe. Thanks for catching my dog." I willed my voice to stay calm, but I could barely hear myself over the pounding in my ears. All my alarm bells were clanging.

Joe's mouth formed a smile.

"This isn't your dog."

I forced myself to take another step forward. I felt Baxter leaning into my leg, his chest vibrating with a growl that began deep in his throat. "I'm taking care of him for the owner."

"The owner is dead." Stark put Tuffy down. The dog snarled and bit into Stark's ankle. Stark's other leg came around and caught Tuffy in his back leg. He let out a yelp of pain and the little furry body flew several feet before landing still and silent just a yard or two from where Seth was hiding. Stark bent down to his shovel, and when he stood, he had a gun in his hand pointed directly at me.

Baxter growled and pulled on the leash, I held firm with both hands. The hair on the back of my neck stood up and I heard loud breathing to my left.

I felt Seth grab my gun from my waistband. I turned and saw him, his face streaked with tears, aiming my gun with a shaky hand at Stark.

Stark let out a bark of laughter. "Call off your bodyguard, Ms. Fortune."

"Seth, put the gun down." I took a step toward him, but Stark shook his head and motioned with his gun that I should stay put. My body felt like ice as I watched Seth grip the gun, my mind playing out every sort of horrible outcome. The safety was still on, and Seth didn't know how to shoot, as far as I knew. But Stark didn't know that, and he'd already killed two people who'd gotten in his way.

"Seth, listen to her," said a new voice. Milo stepped out of the trees toward Seth. He didn't even glance at his stepfather. "Seth, you don't want to do this. It will follow you for the rest of your life, believe me. Put the gun down and no one will get hurt."

"Tuffy's already hurt!" Seth said.

Milo inched closer to him. "Seth, you're not a killer. Put it down."

Seth glanced at me. I nodded. Baxter moaned as if to join in the chorus of reason.

Seth let his arm drop, and Milo stepped forward to take the gun. He put his arm around Seth, who shrugged him off and ran to where Tuffy had fallen.

"You shouldn't come to the woods at night, Ms. Fortune. You never know what might happen," Stark said.

This was it, I thought. In my effort to protect my family by sending them on a wild Milo chase, I had left myself open to danger. And since Seth was always with me these days, he was in danger, too. In the distance, I heard something crashing through the forest. And a siren.

"Stark, put the gun away. It's over," Milo said. He pointed my gun at Stark.

I heard a *ka-chink* to my right. Cecile held a hunting rifle up to her shoulder, aimed at me. I wasn't shocked, based on Tish's diary entry, but was angry at myself for momentarily forgetting that she was just as dangerous as Joe.

Stark laughed and shook his head. "It's not over for—" he began.

His next words were drowned out by the sound of a car approaching through the trees, the siren flashing and wailing on top. Tom pulled the wheel hard to the right but too late to stop it from crashing into a huge oak at the edge of the clearing. We were all momentarily distracted by its arrival. The driver's side was blocked by the tree, but the passenger door flew open, and Mac climbed out. He took a step toward us, his arms outstretched just like in my dream.

I turned to warn him to stay back, and my hand loosened on the leash, which was all Baxter needed. I felt Baxter's low growl, then the leather leash ripped into my hand as it was pulled out of my grasp. He launched himself at Stark with a deep bark. Joe put his arm up to protect himself and, just as Baxter was about to land on him, the gun fired. Dog and man went down in a pile of fur and stringy hair. Stark rolled out from under Baxter and started crab-walking away, but the dog didn't move. I heard a deep howl begin off to my left. Tuffy had come around and made the most mournful sound I had ever heard.

The howl was deafening in the otherwise quiet clearing. The car engine hissed, and the headlights lit up the woods to the north of us. The bubble on top spun, and the flashing lights revealed Milo wrestling with Stark for possession of the gun. I caught a glimpse of Cecile running into the trees, but I couldn't deal with her until I knew Seth was safe and I had checked on Baxter. I signaled Seth to stay on the ground near Tuffy. I saw Stark's gun drop to the forest floor as Milo slammed his knee into Stark's gut.

I crawled toward Baxter. He still had not moved. I reached his long body and ran my hand along his chest. It was wet. I looked up to see Mac running toward us, and back at my hand, covered in blood.

Mac ran past me and pulled Stark away from Milo. Stark's gun lay glinting in the moonlight just a few feet from me. I grabbed it. Seth had moved closer to Baxter, and Tuffy continued his keening. As Mac clicked the handcuffs onto Stark's wrist, Tom finally climbed out of the police car. Alex and Diana emerged from the trees.

"I tried to text you about Cecile," Diana said, as she ran over to where I sat with Baxter. "We saw her headed this way with a rifle."

Stark's gun lay in my hand, and I could see Sara and then Tish falling to the ground. I shook my head to clear it, and then focused on the section of woods into which Cecile had disappeared.

Alex had already moved to check on Seth and Tuffy. They seemed to be examining Tuffy's back leg.

I stood and told Seth to stay down near the dogs. I gestured at Diana to check on Baxter, although the hopeless dread was already settling around my shoulders. The red and white lights of the cruiser reflected off the closest trees, leaving the rest of the woods in darkness. I wondered for a moment if Cecile could be out there hiding and decided she had probably run toward the road to get away. I was up and headed into the woods before I had time to reconsider.

"Tom, Baxter needs help!" I ran past him into the darkness and heard Mac's voice calling me as I slipped between the trees.

I tried to calm down and focus. Tuffy's howl was masking all other sounds in the woods and, with my back against a tree, I tried to listen past his racket to anything that might give away Cecile's location. I continued toward the road, pausing every minute or so to listen. Tuffy finally stopped his noise, which had me concerned. Was Baxter dead? Was Tuffy hurt and unable to continue?

As I got farther from the clearing, the lights from the squad car no longer penetrated, and I moved through the trees with only weak silver moonlight to guide me. It was eerily quiet. No animals were moving about, no owls hooted. Then I heard it.

Scuffling and swearing and thumping. I followed the sound, being careful to stay under the cover of the trees. I saw two people struggling on the ground. Long white hair blended with blonde spiky hair as Cecile and Vi rolled around on the mossy forest floor. I entered the melee just as Mom cocked Cecile's gun, which caused the rumpled twosome on the ground to freeze.

"Vi, what are you doing?" I said.

"I'm subduing a suspect." She sat up and moved away from Cecile, who stayed on the ground. Both of them had dirt streaks on their faces and twigs and leaves hanging off their hair and clothing.

Mom walked closer and pointed the rifle at Cecile. I went to help Vi get up. She struggled to stand and favored her right leg. I grabbed her elbow and pulled her up out of her crouch. She leaned against me and began brushing leaves off her skirt.

"What should I do, Vi?" Mom didn't glance our way but continued to point the gun at Cecile.

Cecile lay perfectly still, mesmerized by the barrel of her rifle. She wisely chose not to speak. Her eyes flicked from Vi to me to the gun. Her hope of escape evaporated when Mac burst upon us.

"What the—?" he said as he took in the scene: Vi and me covered in dirt and leaves, Mom holding a gun on Cecile, who also looked like she'd been dragged through the forest.

I tilted my head toward Cecile, and Mac went to her and pulled her to her feet. Mom lowered the weapon.

We trudged back through the woods. Vi leaned heavily on me, and I half carried her most of the way. Mom and Mac flanked Cecile, who walked with her head down, refusing to speak.

The next hour was a blur filled with flashing lights from the police cruiser and Tuffy's howl. The little dog had started up again and didn't stop until he and Baxter had been taken away to the emergency vet clinic. Andrews had radioed that shots had been fired, and when the ambulance arrived, Mac bullied them into transporting the dogs to the vet. I remembered Seth's face, young and scared, wet with tears, as he asked if I thought Baxter would be okay. I said I didn't know, because if I told him what I really thought, we would have stood there all night crying.

The Starks were taken into custody for the murders of Sara, Tish, and Mike Jones. I had figured out that much on my own, but I still had a long list of questions. Milo admitted he was in town to find evidence that his stepfather had killed his father in the hunting accident. He'd been digging for the rifle all this time. He filled us in on the rest: Tish had seen Cecile leave with a gun and come back without one on the night of Mike's death all those years ago. She'd been babysitting that night and had suspected they had killed him, but she was just a kid, and no one would listen to her.

Tish kept the secret as she grew up. No one had believed her when she tried to tell them about what she saw, and then she got scared that her knowledge would put her in danger, so she let it drop. Then, two years ago, she ran into Milo in Chicago, and he asked her to do a reading for him. He said he was interested in learning about his past. She faked the reading and told him that his father's murderer had buried the gun in the woods. Milo launched a plan to get access to the land and dig up the gun to link it to the murderer. They'd been arguing recently because she finally told him that she had faked the reading and only assumed the gun had been buried out there. They both thought Joe was the killer.

According to Milo, Tish said she had lost the ability to do readings after the fake one. Either it was guilt or some cosmic consequence, but her practice fell off. She was desperate to fix things.

"It makes sense now," Mom said. "Tish had been irritable and stressed for months. She went to tons of conferences to try to improve her skills. Whenever I tried to talk to her about it, we ended up arguing."

Sara's séance accusing someone of being a murderer pushed them all over the edge. Tish thought it could have been the Starks Sara was referring to, Milo thought it was his stepfather, and Cecile thought Sara actually had knowledge about Mike's death. I secretly wondered how much the newspaper stories had to do with Sara's séance. She may have been playing a very dangerous game of trying to draw out the murderer. I wasn't sure we'd ever know what really happened that night, except that it triggered everything that had come after.

I left it to Mac and Tom to sort out all the conflicting stories. I barely had time to thank Mac for coming to the rescue before he headed back to the station to begin the long process of building a case against Cecile and Joe. Alex offered to take Seth and me to the vet clinic, and we gratefully accepted.

29

I opened my eyes the next morning and squinted at the brightness. Every muscle ached from having been dragged around the woods by Baxter the night before.

Baxter. I tried not to think about him. He had been so brave. I wished I could take back even one of those times I had pushed away his wet nose. I would have placed a large bet that Baxter would have run for cover before ever protecting me, and I was thankful I had been wrong. He'd been my very own secret service dog and now he was . . .

I got out of bed, pushing all thoughts of Baxter out of my head. It would be even worse dealing with Seth if I was teary-eyed. I went downstairs in search of coffee and news.

In the kitchen, Mom came up to me with tears in her eyes and hugged me.

"It's okay, Mom." I patted her back and tried to pull away.

"No, it's not. You could have been killed." She squeezed

once more and released me, but gripped my hand. "It was bad enough when you were in Ann Arbor and I imagined you to be in danger all the time, but for it to happen here, right under my nose." Her lower lip quivered as she fought for control.

"Mom, it just got out of hand is all." I sat at the table and focused on the coffee she slid in front of me.

"It wouldn't have gotten 'out of hand' if you had known what to expect going in." She stood in front of me, arms crossed. "Clyde, you wouldn't go into a building on a police call without assistance, would you? If you were expecting trouble?"

My mind flashed again to Jadyn. I remembered the adrenaline racing through my system as we caught sight of him and chased him through the alleys behind the apartment building. I knew I wouldn't have done that if my partner hadn't been with me. I would have called for backup; the kid would have gotten away.

"No," I said.

"Then why do you go through life without using the support that has been given to you?" She had her hands out, pleading. "Why do you insist on ignoring your gift when it could save your life?"

"It wouldn't help, it never helps. In fact, I *did* know something about last night. I had a dream about it. It didn't help in the least, except I thought it was Mac who was going to be shot."

"Is that why you started avoiding him?" She sat across from me.

"What?"

"He told me. He said things were going just fine between the two of you, and then you withdrew for no reason. He didn't understand it."

"I thought I could protect him if we stayed apart," I said without meeting her eyes.

"The thing about your gift, Clyde, is it will never be of any use until you learn how to understand it. You can't pay attention to some of it and not all of it. You have to know what you're doing, or you're going to end up getting hurt."

"Mom, when was Mac here?"

"He came by looking for you after Tish's funeral. He spent some time with Vi and then left."

"Who spent some time with me?" Vi clumped into the kitchen using Mac's cane. She clearly hadn't slept much and was covered in scratches from her brawl with Cecile.

"Mac," we said in unison.

"Yeah, he had it all figured out." She flicked her hand and made her way to the table to sit with us.

"What are you talking about?" Mom said.

"He said he needed me to keep everyone interested in Milo so no one would get hurt." She gestured around the table. "You can see how well that worked out."

"Start at the beginning, Vi," I said.

"He came here after Tish's funeral and said he'd been looking into old cases. He suspected that Joe or Cecile or both of them had . . . killed Mike all those years ago." Her voice trailed off, and she stared past me out the kitchen window.

"So, why didn't he arrest them and save us all this trouble?" Mom's brow was furrowed, and a storm was brewing in her eyes. She got up and went to the coffeemaker, a reflex when she expected a long conversation.

Vi pulled herself together and summarized Mac's investigation. Mac had followed leads that were on Sara's computer. She'd been investigating Milo. When Milo came to town, Sara's lawyer instincts kicked in, and she decided she should know more about this guy who was trying to change the town and was causing trouble between her and Gary. In researching Milo, she found the newspaper reports about Julia, and that led her to the older reports about Mike Jones. Joe and Cecile were big believers in psychic phenomena. Mac assumed that, when Sara had accused someone at the séance of being a murderer, they thought she knew more than she did.

"What a mess." Mom put the coffeepot on the table with milk and sugar. "But why kill Tish?"

"I think I can answer that," I said. "Tish knew all along that the Starks had been involved somehow. She either let it slip that she knew or . . ." I stopped, remembering Cecile hiding in the bushes while I told Tom that I was sure Tish knew something.

I put my head back in my hands. Cecile must have gone straight to Joe and told him Tish was a threat.

"Mac thinks that Milo told them he was on to them and why," said Vi.

My head popped up and I looked at her.

"According to Mac, Milo had been very up-front with Cecile about what he was doing in town. He wanted to find the gun that killed his father and prove it was Joe who had pulled the trigger." Vi stirred her coffee.

"But he never suspected that his mother was involved as well, because Tish never told him that part." I finished the tale. Maybe it wasn't what Cecile had overheard that caused Tish's death, but it probably didn't help.

I put my head down on the table, thinking about the mess we had made, and how I had put my family in danger.

Vi patted my arm. "You know, we were all in it together. We all wanted to catch the killer."

Tuffy and Seth shuffled in looking for breakfast, and we were distracted by looking at Tuffy's cast. We'd called Gary from the vet clinic the night before to get permission to treat his broken leg. When Gary heard how much it was going to cost, he offered to let me keep the dog. He admitted that he and Tuffy had never gotten along, and he was almost bankrupt from his gambling debts. Seth was now the proud owner of a shih tzu. Grace was not going to be thrilled. The vet said Tuffy would have to wear the cast for about a month and would need lots of care during that time. Seth had already become Tuffy's servant, so not much had changed on that front. We all purposely avoided talking about Baxter.

The doorbell rang, but Tuffy didn't have the energy to bark. He looked at Seth from underneath his messy fringe and sighed. I followed my mother out to the front hallway and caught a glimpse of Milo as she pulled the door open. He was standing next to a pretty blonde woman who could only be—

"Julia?" Mom said as she stood there gaping.

"I knew it!" Vi said from behind me.

While the ladies stood staring, I gestured for Milo and Julia to come in.

"Clyde, I'd like you to meet my fiancée, Julia Wyatt."

"She's not dead?" Seth had come out of the kitchen to see what was going on.

"Seth!" Mom exclaimed.

Julia laughed. "No, I'm not dead."

Mom hustled them into the living room and then headed off to the kitchen for more coffee. We sat and continued to stare at Julia. Milo reached over and took her hand, and she smiled.

"So, tell us!" Vi said, and rapped Mac's cane on the floor.

Julia jumped and looked at Milo.

"Julia drove in from Chicago last night. We're heading back tomorrow as long as I'm not needed at the police station," Milo said.

Mom bustled in with a tray of coffee mugs and cookies.

"What did I miss?" she asked as she sat next to Vi on the loveseat.

"Not a thing, Rose," Vi grumbled.

"Mac thought it would be a good idea for us to stop by and talk with you. He thought it would clear the air a bit." Milo sipped his coffee and seemed to consider how to proceed. "I helped Julia run away right after high school. She was eighteen and legally an adult, but we wanted to be sure no one would look for her." Milo glanced at Julia, who nodded. "Her father was a vicious drunk, and after Julia's mother died, he drank even more."

He squeezed Julia's hand. She looked at her lap.

"I'm not going to go into detail, but she needed to get away from him before something truly terrible happened."

I remembered all those times trying to "see" Julia that summer she disappeared. All I saw were bruises and tears, which must have been why she decided to run.

"Now that my father is gone," Julia began, "we thought it would be safe to return here. But, after everything that has happened, we're thinking we'll just stay in Chicago. There are too many bad memories here." Her voice was soft and, when she finally looked up, it was to nodding heads and sniffles from Mom.

Milo went on to tell us that Mac knew about it even all those years ago. As a new police officer, he'd gone out to the Wyatt house on domestic disturbance calls. But there was never enough evidence, and until Julia was eighteen, she would have nowhere to go, so she didn't press charges. She just tried to stay out of trouble and avoided her dad if he'd been drinking. Milo hatched the disappearance plan after a particularly violent outburst from Julia's father when she'd talked about going away to college.

Although they couldn't get married because Julia didn't want any paperwork to trigger a renewed search, they'd been living happily in Chicago. Then, Milo talked to Tish and began his quest to reveal his father's killer.

After Milo and Julia left, I sent a text to Tom to see how things were progressing at the station. Rather than text back, he arrived on the doorstep ten minutes later. We had all reconvened in the kitchen, and I led Tom there to fill us all in at the same time.

Vi greeted him as he sat down at the table. "What's the news, Tom?"

Tom shook his head. "It's all sort of confused right now, but everyone is busy trying to compile the evidence and avoid Mac. He wants the case against Joe and Cecile to be airtight, and he wants it yesterday."

"Have they confessed?" Mom asked.

"No, they asked for lawyers the minute we got them to the station, so a confession is unlikely. We did just get a report back on the gun Stark had with him in the woods. It's the same gun that killed both Tish and Sara. Unfortunately, it has all sorts of fingerprints on it, including yours, Clyde."

"They must have other evidence against him," I said.

"Mac has a couple of people in the woods digging in the area where Joe had started. I'm not sure what he's looking for. . . ."

"He probably thinks Joe was digging up the rifle that killed Milo's dad." Seth's head was down, examining Tuffy's cast, but he was apparently paying attention.

"What about Gary?" I asked.

"He's off the hook. He came down last night to volunteer the information that he had been threatening Sara on her website. He wanted to scare her into selling her land to Milo so he could get the money to pay off his gambling debts." Tom nodded thanks as my mother slid a mug of coffee in front of him.

"Poor Sara. She probably would have given him the money if she knew he needed it." Mom pushed the cream and sugar toward Tom.

"What about Clyde's car? Who cut her brake line?" Seth asked.

"Once we got fingerprints from the Starks, we checked them against a partial print found under the car. It matched Cecile."

"I knew it!" Vi slammed Mac's cane against the floor. Tom jumped. "Cecile would be mortified if anyone knew that she used to work in her dad's garage. She could probably cut a brake line in her sleep."

Seth and Mom nodded. Tom looked confused.

"Thanks for coming to the rescue in the woods, Tom." I smiled at him. Seth sighed, and I imagined the accompanying eye roll.

"I wish I could say it was my idea, but Mac knew you were in danger once we saw that the Starks weren't at home. I don't know how he figured it out."

"Tish had reported them back when she was a kid. No one listened to her then, but Mac must have found the report and put it together with the articles we found at Sara's," Seth said, and all eyes shifted to him.

"What?" Seth said.

"How did you know all that?" Tom said.

"It's obvious, now that we know who did it."

"Oh, this is for you." Tom slid a folded piece of notebook paper across the table.

I opened it with shaky hands. *Meet me at the bridge tomorrow. Ten a.m. Please?*

"What? What is it?" Mom said, as I slipped the note into my pocket and smiled.

The rest of the day was quiet. Vi had called all my Friday clients and cancelled. Not one of them had an issue with the lack of a dog walker, but they all wanted details of the arrest in the woods. Alex and Diana stopped by to check on everyone. They said the gossip in town was that I had led the police to the killer using my psychic ability. Mom fielded phone calls and gave me pointed looks as she told people I was not open for business.

30

On Saturday morning, I waited on the bridge for Mac. The sun was bright, but the light filtered through the trees on the water below. The stream bubbled brightly under the bridge. It had been a long time since I'd felt this light and free. I realized I was happy. I was going to see Mac, and the dream that I thought predicted his injury or death had been wrong. I had been wrong. He was going to be fine.

I spotted him coming along the path. He wasn't using his cane, since he'd given it to Vi, and seemed to be moving more easily without it. He walked up to meet me at the top of the small rounded bridge. He put out his arms and smiled. It was a smile I had seen so many times before, mostly when I was asleep.

"Hi," he said.

"Hey."

I went to him and he folded me into his arms. I breathed in his pine-and-lake-breeze scent. We stayed like that for a long time.

"Mac, I need to tell you something." I pulled away to look at his face.

"Do I want to hear it?" He smiled down at me.

"That letter you wrote. The one you gave to Tish?" I wasn't doing this right. His smile faded.

"We don't need to talk about it. Let's just start from here."

"But you need to know."

"Ancient history." He drew me back into his arms.

"The thing is . . . I just got it." I felt his arms stiffen.

"Just got what?"

"The letter. It was part of Tish's will. She left me your letter and said she was sorry to have kept it, but the time wasn't right for us."

Mac let go of me and turned toward the bridge wall.

"So, all that time I thought you had chosen your psychic life over me—"

"I thought you were mad that I didn't tell you about Dean," I said to his back.

His shoulders started to shake. I panicked for a moment—I'd never seen Mac cry. I didn't think I was ready for that. I looked around, trying to come up with a distraction so I could pretend I hadn't seen.

He turned, and I saw that he was laughing. Laughing so hard he was crying.

I stamped my foot. "I don't know what's so funny about wasting eight years when we could have been together."

"It's not that. It's just, well, we can't fix the past." He

shrugged. "I wasn't mad about your involvement. I just didn't know how to handle it." He rubbed his eyes and appeared to be trying to pull himself together. "When you told me that you had dreamed we would be married, I knew we would have to get away from here if we could ever live a normal life without the psychic influence."

"Why didn't you ever call, or come back?"

"Well, I wrote that letter and thought that if you wanted what I wanted you'd come to me. I was a coward." Mac turned toward the stream again. "I didn't want to tell you in person and risk watching you choose this place over me." He turned toward me. "I won't make that mistake again."

"I'd have had a few things to say to Tish if she were still alive." I crossed my arms and glared at the stream, which now seemed brightly irritating.

"I brought something to show you." He put his arm around my shoulder and turned me toward the path.

We looked back down the pathway in the direction of the parking lot. I didn't see anything. Mac whistled. A large brown dog turned the corner onto the trail. I recognized his dark droopy face as he came limping along the track through the trees. His left front leg was wrapped in white, and another bandage crossed his chest. Andrews waved from the other end of the trail. Baxter sped up a bit when he saw me, and I ran down the path to meet him. I was so happy to see him I didn't even mind the drool. He slobbered and wagged his tail so hard his whole body moved with it. I buried my face in his fur and didn't let go until my entire sleeve was wet. We walked slowly back to Mac, Baxter limping and flashing his doggy smile at me.

"Thank you," I said.

"I should be thanking Baxter. He did the one thing I was trying to do all along."

Suddenly I was in his arms and I felt all the pain and stress fade away. It felt better than I remembered. It felt like home.

FROM

LINDA O. JOHNSTON

The More the Terrier

A PET RESCUE MYSTERY

When shelter manager Lauren Vancouver finds out that her old mentor, Mamie Spelling, is an animal hoarder, no one is more shocked, and she jumps in to help rehome the cramped critters. But Mamie's troubles don't end there. She's accused of murder when the CEO of a pet shelter network is found dead. And Lauren's dogged determination to clear her former friend of murder may put a killer on her tail.

facebook.com/TheCrimeSceneBooks
LindaOJohnston.com
penguin.com

M998T1011